INTIMATE DISTANCE

by

Karla Brandenburg

Intimate Distance
Copyright © 2005 by Karla Lang
All rights reserved
No part of this book may be reproduced or transmitted in any form or by any means, graphic, electronic or mechanical, including photocopying, recording, taping, or by any information storage retrieval system, without the permission in writing from the author

For Information, contact Karla@KarlaBrandenburg.com

Any resemblance to actual people or events is purely coincidental.
This is a work of fiction

ISBN 978-1-4303-2448-5

Acknowledgements

My thanks go out to the folks in my critique group who labored through this with me. To my family that did the test reading (also waving to Joy), thank you for your support. Most of all, to my husband and my kids who let me bounce ideas around and, although they haven't read a word, have the confidence in my stories to promote them – I couldn't do it without you. And to Bill (*He says his name's William but I'm sure He's Bill or Billy or Mac or Buddy* – Wyn Cooper), a friend who helped me through a difficult time while I was writing this and helped point my compass north in the middle of a magnetic field.

"It is easy to be brave from a safe distance." – Aesop

"...love from one being to another can only be that two solitudes come nearer, recognize and protect and comfort each other." – Han Suyin

CHAPTER 1

Julianne lay on one side in her futon bed staring at the digital alarm clock while it clicked off another minute. Across the room, the computer sat on a desk in the corner, beckoning. She shivered and blamed it on air conditioning.

All she had to do was sign onto the program. She knew he'd be there – on the other end of the Internet connection.

It was a losing battle. She hadn't anticipated this obsession. Online afforded a false sense of intimacy; she recognized the feeling and consciously made an effort to avoid falling into that trap. Jack had become a lifeline. And he never asked to breach the faceless void between them.

She flung back her covers, kicked her feet over the side of the bed and tip-toed to the door, peaking into the other bedroom.

Steve's back was to her, a shapeless blob on the far side of the bed making irritating half-snores.

Julianne pulled her door closed and turned on the lamp over her computer desk. The light reflected in the eyes of the gargoyle hanging over the shelf, watching her approach.

She sat down in front of the computer as she had done more and more frequently since Steve moved in, and it occurred to her for the first time in the six months they'd been living together that she actually preferred the time spent with her online community to the man sleeping in the next room.

The computer purred to life, following its programming to take her where she wanted to go. All she had to supply was one mouse click to accept her destination. Minutes later, she stared at black words scrolling across the gray background on the monitor like ants marching to a picnic.

A quiet ding welcomed her into the advertising forum and Julianne felt the fellowship of friends.

When his screen name, JGGuilder, stood out blue in the message box he sent out to greet her, Julianne smiled. She guided the mouse, pulling down his profile once more to personify the statuette hanging over her computer.

There was his name: John "Jack" Gryphon Guilder. Julianne nodded an acknowledgement to the gryphon over her desk and then returned to the waiting screen.

Outside, a police car sped down the highway with its siren blaring. Julianne cringed like a hiding criminal. Was her online relationship with Jack Guilder disloyal to the man she was engaged to? She heard Steve roll over in the next room and considered exiting the forum until another instant message invited her back into her cyber world.

"Not even a graduate yet and your ideas are making me money," his message read. And then a second later, "I got the Preston account. Don't be surprised if you recognize part of the slogan."

She smiled, laying her fingers to the keyboard. "Too bad it won't go toward my final grade. I need you to come back to the class so I can be sure to get that 'A'."

"They'd only call you teacher's pet. And I doubt that you need my help," came his answer moments later. "One more big fish to fry. Any ideas for selling sweats?"

"I'll work on it."

"I can't wait to get back to Chicago. L.A.'s like another planet."

She looked over her shoulder at the moon hanging in the sky outside her window. "Weather's lousy here, rain predicted and getting colder. You might want to reconsider and stay in California." Julianne shivered again, irritated at the air conditioning. If she lived alone, it wouldn't be on.

"It must be like 2:20 there, isn't it?"

Julianne checked the clock on her computer and mentally subtracted two hours to get to his time zone before he drew her back with his next line of type.

"What's keeping you up?"

Her fingers hovered over the keyboard. Where to start? Her doubts about the man in the next room? She'd made her choices: right or wrong. "Just restless," she finally spelled out.

"I'd pick you up for coffee if I weren't halfway across the country."

Julianne laughed. He always made the offer when he was out of town. "Maybe when you get back," she typed out of habit.

How easy it was to romanticize the online relationship. She scarcely remembered what he looked like. All she could make out of his face from the photo on the Perkins & Stone website were his large, round eyes and a face covered with hair. Although neatly trimmed, his beard covered most of his features like the picture on the old Dan Fogelberg record she'd seen at her mother's house.

"Doing your homework?" she read as it came across the screen.

"I do my best work at night."

"Ambiguous," came the next line, and then below it: "When do you sleep?"

Her lips curled into a smile, caught up in the innuendo.

"Between 'Johns'," she typed, referring to John Thomas, the employer that occupied her days, and John Guilder, the man she spent most of her nights conversing with online.

"So long as you're not under one of them. LOL."

She "laughed out loud" along with his acronym. Allowing her arms an exaggerated stretch, she reached for the grotesque statuette above her and then pulled back, suddenly afraid to touch what it represented.

Steve's radio alarm began playing in the next room, waking him for his 3-11 shift.

It was as if Jack heard the alarm halfway across the country. "Don't suppose Steve would let you slip out anyway."

"Not sure he'd notice," she replied with a sigh.

"How long before the wedding?"

"Six weeks." It was like a noose tightening around her neck every time she thought about it, but she couldn't pass that along across a computer screen. Jack Guilder probably didn't care any more about her wedding than he did about the class he taught at the college. Still, she had to wonder why he spent his nights in front of a computer screen chatting with her, or why she sat answering him at 2:30 in the morning instead of getting much-needed sleep. She needed to kick the habit.

"Let's go to bed," she typed and watched it scroll across the screen.

"I'll turn back the sheets."

"Good night. . . " she sent her final message and then disconnected.

Julianne fell into bed, unable to shake Jack Guilder from her thoughts. When he had invited the students in her class to join in the Perkins & Stone forum online, she never imagined he would be there as well. She had been so intent on her studies that she didn't take much notice when he was the substitute teacher in her classroom, but since joining the forums, he had become a part of her daily life. A much bigger part than she had anticipated.

A wave of guilt drove the smile from her face. Her nightly discourses with him were no better than Steve's trips to the arcade every day. If he was meeting other women there, was she any better, meeting another man every night in the privacy of her bedroom?

Julianne fought back her doubts one more time. People didn't marry people they didn't love, and everyone had their lover's quarrels, especially this close to the wedding. In a few more months she would have her degree. She would have no more use for an advertising teacher/ mentor.

But she had come to look forward to their nocturnal meetings of the mind. She sparked more than a few creative ideas. Hadn't Jack given her credit for helping him land the Preston account? It was her slogan, after all, that he claimed won over the client.

"Don't kid yourself," Julianne muttered to herself. She grabbed her covers tight around her neck and rolled away from the glare of the alarm clock. Jack Guilder was handsome and successful. What practical use could he have for a struggling student?

Her vivid imagination would be her downfall. It had to be pre-marriage jitters. Why else would she feel closer to a man she had met in person only twice? With one last glance over her shoulder, Julianne looked at the gryphon hanging over her computer. "Good night," she whispered in the dark.

CHAPTER 2

Megan Reilly walked into the elevator beside Julianne, overdressed in a brown tweed suit. A perm gave the illusion of flawless curls to her heavily streaked hair, the dyes making it impossible to guess the original color.

Feeling plain in her own simple cotton dress, Julianne smoothed out the skirt. "How's life in marketing?"

"I really love the move. Best choice I ever made."

"I think Mark would be hard to work for."

"He's not so bad." Megan's tone of voice implied the truth the way her hair showed its color.

Julianne smiled. "I'm glad I work for JT," she said. "Mark's so high strung. I think he'd make me nuts - he has made me nuts - in a very short period of time."

"I'm just glad I don't have to deal with all those petty women on a daily basis any more."

Julianne nodded. With Megan gone, there was one less among their number.

The elevator doors opened to the offices of Kimball Brothers. The women each greeted the receptionist before heading down opposite corridors.

"Morning Julie," JT greeted her as he swept past.

He always greeted Julianne, something he seldom did with those beneath his status unless he had some ulterior motive. It was a sign of respect and issued Julianne a small degree of prestige among her peers.

She did like working with John Thomas: "JT." He was the youngest senior executive with the company and highly motivated. He had a deceptively boyish quality that made people open up to him. But beneath the exterior lay a lethal cunning.

He was five foot ten and built like a basketball player - muscular and lean to the point of being almost too thin. Always dressed in a suit, Julianne felt sure he could charm bears away from honey. That same quality was what put the other women in the office on their guard. A general feeling of distrust surrounded him where they were concerned.

Black hair fought against a cowlick on the top of his head and there was a pimple on his chin. That was part of his charm - he wasn't perfect.

"Stop in when you get settled," he called out before disappearing into his office.

Julianne rolled her eyes. She took her seat at her desk and stashed her purse. The light on her phone told her she had voicemail messages but she had the feeling JT wasn't in the mood to wait. She powered up her computer, grabbed a pen and a pad of paper and made her way back to JT's office.

"Hey," he acknowledged, looking up from the report lying open in front of him.

"Hey," she answered back and took a seat on the opposite side of his oak desk.

"Close the door."

Julianne reached across and did as he asked, then crossed her legs and waited for her boss to state his purpose.

JT turned over another piece of paper before he pushed the report to the side. He folded his hands and leaned forward. "We've had this conversation before."

"Then why are we having it again?"

"We need you in the new marketing department."

"You have someone in the marketing department."

"You could supervise Megan, Julianne."

Julianne gave a short laugh. "Oh that would go over real well."

"You know you were our first choice."

"As you pointed out, we've had this conversation before."

"It's a promotion from the secretarial ranks. Don't you want to advance? And aren't you going for a marketing degree?"

"I have other goals in mind."

JT took a deep breath. "You know I want what's best for you. They want me to move over into that department, too. So if it's loyalty to your boss that keeps you in this position, then you'll have to move with me."

"That's suicide," she told him. "The promotion to head the marketing division could only result in ultimate failure. It's like any new division they open. How many business developers have you seen come and go? They should hire a marketing department, or outsource it. Not try to build one with people who don't know what they're doing."

"But you should know what you're doing. That's what you're working for. We want to help. We want you to continue to be a part of Kimball Brothers' success story. You'd be writing your own along with it."

Julianne pursed her lips. "It would result in being underpaid, overworked and, after putting in the effort to build a respectable beginning, they would finally bring in someone 'with experience' to take it over. No thank you."

"Part of every success story is attitude," he argued.

"And our lives are made up of choices. I don't feel this would be a good choice for me."

He squinted at Julianne, short one comeback.

"Anything else you want to address this morning before I get started?" she asked.

JT pulled the report back to the center of his desk. "I wish you'd reconsider."

"I'm flattered. But I don't think it's the right choice for me."

"This stays in this office." He looked directly at her to emphasize his point.

"Don't worry."

He nodded toward the door. "I'm going to need to deliver that proposal by 10 this morning."

Julianne paused, her hand on the doorknob and then turned back. "Thanks, JT. I appreciate what you're trying to do."

He waved her off, his attention back to the project in front of him.

Another secretary leaned forward from her desk behind Julianne's when Julianne sat back down. "Did you see Megan's suit?"

"I rode up the elevator with her," Julianne answered without turning to face Andrea.

"She's a little too wide in the hips if you ask me, and she doesn't have the chest to fill out that style of jacket."

"Doesn't do her any favors," came Caroline's voice. The third woman leaned around her fabric-covered half-wall. "I don't think she's all that pretty."

Julianne forced a smile and turned to address her co-workers. "She's pretty, whether we think so or not. Did you hear that new guy the other day? Walked into her new office and said it right out - 'Pretty lady.'"

"I heard him. I wanted to throw up. She thinks she's so hot now that she has her own office," Caroline said.

"I just want to know who she had to sleep with to get that job," Andrea said.

"Why? You want to give him a go?" Julianne teased, turning back to pick up her telephone. She wondered if they would be saying the same of her if she had taken the position.

Julianne scribbled down notes from her voicemail message before she turned her attention to her e-mail messages. She took guilty pleasure at seeing the name JGGuilder on her list of unread messages. Was she disloyal to Steve?

She enjoyed having someone to talk to on those long nights after Steve left for work, someone to share ideas with on-line. Too many nights she felt alone, even with the man she was going to marry asleep in the next room.

The truth of the matter was JGGuilder was better company, even from a distance. Just the sight of his name sent prickles of anticipation along her skin.

Julianne took a sip of tepid water left on her desk from the night before. JT's proposal stared at her from the corner of her desk. Gathering it up, she took it back into JT's office.

"The proposal," she informed him, laying the papers on the desk.

"Hey," he halted her. "I should have asked, how are things going with the wedding?"

Julianne couldn't prevent the shudder and squared her shoulders to push it back. "I think we're about ready."

"Haven't changed your mind yet?"

That familiar feeling of dread crept over her, and still she managed a smile. "You don't plan something for a year only to change your mind at the last minute."

"It's never too late to change your mind," he pointed out. "You can still take the vacation time, you know." JT leaned back in his chair, narrowing his eyes. "This wedding thing, does it have any connection to why you won't take the job in marketing?"

Julianne let out an exasperated sigh. "Look. I really like my job at Kimball Brothers. But you don't want an experienced person in that job or you would have hired from the outside. You want a workhorse that you can scapegoat later so you have an excuse to hire a professional."

"You could be that professional. Then we wouldn't have to hire anyone else."

"You guys wouldn't take me seriously. You'll put your blinders on and you'll never see past the secretary that I am now."

JT's eyes strayed to a woman hovering just outside the office door. "You're wrong," he told Julianne more quietly.

"You know I'm right," she insisted. "One of the things you like about having me for your secretary is my ability to see through the bullshit, isn't it?"

He shook his head. "You're too smart for your own good, Julianne DeAngelo." He looked straight at her, demanding her attention. "That's why I don't understand why you would marry someone like Steve Montgomery."

"Hey, he was there for me when my dad died."

"Yeah, but is that a good enough reason to marry him?"

Julianne shrugged her shoulders. She wasn't sure anymore. "Life's a series of trade-offs. Pick your poison."

CHAPTER 3

He was late again.

Julianne looked at the clock at the end of the galley kitchen and put her plate into the sink. She rinsed off the remnants of the tasteless microwave dinner she prepared for herself. The other dishes in the sink proved that he had been home at some point during the day.

She turned up the radio on top of the refrigerator and reached down to open the dishwasher. She started out humming and then tapped her foot to the pop song that filled the small kitchen. Singing into a spoon she danced out into the dining room that still lacked for furnishings.

She stopped short, nearly bumping into Steve in the open doorway of their apartment. Lowering the spoon, her hands went to her hips.

Steve leaned in to kiss her forehead. An aura of stale beer and cigarettes surrounded him. "Hey."

She bit her lip, glad he'd only offered the peck on the head. "Should I ask where you've been?"

"I just went to play a few games with the guys."

"You know if you stopped playing those stupid video games every night we could afford to buy a house a little quicker."

"This'll be okay for a while, don't you think?"

Julianne folded her arms across her chest. Still in her high heels, Julianne stood two inches taller than Steve. His sandy hair lay perfectly, never out of place. His face was long and thin. His brown eyes, indifferent, were dark against his fair features.

Steve turned away from her scrutiny and started toward the bedroom. "You don't have any classes tonight do you?"

Julianne shook her head and walked the opposite direction into the living room. She came to a stop in front of the sliding door that opened onto the balcony. "Maybe I'll watch some TV or check out the on-line conferences."

"You and those damn on-line conferences. Why don't you just come to bed with me?"

"Because I'm not tired," she lied.

"Who says you have to be tired? We're not even married yet and already you're hanging up the do not disturb sign."

She knew she had been avoiding him. The intimacy between them always seemed forced. He always pushed the limits, even after they agreed to wait until after the wedding. Then there was always that doubt that she wasn't the only one. Would she ever trust any man?

"You don't mind if I go to bed, do you?" he asked.

She saw his reflection in the patio door, peaking around the wall at her, and then she redirected her gaze to the sunset blazing from behind a line of trees.

Steve walked up behind her and slipped his arms around her waist.

Julianne wrinkled her nose, detecting the scent of stale perfume when he leaned around to kiss her cheek. "So who was at the bar?" she ventured.

Steve immediately pulled back and retraced his steps toward the bedroom. "The usual guys."

"Maybe I'll go with you next time." She closed her eyes, shutting out all the visual distractions and listening for the answer she knew he would give.

Several minutes passed before he spoke. "You know you hate playing those games."

"No," she corrected him, "I hate wasting the money. And that's not why you don't want me to go."

He stood in the doorway in his jockey shorts, spindly legs stretching out from his slight frame. "What?"

"It's going to change, isn't it, Steve?"

"What's to change?" He walked halfway back into the living room. "You don't want me going out with the guys?"

"It's not the guys I'm worried about," she admitted.

"Julie, you know I love you."

"There's more to marriage."

"You're the one I want to grow old with," he assured her, keeping his distance. "I want to spend the rest of my life with you. Now stop worrying about other women."

"I will, when you stop chasing them."

"I'm going to bed. I have to get up for work in a couple of hours."

* * *

The computer conference was like one of her college lectures. Julianne sat watching the protocolled discussion scroll down the screen, line by line, not really seeing the words.

She ran her mouse back and forth across the mouse pad, watching the pointer chase across the screen and then she pulled up the profile of her on-line host again. John Gryphon Guilder, Partner, with the advertising firm of Perkins & Stone. The personal information was sketchy.

She looked at the small gargoyle that ornamented the top shelf of her desk, her attention distracted back to the man it had come to represent.

He was in Chicago, half an hour on the expressway. The offices of Perkins & Stone would be in the Loop. She could get there on the train. Would he ever ask her to coffee while he was in town? Would he hire her after she got her degree?

"JulianDe?"

She saw her name on the screen and sat up straight. "Had to answer the phone, give me a minute to catch up," she typed and then scanned the last couple of lines of dialog.

The conference room was reserved hourly and their time slot was nearly exhausted. It was her reprieve. "That's not something you can summarize in five minutes," she sent out. "It comes down to an intangible quality that you have to exploit for people to notice and imitate."

"Perfect summary," he responded. "That kind of ties up everything we've discussed tonight. I'm going to end protocol now."

Julianne yawned. She exited the conference room, determined to leave him tonight. She was getting married in a couple of weeks. John Guilder had no personal interest in her. He was a habit she would have to break.

But an instant message stopped her. "Have a favor. Can you pop into a private room with me for a minute?"

Without hesitating, she replied yes and waited for him to open one. There was something intimate about a private chat room, a one-on-one meeting, a confidential rendezvous.

"Whatcha doin?" Steve asked, peering into the second bedroom from the hallway.

Julianne jumped and felt the heat rising in her cheeks. "On-line conference," she answered, her breath coming short. "What time is it?"

"Ten."

"What are you doing up?"

"Bathroom. Going to bed soon?"

"Mmm."

The scent of another woman's perfume, almost indistinguishable and yet clearly separate, faded in the wake of Steve's departure. The guilt evaporated like alcohol as she clicked into the chat room JGGuilder set up. "What's up?" she typed.

His first line caught her off guard. "I need a wife - big interview with potential client. Can you step in for me?"

Her heart beat like a trip hammer. "I don't think that would be a good idea," she answered. "There must be someone else you can ask."

"Just a lunch," came his reply. "And I'd be willing to bet you know me as well as most of my friends, maybe better."

She stared at the screen in disbelief. "I don't know you at all."

"Don't you?"

She mentally sifted through all the on-line conferences, all the chat sessions she spent with JGGuilder and an assorted cast of other parties that had come and gone over the past six months.

There was no question she wanted to go. But was it the right thing to do? What if Steve found out? Julianne pursed her lips. She wasn't sure she cared if Steve found out, truth be told. Another line of type scrolled up. "Free lunch. An hour and a half. Two tops. Besides, I owe you for your help with the Preston account."

Julianne blew out the breath she'd been holding. "That's a tough gig to pull off," she typed to allow herself time to think. "What if this client asks personal questions?"

"What do you want to know?"

She laughed in spite of herself, excited by the possibilities.

"What's so funny?" Steve called from the adjoining bedroom.

Pulling herself upright in the chair, Julianne scowled. "Just a joke," she called back.

She wasn't married yet.

Maybe she did know JGGuilder, at least she knew him a little. She also knew this might be her last chance to see him. And they would be on neutral ground. Maybe seeing him in person one more time would set aside this silly fascination she had with him once and for all.

"How much time do I have to consider?" she typed.

"Thursday - 11:30 at Berghoffs. Can you make it?"

Two days away. She let out a low whistle and clutched her stomach when it lurched in eager anticipation. "I shouldn't," she whispered out loud.

"Maybe Steve would be uncomfortable with the idea?" the screen responded as if he had heard.

She gave a derisive laugh. "Screw Steve," she muttered. "Everyone else does."

"When are you going to get off that damned computer?" Steve called from the bedroom.

She could courier into the city for Kimball Brothers. Getting downtown for lunch wasn't an issue. She told herself she could position herself for a job with Perkins & Stone. "I'll be there," she typed. Even as she hit the send button she quivered.

"You're a lifesaver," JGGuilder returned. "I'm looking forward to seeing you."

"Not half as much as I am," she whispered. She escaped out of the chat room before she had a chance to change her mind. "I'm not married yet," she repeated.

CHAPTER 4

The city was hot, the sticky humidity thick enough to cut through. Smog insulted Julianne's nostrils. Gusts of oppressive September wind swept down from the tops of the skyscrapers to the crowded streets below.

Putting her head down, Julianne pulled at the bottom of her jacket one last time and forged into the German restaurant.

She twisted the unfamiliar wedding band on her finger. The proper jewelry. Was it bad luck to wear your wedding band before you were married?

A maitre d' greeted her and Julianne took a deep breath. "Can you tell me where Mr. Guilder's table is?"

The German host nodded and invited her to follow him with the sweep of an arm.

The scents of garlic and roasted meat made Julianne's nervous stomach lurch. Still she carried herself confidently, straight and tall.

Second thoughts assaulted her. Julianne never did anything impulsive. Guilt buckled her legs and Julianne reached for the back of an empty chair to steady herself.

"Madam?" The irony of a German waiter calling her Madam brought a nervous titter from Julianne. She brushed back her hair and forced a smile as she prepared to look into the face of the gryphon.

Three tables away, he stood more than six feet tall when he rose to greet her. She could see nothing but enormous, brown eyes, their size exaggerated by the close, brown beard that hid most of the rest of his face.

His shoulders were broad, draping his gray-pinstriped suit coat loosely down to where his body narrowed over trousers hung neatly over long legs. He was much more attractive than she remembered from night school.

Nerve endings sent sparks all through her body. Too late to turn back, she took a deep breath and pressed forward. "J-John," she greeted, holding out her hands, fighting to control the shaking. "I hope I'm not too late."

His head tilted, assessing her curiously just before slipping into a professional smile. "Julianne." His deep voice carried the seductive quality of a midnight disk jockey. Jack Guilder kissed her cheek and turned politely to the prospective client who rose to greet her. "Let me introduce you to Ben Hayden. Ben, my wife."

His wife. It didn't seem such a foreign concept. In fact she rather liked the sound of it, like a school girl writing her boyfriend's name all over her notebook. The flush coursed down through Julianne's body. She took a deep, calming breath, closed her eyes and turned on that part of herself carefully trained through presentation classes. Julianne thrust out a hand to the portly gentleman standing beside her.

Ben Hayden had sparkling blue eyes under a crop of white hair. Beside Jack, he seemed almost dwarfed. "Julianne DeAngelo," she introduced herself.

"DeAngelo?" The older man asked.

She looked nervously to Jack. "Professionally I go by my maiden name. I do a lot of subcontracting. Name recognition accounts for a lot of my referrals."

Jack smiled at her, the corners of his mustache raised by distractingly full lips. He pulled out a chair with a sweeping gesture for her to sit. Julianne returned the smile, feeling another swell of warmth course through her body.

"What kind of work do you do?" Mr. Hayden asked, resuming his seat.

"Presentations," she unfolded her napkin. "I dress up proposals - add graphics, colors. I also subcontract idea development."

"Why aren't you on staff at Perkins & Stone?"

"John does so much traveling," she waved her hand in front of her face. "We hardly see each other as it is without me chasing off around the country in the opposite direction. At least this way I can count on seeing him when he's home."

Mr. Hayden chuckled. "I see your point. Do you always call him John?"

She looked across the table at JGGuilder in alarm. She had become so accustomed to thinking of him by his full name that she forgot he introduced himself to the class as Jack. "That is his name, after all."

"She's a lovely woman, Jack."

Jack put an arm around Julianne and gave her shoulders a squeeze. She smiled like a giddy school girl, trying to ignore a sudden prickling of guilt.

Julianne picked up her menu to browse the entrees.

"Can I get you something to drink?" the waiter asked, appearing beside the table.

"A glass of Rhine wine," Julianne ordered, seeking to soothe her churning insides.

"I'll have a stein of that German beer," Hayden added.

"Rhine wine," Jack ordered.

The waiter nodded. "I will be back for your order."

Julianne reached a hand to her waist to ease the nerves. When the waiter returned with their drinks, she sipped the wine eagerly letting its calming effect trickle down.

Jack transitioned right from their lunch orders into his solicitation to represent Hayden's casual wear. Julianne twisted the superfluous ring around her finger while Jack presented the qualifications of Perkins & Stone and provided his own resume of relevant experience. He spoke in an evenly modulated cadence that added to the relaxing influence of the wine.

Julianne raised her eyes to look at Jack and found him studying her as he finished his sales pitch. Hypnotized by the sound of his voice, she felt pinned to her seat.

"It's a woman's line," Ben Hayden told him, "and I have been talking with another firm represented by a woman's point of view. I'm not sure you could give me that same perspective." The old man looked directly at Julianne. "What do you think, Mrs. Guilder?"

Her eyes popped open wide, brought out of the trance she was falling into. "I'm not sure I understand what you want me to say. John is very good at what he does. Of course I'll share my ideas with him."

"How much do you two work together?"

"She's been the brains behind more than one of my presentations," Jack said.

Mr. Hayden nodded, taking a swallow of beer. "That's kind of what I was hoping you'd say." He leaned heavily across the table. "Look, if you two can work together for me, I'd be willing to take a look at your presentation. Jack, you have the firm I want, but I need that woman's touch. I believe that will be the crucial element to the success of this line of clothing."

"We have women on the creative staff . . ." Jack began.

"No, I want you, Jack. And your wife, here. No, I'm sure of it. Hire her, subcontract her, whatever the proper term is, and then show me what you come up with. Can you do it, Mrs. Guilder?"

Julianne nodded uncertainly, taking another sip of wine for fortification. "I'll see what I can do." Hayden's insistence on addressing her with Jack's surname didn't go unnoticed. It sounded odd, and at the same time Julianne felt that same school-girl thrill.

"My account is worth quite a lot, Mrs. Guilder. It would be worth your while to make room on your schedule."

Julianne looked at Jack helplessly. "I could e-mail you my ideas."

"E-mail?" Mr. Hayden interrupted.

"With John gone so much, we communicate a lot electronically," Julianne covered, struggling for a plausible explanation. "It's the next best thing to being there, and it provides instant access. I can depend on the fact that he'll see what I've written without the interference or dilution of a third party."

"You do live together, don't you?" Hayden asked.

"We don't discuss work during our personal time together," Jack answered. "We have so little of it that we like to make the most of it."

Hayden nodded his head. "As it should be. That must be what keeps the spark in your relationship." He winked. "You two have been making goo-goo eyes at each other ever since she got here."

Julianne saw her surprised mirrored in Jack's round, owl eyes. Jack cleared his throat and laughed nervously. "Well what's the point in getting married if you aren't in love?"

Julianne's heart fluttered in her chest. She struggled to reconcile her increasing reservations about her forthcoming nuptials. Guilt produced a physical stab of pain reminding her how Steve had been there for her through her father's illness and then after the funeral, holding her hand, comforting her. But did she love him?

"Marriage is too temporary these days." Hayden downed the last of his beer. "Think I better go let some of this beer back out." He smiled and rose from the table.

"You're brilliant," Jack enthused. "I believed everything you said."

Julianne blushed under his praise, forgetting her discomfort. "So what about this presentation?"

"I would like your input. Do you think you could arrange to be there?"

The distance between them seemed to close tight. "I, uh, have a lot going on in the next couple of weeks," she stalled. "It all depends on when it is."

"I'll try to work around you. I really think it's important." He was staring at her, his enormous eyes squinting into ovals. "Is something bothering you?"

"What do you mean?"

"In person isn't quite the same as on-line."

She laughed. "No, I'm fine."

He reached for her hand across the table. "Julianne, I know you're engaged. I don't want to put you in an uncomfortable position." The edges of his mustache lifted into a smile. "Although I doubt I could have selected a better wife."

She smiled wryly. "Yeah. Someone else's." She wiggled uncomfortably in her seat, the guilt effervescing like the bubbles in Ben Hayden's beer. Julianne pulled her hand out of Jack's and looked around the restaurant, anywhere but at the handsome man seated beside her.

And then she saw him. In a moment of recognition, her brain went numb. Julianne struggled for her next breath only to realize she had been holding it. Seated at a table near the street-front window, Julianne spotted Steve holding her sister's hand.

Suzanne DePalma was smaller than Julianne and her coloring was darker. Her dark eyes were accented by heavily applied makeup, her skin an unnatural shade of tan. Even through the make-up, Julianne could see the blush in Suzanne's cheeks while she placed her other hand over Steve's.

With a wave of nausea, Julianne held her breath and pushed her tongue against the back of her teeth to constrict the muscles of her throat.

Jack reached for her shoulder and Julianne nearly jumped. "What's wrong?" he asked.

She blew out a slow breath, taking in another deep gulp of air. At that moment, Julianne wasn't sure if she was more worried about being seen or about seeing Steve. "I'm not feeling very well," she whispered to Jack, leaning in so that he obstructed her from Steve's view.

"Can you make it through lunch?"

"Would it be terribly awkward if I left now?" she asked, fighting to maintain her composure.

"What'd I miss?" Hayden asked, returning to the table.

"Julianne's not feeling well," Jack explained hastily, helping her to her feet. "Maybe I should get her home."

"You do look a little green around the gills," Hayden observed. "Look, you take care of her, Jack. I'll take care of the check."

"No," Julianne piped in, rising to her feet, "I don't want to spoil your lunch. Why don't you two go ahead and iron out the details." Leaning forward, she let her hair cover part of her face and extended a hand to Ben Hayden. "I'm sorry to leave like this, but I am looking forward to working with you."

Jack rose beside Julianne, taking her shoulders. "Are you sure you're going to be all right?"

Julianne flashed him a nervous smile, hazarding a glance to the table by the window. Jack held her close and for a moment, she forgot about being seen, reveling in the warmth of his embrace. "I'll see you at home," she said for the benefit of the client and with a wink, she hurried out of the restaurant.

The oppressive humidity choked her after the relative cool of the restaurant. Julianne coughed and took a misstep, catching her heel in a grate in the sidewalk. Throwing her briefcase to the ground beside her, Julianne yanked off her high heels and traded them for the tennis shoes in her bag.

Tears streamed down her face as she forged her way through the crowd back to the train station. It wasn't until she was safely seated on the Metra that she realized that seeing Steve and Suzanne together hadn't upset her nearly as much as her own sense of guilt and the mortification of nearly getting caught with the man who was coming to mean more to her than her own fiancé.

On-line, she could embrace Jack Guilder, tell him things she didn't share with anyone else. No one had ever made her feel as comfortable as Jack Guilder. Seeing him in person again she felt like a stupid school girl: clumsy, awkward and guilty of sneaking out.

The train whistle blew for the first stop and Julianne reached into her briefcase for a tissue. If nothing else, at least she was sure of one thing: she wasn't going to marry Steve Montgomery. And she wasn't the only one who was guilty of being somewhere they shouldn't have been.

CHAPTER 5

Somehow she had pinned more hopes on her meeting with Jack Guilder than she expected.

Did she believe he would fall instantly in love with her when she walked into the restaurant? That the intimacy they shared on-line would translate immediately into happily ever after? Had she actually expected him to swoop down with great gryphon wings and carry her off into the sunset, to protect her from all the hurt and disappointment in the world? Now Julianne had to face the crash back to reality.

Curling up on her bed, tears streamed down Julianne's cheeks. Everything was not going to work out and she was more certain than ever that she had to break things off with Steve. One more failing her mother would find in her, one more relationship she lost to her sister.

Julianne wrapped her arms around herself wanting – needing – comfort. Once more, Julianne's mother would give her the laundry list of her shortcomings. The degradation was ingrained enough without benefit of hearing it.

Then there was Steve. A brilliant actor, he was very good at hiding the truth without actually lying. And Julianne had turned a blind eye. She had so desperately wanted to believe in him that she overlooked all the inconsistencies. There was no more denying the existence of other diversions. It didn't even matter if his lunch with Suzanne was innocent.

Suzanne would say she was only trying to protect Julianne from making a mistake. Not that Suzanne would ever want Julianne to be happy. There were times Julianne had been grateful for her sister's interference. If her dates chose the outer beauty over the intelligence, there generally wasn't much depth to them.

The gap her father's death left felt like a chasm. Julianne had never felt so alone. She realized that was how Steve had gotten a foot hold in the first place, taking advantage of the void left by her father's death. It wasn't love. It was comfort. Julianne wouldn't make that mistake again.

She sobbed into her pillow, pulling it around her head to drown out the outside world.

When she felt the hand on her back, Julianne reluctantly let go of her pillow and wiped at her cheeks. Steve sat silently on the edge of the bed, his face an infuriating mask of concern.

"What's the matter? Are you sick?" he asked.

She retreated back into the corner of the bed and leaned against the wall, curled up into herself. The safety of denial was gone. It wasn't just another woman, he had been with her sister.

"Julianne?"

"I saw you at lunch," she told him in a menacing whisper.

He shook his head, not believing her at first and ready to deny it if need be. "You're not yourself right now. I can see that." He leaned across to take her hand, but Julianne tightened her grasp around her knees. "Julianne, you're scaring me."

She considered that he probably thought he was concerned, but she knew better. The concern was for his meal ticket, not his girlfriend. "At Berghoffs," she continued in order to make her point.

The mask on Steve's face slipped for a moment and Julianne saw real fear for a moment. "It wasn't like we planned it, she saw me in the restaurant so we had lunch together." She suspected it was what he thought she'd want to hear. He was adept at saying the right things, but she wasn't buying into it anymore.

"How often do you have lunch at Berghoffs?" she pressed.

The color was draining from Steve's face. "I, uh, I, uh, just thought it sounded good today."

"It isn't exactly fast food. And you never stop for lunch. Isn't that what you always tell me?"

"Look, Julie, you're making more of this than there is."

She took a deep breath and let it out again slowly. "I can't do it," she said.

"Can't do what?"

"I can't marry you, Steve."

A flash of anger marred his features, and then his mask slipped back into place. It was so transparent now that Julianne wondered how she hadn't seen through it long ago.

"And what were you doing at Berghoffs?" he asked, trying to deflect her attention.

"I had a job opportunity, a business lunch."

"And how did that go?"

"I don't really know. I had a little trouble concentrating."

He inched closer and Julianne tried to withdraw farther into the corner, but she was already wedged into it.

"It's over, Steve."

"You don't mean that." He fidgeted and she knew she'd caught him off guard.

"I'm dead serious."

"You're just upset about what you think you saw."

Julianne pushed up on her hands and leaned forward. "You're right. You know how things are with me and Suzanne. But that's only a fraction of it." She wanted to hurt him the way he'd hurt her. At the same time, she wanted him to deny it all, but she knew that would be a lie.

Steve pressed his lips together in a scowl. He sat silently, staring at her while she watched him attempt to think up the appropriate response.

Finally he sputtered out, "I can't talk to you when you're like this. And while we're on the subject, you expect me to believe you had a job interview over lunch?"

"It was business," she told him.

"What's the job?"

She glared at him. "What am I studying?"

He turned around, throwing his arms into the air. "Shit, Julie. I don't remember. I thought you were just going to stay at Kimball Brothers. How am I supposed to know what you're doing?" He spun around, ready with his next accusation. "There's another guy, isn't there? Someone you met at school? Is that what this is about? Found someone else to take you in?" He grabbed her shoulders. "You're mine, Julianne, and don't you forget it."

Julianne wrenched away, clenching her hands into fists. "I'm not the one screwing around," she reminded him.

His mouth curved and he shook his head as if trying to reason with a disobedient child. Steve got up off the bed, raised his arms up in the air and walked out of the bedroom.

Julianne exhaled a shuddering breath, still struggling against the sobs that threatened to rob her next mouthful of air. She grabbed for the pillow once more and held it tightly, needing to feel the solidity of something she could wrap her arms around.

Reaching for a tissue, she jumped at the sudden slam of the apartment door. She leaned against the wall, loneliness closing in around her. The computer beckoned – the community of friends she had come to know all those isolated nights while Steve slept.

To clear her thoughts, Julianne shook her head and pushed herself upright. During the past six months Jack had been there for her nearly every night, if not on the other end of the modem, in the body of an e-mail. They talked about work, they talked about life, they talked about their dreams.

Steve, on the other hand, went to the arcade, went to bed and went to work without ever stopping to ask about her day. He never asked about school, didn't want to hear about the promotion they'd offered her at Kimball Brothers, didn't even blink an eye when she told him Perkins & Stone had used one of her ideas in an ad campaign. When had he stopped caring?

That knowledge made her take a deep breath. The tears stopped and she sniffled.

Julianne resisted the urge to go to her computer, to reach out to the friend who had been there for her every day. Maybe chatting online hadn't meant as much to him. Maybe he didn't like the way she looked. She probably wasn't his type.

She crossed her legs underneath her and pulled her hands through her tangled hair. Squeezing her eyes shut, Julianne made an effort to push the pain aside. Daddy wasn't here to hold her anymore and in spite of what her mother tried to tell her, she could take care of herself.

Her resolve set, Julianne pushed herself off the bed and walked out into the living room of the apartment. With a cursory sweep around the apartment Julianne realized there was no hominess about it. The apartment felt cold and stark, like her feelings for Steve. Julianne shook her head and wondered what she'd ever seen in him in the first place. What had possessed her to ask him to move in – to agree to start a life with him?

He'd been there when her father died.

But somewhere along the line he stopped comforting her and it became more of a habit. There hadn't been a relationship for a long time.

"What a waste," Julianne muttered. As long as Steve had a set of keys to the apartment, she'd have to find another place to stay.

She reached for the suitcase on the top shelf of the coat closet and dropped it on her head when she heard Steve's voice suddenly beside her, deep and deadly. "What are you doing?"

"Do you want to give me back the keys to my apartment?"

"Very funny."

"The whole reason we moved in together was to spend more time together – plan for the wedding. I don't see any more of you now that I did before, and we hardly saw each other then." Julianne retrieved the suitcase and rubbed her head, carrying it into the bedroom and laying it on the bed.

Steve followed, his voice threatening. "Where do you think you're going? To him?" Julianne suppressed a shudder and wished there was someone else – anyone else – in the apartment with them, but she was ready for the inevitable argument.

"Don't put this off on me," she argued.

"I told you, Suzanne just stopped by the restaurant," he answered. "I didn't ask her out. I know how your sister is. You think I'm some kind of idiot?"

"It doesn't matter anymore." Julianne opened the suitcase.

Steve reached for the suitcase and closed it before she could put anything into it.

"I'm done, Steve. I'm moving out."

He sat down on the edge of the bed and grabbed her hand. "C'mon, Julie. Is this about the arcade? I know you want to buy a house. What is it?"

Julianne pulled her hand away. "It's about you and me. When's the last time we spent any time together? Seriously. We weren't spending any time together six months ago, so we thought we'd try the moving in thing. I see less of you now. We don't have a relationship, Steve. We haven't for a long time."

"So, what, you're saying you don't want to live together anymore?"

"I don't want anything anymore."

"But the wedding . . ."

Julianne put her hands on her hips. "I don't want to marry you, Steve."

"Next you'll be telling me you're in love with someone else." Steve stood up and advanced toward her, backing Julianne into a corner.

She pushed against his chest with both hands, fighting her way out of the corner. "If I followed you to the arcade, how many women would I see waiting for you?" She waved in the air. "It doesn't even matter about Suzanne."

"I already told you that wasn't what you think."

Julianne continued to back Steve away. "When you come home reeking of perfume is it because you were trying to buy a fragrance for me? Or do you just like trying on women's perfume?"

The panic reflected in his eyes while his brain struggled to invent a plausible excuse, but Julianne cut him off. "I don't want to marry you. And I don't believe you want to be tied down to one woman for the rest of your life. At least not this woman."

"You don't mean that." He shifted his weight from one foot to the other, his eyes darting all around the room.

"I'm dead serious. I want a faithful husband. I don't think you can do that."

Steve pressed his lips together in a scowl. He stood menacingly in the bedroom door. "Maybe if you said yes once I wouldn't be so interested in looking for it somewhere else."

His attack to her values felt like a slap across the face. "You said you could wait until we were married. You said it didn't matter and you'd respect my wishes."

"So you give it away to someone else? How do you just happen to go into Chicago for lunch?"

"I had a job interview. I've already told you that."

Steve waved an arm around the bedroom. "So you were just going to sneak off? Without telling me?"

"We covered this territory already. One of us has to go. Do you want to give me my keys?"

"You just need some cooling off time," he suggested. "I'll go."

Julianne rolled her eyes. "Right. Where you gonna go – room with the 'rat sniper' at work?"

"I was doing fine before I moved in here," he reminded her. "I don't need to room with anyone. Where do you think *you're* going to go? Your mother's?" He smirked and Julianne shuddered in response to the suggestion.

"I'm the one with the apartment," she pointed out. "I'm sure I could find another one."

Steve sighed and shook his hands. "Just give it a little time," he pleaded. "You're just mad at your sister."

"This isn't going to go away," Julianne told him. "I've been ignoring too much for too long. I'm done."

"It's wedding jitters."

Julianne's hands went to her hips. "It's facing the facts. Are you going to give me my keys or shall I get back to packing?"

Steve scowled, standing toe to toe with her. "I'll find a place to stay. I'll give you back your keys in a week if that's still what you want then."

"I don't trust you. I'm not staying here while you still have keys."

Steve stared at her, his nostrils flaring and his eyes menacing. "Suit yourself," he finally growled. He spun on his heels and stormed out of the apartment once more.

Julianne followed this time, turning the deadbolt and pulling the chain lock across the door behind him.

CHAPTER 6

The sun dipped below the horizon outside the balcony doors. Julianne slouched in the easy chair with a glass of wine in her hand watching the clouds burn various shades of red and yellow and orange while the sun disappeared. She hoped the wine would numb some of her frayed nerve endings.

Through the pleasant fog that settled around her brain, the telephone rang. With a sigh, she rose from her chair and walked wearily into the kitchen to answer the call.

"Hey, Jewel. You okay?" The sound of her brother-in-law, Bill's, voice cheered her.

"Better than I've been for a while."

"What happened with Steve?"

Julianne plopped onto a kitchen chair. "How much do you know?"

"She said she was trying to prevent you from making a mistake with your life."

Julianne rolled her eyes and chuckled. "That's original."

"I'm sorry, Jewel."

"Doesn't matter. We were already headed that way. She just helped things along."

"What happened?"

Julianne took a deep breath to repeat her story. "I had a job opportunity – a meeting at a restaurant in the City, trying to set myself up for when I get my degree."

"Wow! How'd that go?"

"I don't know. We're supposed to have another meeting, but I was so distracted when I saw them that I don't know what kind of impression I left. Mostly I'm just embarrassed."

"Yeah well, she was only trying to help, you know," Bill laughed. "Maybe I did marry the wrong sister."

"No, you wanted the flash. Now you have to live with it."

"I'm sorry, Jewel."

"Don't be silly."

"So this guy she saw you with?"

Julianne hesitated. "I told you about that teacher at school?"

"He was the job offer?"

"That remains to be seen."

Julianne could hear Suzanne's voice carry in the background. "Suzanne just told your mother he looks like an owl."

Julianne eyed her glass of wine sitting on the table in the living room where she'd left it. "Then maybe she won't bother to save me from him."

"You're a beautiful girl, Julianne. Not every man is going to find Suzanne more interesting. Don't sell yourself short."

"I didn't mean it that way."

Bill hesitated a moment, then asked, "And Steve?"

"Guess it all worked out for the best in the end."

"You're sure this is what you want?"

Julianne nodded, then took hold of her head when the effort made her dizzy. "It was a mistake from the beginning. I kept thinking things would change after we were married, but I don't believe that any more. Living together I got a glimpse of my future with Steve - stuck in a go nowhere job with a good for nothing husband whose bad habits I'd have to support. It's like someone turned on the lights."

On the other end of the phone, Julianne could hear Suzanne yell something at Bill. He laughed and told Julianne, "I took away her car keys." His voice became muffled as he addressed Suzanne. Suzanne made a rude remark that Julianne couldn't quite hear and then Bill talked to Julianne again. "I told her to let you live your own life."

"Bill. . ." Julianne hated listening to them argue. And she hated being part of their arguments.

The two sisters had been together, side by side, when Bill DePalma met them. Julianne had shown her interest in him first, but Suzanne picked up on Julianne's casual flirtations and stepped up to the plate. Suzanne, perfectly made up as usual, with her dark hair and dark eyes. Julianne rarely wore make-up. Taller and slighter than her sister, she felt more angular and less attractive. The poor guy never stood a chance. There hadn't really been a choice when it came down to it. Julianne backed off. She always backed off.

"Jewel," he whispered, "I don't know if we're going to make it."

"You'll find a way to make it work, Bill."

Bill sighed into the receiver. "What about you? What are you going to do now?"

Julianne rubbed her head where the headache was starting to take over. "Well I think using my degree would be a good start."

"Who says marriage isn't still out there for Julianne DeAngelo - career woman?"

"You know what my mother says: Men are intimidated by a career woman."

Bill laughed. "Some men find that a very attractive trait."

"I guess we'll find out."

"Do you like this guy?"

Julianne gave an exasperated sigh at Bill's inept matchmaking attempts, but he continued quickly. "Because if you do, Julianne, you should let him know. If you back off, so will he."

Julianne hesitated. Yeah, she liked Jack Guilder, but what chance did she have with him, a powerful ad exec? "It was a business lunch, Bill. That's all."

"You forget who you're talking to. I've heard you talk about this teacher. Trade one man for another."

"How often have you seen me do that?"

"I'm kidding. No one would see it that way."

"I need to focus on my priorities. Right now that means getting this degree. I don't need any other distractions and I don't want to have to rely on some man as a crutch. I can take care of myself."

"We all know you can take care of yourself, Julianne, much to the chagrin of your mother. Maybe if you stopped expecting to lose you might win," he suggested.

"What's that supposed to mean?" The tears were threatening just below the surface again.

"Love is a game, Julianne. Maybe you should try saying yes once."

"If love is just a game, I think it's time for a time-out. I said yes to Steve and look where that got me."

Suzanne's voice was shrill across the phone line. "Are you on the phone? Who are you talking to? You're talking to her, aren't you?"

"I better go," Bill whispered. "Call me if you need anything."

"I'm fine," she assured him. "Go make up with my sister."

CHAPTER 7

At 3 a.m., the illuminated numbers of Julianne's alarm clock stared back at her, daring her to ignore their beacon. Julianne rose from the bed and made her way to her desk, unable to resist any longer.

She sat down in front of the computer and leaned back in the chair while the modem screeched. Moments later she was among her on-line community of friends. In the dark of the apartment, the glow of the monitor reached out to draw her in.

Julianne laid a hand on the smooth, cold surface of the computer mouse to open an e-mail from JGGuilder.

"Hope you're feeling better. Don't want you to feel obligated to the Hayden deal. I'll see it through. J."

The Hayden deal. Without it, she might as well marry Steve and stay in the mire of her job at Kimball Brothers, competing with all the other secretaries for who could type faster and run harder than the rest to win the position of indispensable, under-appreciated assistant.

As if she needed confirmation that their lunch had been a flop. Evidently one meeting with her was enough to satisfy Jack Guilder's curiosity about the woman he spent his nights with on-line.

Julianne sat up and navigated the screens. He was always online somewhere this time of night. With a glance at the stone statue hanging over her computer, she typed in his screen name and sent out the query.

"JGGuilder is not on-line," came the response seconds later.

"Naturally," she said quietly. She returned to his e-mail and began typing a return message. Closing her eyes, she took a deep breath to compose her thoughts into an unemotional business memo.

"I would have thought you'd be sleeping." The message from JGGuilder popped up midway through her second sentence.

"There you are," she said out loud.

"Chat?"

She opened up a private chat room and invited him in. "I want to do the Hayden presentation," she typed, waiting to send until she saw his name appear in the participant box.

There was no response for several seconds. "I know how busy you are with the wedding and all. We could probably just do this the way we did the Preston deal."

Julianne stared at the screen, shaken by his disinclination to see her again. "So I keep feeding you ideas and you get all the credit?"

"You met Hayden. You know you'll get credit on this."

Her fingers banged sharply against the keys while she typed out her next response. "Then why are you pushing me out of the meeting? He asked me to be there."

The screen sat silent, the cursor blinking out the minutes until his reply came up. "Doing it this way has worked pretty well for us so far."

Her cheeks flushed hot with indignation. "Then why'd you ask me to go to lunch in the first place?" Her breathing went shallow, afraid of his next response. Every nerve tingled in anticipation, waiting for the brush off personally, professionally: both.

"Bad luck to borrow a woman who's spoken for."

"And if I wasn't 'spoken for'?"

"Rhetorical."

She struggled between telling him she'd called off the engagement and the principle of the matter. Whatever he thought of her, whatever she hoped for from him, suddenly the most important thing was making that presentation to Ben Hayden. It was her entrée into the business.

"I want to do the presentation." She typed deliberately. "I *need* to do the presentation," she said out loud.

"I'd rather lose the deal."

She stared at the screen with her mouth gaping open and fell back against her chair.

Interminable seconds passed before another line of type appeared. "You're the one that said you had a lot on your plate."

"How are you going to tell Mr. Hayden you lied to him?" she typed.

"I'll sell him my ideas as yours and explain to him how you're still recovering from the flu."

Another lie. "He said he wanted me at the presentation."

"He'll excuse you under the circumstances."

Julianne sat straight again and placed both hands back on the keyboard. "He's not the type to be easily fooled."

"He believed we were married, didn't he?"

Julianne's mind raced with the development of an idea. She knew how to find out when the meeting was and she intended to be there. "You can help me or not, but I'm part of this now. This presentation is important to me."

"Send me what you've got. I'd be happy to present it."

"Oooh!" Julianne muttered in frustration. "Maybe you don't like the way I look, Jack Guilder, but I sure as hell appealed to Ben Hayden," she shouted at the screen.

She exited the chat room and moved into the advertising forum. She prepared presentations dozens of times in her marketing classes. Although she knew she lacked seasoned professionalism, she believed Ben Hayden would forgive her any amateurish blunders.

* * *

Julianne checked her watch again, anxiously waiting for 5:00. It was the longest Friday she could remember for a long time. All day she'd been distracted, writing down ideas. She planned to spend the entire weekend holed up in the apartment developing her presentation.

She began the day with the call to Perkins & Stone.

"May I speak with Dorian, please?" Julianne asked in her most officious voice. When she was connected, she continued her charade. "Hello, this is Mr. Hayden's secretary speaking. I'm so sorry to trouble you, but it seems Mr. Hayden forgot which day he made his appointment with Mr. Guilder. Do you have Mr. Guilder's calendar?"

"Yes, of course," the woman replied. "Mr. Guilder has Mr. Hayden down for 9:00 next Thursday morning."

"He couldn't remember if it was Tuesday or Thursday and then he was worried about a meeting he'd already scheduled on Tuesday. Thursday's no problem. At Perkins & Stone?"

"With Mr. Guilder and Mr. Stone," Jack's secretary confirmed.

"Thank you so much." Julianne hung up the phone, smiling at her simple deception. She had less than a week to prepare an ad campaign for a product she knew very little about. With a little luck, she could also use it toward her final grade and her degree as well.

"Julianne, can you step into my office a minute?" John Thomas asked the question on the way by without waiting for her reply.

She wondered if he noticed she had been staring blankly at her computer for the past 15 minutes. Maybe her request to courier to the Chicago office the following week was crossing his desk.

There was only one way to find out. Julianne rose from her desk, taking a notepad and a pen with her.

"JT."

He sat back, staring at her for several moments before he spoke. "I hear you got sick yesterday when you went into the city."

Swallowing down the lump in her throat, Julianne nodded.

JT leaned forward on his desk, playing with a pen in his hands. He raised his eyes to address her again and waved for her to sit down.

Julianne looked at her watch again and eased into the chair, wondering why he had waited to call her in until the end of the day. JT's modus operandi tended toward distraction and rarely consisted of the amount of eye contact she was getting from him. She squirmed in the chair.

He stood up and walked around her to close the door. His lanky frame inclined toward her, he sat on the corner of his desk in front of Julianne. "Did I hear you called the wedding off?"

Julianne nodded, not meeting her boss's intrusive stare.

"Glad someone finally knocked some sense into you. He was never right for you."

Julianne squinted, raising her head to address his remarks. "And you would be in a position to know who is right for me?"

JT examined his fingernails, picking at one of them. "Let's just say I think you could get more out of life." He looked casually over his hand at her. "I know we've talked about this before . . ."

"JT," she interrupted, but he held a hand up to stall her argument.

"While you were out, I got the transfer. They didn't give me much choice." He leaned forward and took one of her hands. "I want you to transfer with me."

He wasn't exuding his normal little boy charm. In fact his dark eyes made her very uncomfortable. "I like my job just the way it is," she told him.

"I'm trying to give you the chance to make the right decision, Julianne."

JT slid off the desk, crouched down beside her and whispered into her ear. "Transfer to marketing with me." He lingered a moment too long and Julianne realized he was inhaling her perfume.

Julianne rose to her feet and pulled away from JT. "Please tell me you're not implying what I think you are."

"I can make it worth your while." He rose to his full height, a mere two inches taller than Julianne, and ran a finger down the length of her arm.

Julianne shivered and stepped back. "You should stop now."

"You don't really have a reason to turn it down, Jule. The work falls in line with the degree you're working toward, you and I will still be working together . . ." He took a step closer to her and reached for her hand.

"You're walking a fine line, boss."

"You're a smart girl, Julianne. Think it through. We complement each other pretty well in the office . . ." He let the sentence trail into innuendo.

"Let's just keep it that way, shall we?"

His nose brushed against her hair, his voice low in her ear once more. "We could make this new department work, Julianne. You and me. I'm sure there would be travel opportunities for us."

Julianne could feel the warmth of his breath on her neck, could smell his cologne. She shivered with revulsion and pulled her hand away. "There is no you and me, JT."

He remained only inches away from her, invading her invisible field of personal space.

"Back off," she threatened, pushing him away. When she opened the door of his office, her shoulders released the tension. Signs of bustle in the office outside offered protection from his insinuations.

He returned to the chair behind his desk. "Why do you want to courier into Chicago next week?"

Julianne froze in her steps. There was no way he could know, unless Jack had called him . . . "One of the girls downtown asked for some help so I offered to take the courier run that day." She could feel her hands shaking and hoped he didn't notice her notepad quivering. She never had to lie about a day off before.

"There hasn't been much courier activity lately, maybe you can get back before the end of the day." He raised his eyes to meet hers once more. "I have a lot of things to clear off my desk before the transfer."

Julianne nodded, and turned to leave.

"Julianne," he halted her, "you need to think about this position seriously."

He had an odd smile on his face and she knew there was more, but she wasn't going to give him the satisfaction of asking. They stared each other down for several minutes before he finally spoke again.

"With my transfer, there probably won't be a need for your position in this department. The other girls can pick up any slack." To make sure she understood the full impact of his remarks, he added, "and I don't think there are any other openings at the moment."

"I'll try to be back before the end of the day on Thursday," she lied.

She was going to get that job at Perkins & Stone even if she had to go around Jack to do it.

CHAPTER 8

Walking into an office building in the "big city" was always intimidating for Julianne - even the downtown offices of Kimball Brothers where she routinely visited.

The reception area of Perkins & Stone was elegantly decorated in brass and glass. Julianne held her portfolio case tightly to control the shaking of her hands. It was 8:55. She had five minutes to bluff her way into the meeting with Ben Hayden.

The receptionist had a matronly air about her, gray hair over a pleasantly wrinkled face. Her eyes were a washed out blue. "Can I help you?"

Julianne straightened and gave the woman a confident smile. "I have an appointment with Jack Guilder," she began. "I wonder if you could direct me to his secretary? There are a few things I'd like to give her in preparation."

The receptionist's face stiffened only slightly, but enough for Julianne to know she was under suspicion. The Hayden casual clothes that she selected were the least offensive of the line, but Julianne still felt horribly underdressed for a client presentation.

"Mr. Guilder is with a client," the receptionist replied formally.

"I know - Mr. Hayden. I'm here to assist with the presentation." She displayed the clothing she wore with a sweep of her available arm. "Hayden's casual wear. Will you tell Dorian I'm here please?"

The receptionist picked up the phone reluctantly and spoke to the secretary requested. After a few moments, she hung up the phone again and smiled sweetly. "Dorian isn't aware of anyone else expected for the meeting, but *she'll* be right with you."

Julianne flashed her brightest smile. "Thank you." She walked around the reception area, taking in the modern decor. Chairs were lined up, two each against two walls with a coffee table between them. Periodicals lay on the table in wait of visitors whose meetings might be delayed.

Behind the receptionist, a door opened. Dorian Lannon was small and slender, her frosted blond hair permed into tight curls. Dressed in a blue pinstripe suit, she made Julianne even more aware of the casual wear she adopted for the meeting.

"Can I help you?" the secretary asked warily.

"Dorian." Julianne looked at the receptionist who was smiling smugly. "I'm sure Jack filled you in. I'm Julianne DeAngelo." She glided forward to shake Dorian's hand, but Jack's secretary rebuffed her. Julianne's bluff wasn't working.

"I'm sorry, I don't know you." Dorian turned to walk back into the office area, but Julianne allayed her.

"Surely Jack told you I was coming. I know I look underdressed, but it's part of the presentation. Hayden Casualwear?" She looked from the receptionist back to Dorian. "Can we talk in private?"

Dorian's eyes narrowed before she nodded. She opened the security door and invited Julianne into the business offices.

Dorian crossed her arms in the narrow hallway, blocking Julianne's progress. "All right, what do you want to talk about?"

"He hired me to pose as his wife. Ben Hayden represents a family oriented company and prefers a family image. But I'm sure you know all this," Julianne explained. "Mr. Hayden asked me to be at the presentation today." She shook her hands in exasperation. "If you don't believe me, go tell them Jack's wife is here. See what happens. If I'm lying, the worst you'll have to do is apologize for interrupting them." Dorian's face reflected her skepticism, but Julianne persisted. "Mr. Hayden is expecting me to be there. If they don't get this account because you prevented my being at the meeting I don't imagine Jack will be very pleased."

"Look, I don't know who you are, but I'm not going to play your game."

"I'll wait right here until you've talked to them," Julianne promised. "I won't follow you, so I won't know where they are. I'm not trying to impose myself on them. I was invited." She shook her head again, putting forth her best impatience with the situation. "I can't believe they didn't tell you I was coming. Would you wear these clothes if you didn't have to?" She waved a free hand in front of her outfit once more.

Dorian uncrossed her arms. "Come with me." She led Julianne down the corridor to a small conference room. Julianne read doubt in her face but she knew she had broken through. "You wait here," Dorian instructed.

Julianne blew out a breath, clutching at her portfolio with both hands. She was gambling heavily on the first impression she made on Ben Hayden. Dorian would either usher her into the meeting or security would escort her out of the building.

Dorian returned in less than five minutes, red-faced and less composed than when she left. Julianne rose from her seat behind the round conference table. "So am I lying?"

"Mr. Guilder asked me to tell you to go home and rest, that you shouldn't be out."

Julianne stood her ground. She had impressed Ben Hayden, but she had impressed Jack Guilder, too, in a different way. He seemed anxious to wash his hands of his wife. She could feel her pulse racing as her mind struggled for an excuse to stay until she found a way into that meeting.

"But he confirmed my story?" Julianne asked, buying time.

"No," Dorian answered, "It won't take Ben Hayden long to realize that Jack Guilder is not interested in a wife."

"Mrs. Guilder!" Ben Hayden appeared in the corridor with his hands in front of him.

Julianne smiled triumphantly and let out a sigh of relief. "Mr. Hayden. How nice to see you again."

"You know that husband of yours is quite upset about your being out. Are you sure you're well enough to sit in?"

"I assure you I'm quite well. He's naturally a little overprotective."

Mr. Hayden embraced her and then held her out at arms length. "You look wonderful."

Julianne tilted her head. "I was hoping to sit in on the meeting." She looked past Mr. Hayden to see Jack hurrying down the hallway, his expression concealed behind his beard. "I know you'll love John's layout, but I was a little worried he might have modified my input a little too much. I wanted to make sure you found it satisfactory."

"Julianne, I told you to stay home and rest," Jack scolded with a nervous glance at his secretary.

"I'm tired of resting," she argued. "I'm really quite well. I promise to sit quietly in the corner. I was just telling Mr. Hayden that I'm sure he'll love what you've done with the layout." She turned to the rotund prospect one more time and winked. "He really is quite brilliant, you know."

"Come along in then," Mr. Hayden invited. "You might as well sit in since you're here. You don't mind such a pleasant distraction, do you?" he asked Jack.

Jack took Julianne's arm, squeezing it to show his displeasure, and led her back toward the conference room. "Alec was just asking about you," he told Julianne, nodding toward the conference room. "It's been quite a while since you two have seen each other, hasn't it?"

Julianne looked up into Jack's large, round eyes, picking up the lead. "Alec? Why yes. When was the last time I saw him?"

"I should think you'd see him rather often," Mr. Hayden commented, "what with him being Jack's godfather and all."

"Oh, we do," Julianne bluffed, "normally, but with the last couple of months being so busy and all, it has been a while."

The corner conference room held a round table circled with chairs and a white board against one wall. On the table a computer was connected to the projection system. She hadn't missed the presentation yet. The aroma of fresh coffee filled the closed room.

Julianne smiled broadly and walked across the room to embrace a tall, thin man with salt and pepper hair dressed in a glen plaid suit. "Alec. It's good to see you."

Alec looked to Jack, holding Julianne's shoulders tentatively. "How are you, my dear?"

"I'm really doing quite well, although Jack has been coddling me a little too much. As usual." She flashed a sassy smile over her shoulder. "I promise to sit quietly in the corner and not speak unless spoken to."

Alec's smile wavered and she sensed his uncertainty. "It will be a pleasure to have you with us."

Julianne took a seat at the table beside Mr. Hayden, who patted her hand. Alec stood beside a panel of windows darkened by horizontal blinds and crossed his arms across his chest while Jack took his place beside the white board to begin his presentation.

"All women like to know that they are appealing to the opposite sex," Jack began. "The basis of most ad campaigns is grounded in the fact that sex sells." He turned on the display and started his computer program. A series of pictures projected onto the white board as Jack outlined his advertising scheme consisting of men finding a woman dressed in Hayden Casualwear irresistible.

Ben Hayden shifted uncomfortably in his seat. "And these are your ideas, too, Mrs. Guilder?" He interrupted.

"Please, hear him out," Julianne deferred. "He's really the brains in the family. He's blended some of my ideas into his, but I have to give him the creative edge. It's what he's best at." She nodded toward the layout projected before them. "Let him finish."

"I've worked up another layout," Jack offered, "if you don't find this to your liking." He canceled the program he was running and began another screen show.

Midway through it, the round little man stood up. "I'm sorry, Guilder, but I don't see the feminine touch in your layouts. This isn't what I wanted at all." He looked at Julianne apologetically. "I was really hoping for something more."

"We could start from scratch," she suggested. "I brought my original layouts with me. I'm sure with Jack's input, we could blend them a little more to your liking - my feminine approach with Jack's industry savvy, I mean."

Ben sat down at the table once more. "I'd like to see your layouts, Mrs. Guilder. I have a feeling that you let your husband run roughshod over your ideas. I will admit he's a brilliant ad man, that's why I agreed to let him bid on my business. But he's way off the mark with what he's showing me."

Julianne looked across the room to the owl-eyed man at the white board. "I think Dorian has my portfolio. Can you ask her to bring it in?"

His jaw worked beneath the close cropped beard as he picked up a telephone in the conference room and punched in a series of numbers. "Could you bring in my wife's portfolio?" he instructed in a deep voice.

Dorian appeared at the door almost instantly carrying the black leather case. Julianne rose to meet her and, taking the case, unzipped it.

"It's rather amateurish," she submitted, "and I didn't put it into the CAD program like John's." She pulled out the heavy cardboard pictures and put them on the table. Alec sent a significant glance Jack's way. Jack shrugged in response, shifting on his feet as he watched Julianne pull out her layout boards.

"In this first one," she began, "I have a woman sitting alone reading a book. The caption is 'I want to look good when I'm comfortable, even if I expect to be alone.' Kind of Garbo, you know." She looked nervously at Mr. Hayden who was nodding his head speculatively. She turned over the board and showed him the next.

"Or we could follow John's theory that sex sells on a gentler note. A husband comes home from work and his wife is wearing Hayden Casualwear. He says: 'You always look so nice, even when we don't have anywhere to go,' and she responds, 'It's easy with Hayden casual wear. It's so comfortable.'"

"Simple . . . but I like it," Hayden stated. He slapped Jack on the back. "You can still wear the pants in the family even if your wife does good work. These layouts don't need any blending. I think they're top notch."

Jack's cheeks burned red beneath his beard. "I was just going with the trends," he explained.

"Sometimes you have to set the trends."

Alec stepped forward. "Do we have a deal then?" he asked, extending his hand to Hayden.

Ben took Alec's hand, holding it in his own for a minute. "Only if you keep this little lady involved. She has a pulse on my views." He crossed the room smiling broadly. "Not only that, I want you to be in my commercial."

Julianne blanched. "I don't have any modeling experience."

Ben Hayden motioned to the clothes she was wearing. "You're doing a fine job right now. I've never seen my line of clothing look better."

"We couldn't do that," Jack seconded. "We have professionals lined up that I'm sure you would prefer."

"I want Julianne to be my spokesperson," Hayden insisted. "She suits the campaign perfectly. Right to the braid in her hair." He pointed to the layout on the table and motioned to Julianne's auburn hair pulled back into a thick french braid hanging over one shoulder.

"I-I'm flattered," she sputtered, "but I really don't think . . ."

"I'm paying the bills for this deal, and that's what I want. You make the commercial or I'll take my business somewhere else, and I'd hate to do that after what I've seen. You'd be perfect."

Jack and Alec exchanged glances.

"I'll make you a deal," Alec proposed. "We give Julianne three takes, then we bring in one of our actresses. You make the final decision, but give us the opportunity to prove you wrong." He nodded toward Julianne. "Not that we don't think Mrs. Guilder capable, but it really should be done by a professional."

"I agree," Julianne added.

Hayden nodded his round head in agreement. "Alright, sold."

"Why don't we go to my office and iron out the details," Alec suggested, opening the door of the conference room and leading Hayden out.

Jack sat down heavily behind the table and held his head in his hands. Julianne watched, putting a hand to her mouth and trying not to be disappointed by his lack of enthusiasm for her presentation.

"I didn't mean to steal your thunder," she apologized.

He looked up at her, his eyes opened wider than normal in surprise. "You saved the day. He hated my layouts." Jack got up to stand beside her. "I asked you not to come. Why did you?"

"Let's just call it my homework."

Leaning over, he wrapped one arm across her back and gave her a quick hug. "I owe you."

"That's what friends are for."

Dropping his hand, he turned away and looked through the horizontal blinds at the city below.

"I know you didn't want me to come," she began, reading his apprehension, "but this was very important to me."

"Your layouts are very simplistic, very amateurish." He laughed and raised his face toward the ceiling. "And I should be thanking you."

Julianne looked through the open door into the office, catching the curious stares of several employees. "Maybe you can help me there. I was wondering . . . you see, it seems I've created a problem for myself. I almost hate to ask you, but is there a chance Perkins & Stone would hire me?"

He turned to face her again, his voice skeptical. "You want a job?"

She winced, put off by his apparent distaste for the idea, but not sure how much she could tell him about JT and her job at Kimball Brothers.

Jack walked over and closed the door before addressing her request. His eyes squinted into large ovals. "Look, Julie, I'm glad you came, I really am, but I can't. You'll get paid, as a subcontractor. You'll also get paid for making the commercial. I just don't think I could get you in here."

"I know I don't have my degree yet, maybe as a secretary? I really need the job. Look, I realize I'm not quite what you expected. . . "

He turned to face her. "You want compliments? I can't do it, Julie. You're engaged."

The door to the conference room boomed open, Ben Hayden's sparkling blue eyes alight with laughter. "Sorry to interrupt, but I thought of something else I wanted to talk over with you. By the way, Mrs. Guilder, weren't you wearing rings when we had lunch?"

Julianne looked at her naked fingers. "The jewelers," she answered. "They needed to be sized. We were walking past the jewelry store just the other day and I asked John if he'd mind. I've been putting it off for a long time."

"That's right," Jack added.

Hayden studied them suspiciously and then continued. "I've decided to shoot the commercial in Mexico. A little time away from home. Let's schedule it for next week."

"I couldn't," Julianne gasped.

"I can't possibly clear my calendar," Jack added. "Such short notice . . ."

"Nonsense. The fees you'll charge my account will no doubt pay for the inconvenience."

Alec Stone stood behind Hayden holding the unsigned agreement over the client's head. "I can handle anything you can't reschedule," he suggested to Jack. His steel blue eyes shifted to Julianne with a plea as he pointed to the piece of paper in his hands.

"Julie's schedule is extremely heavy next week," Jack argued. "I've already made her put off a lot of her appointments."

"Surely you make enough to cover her losses," Hayden answered. "And she'll be getting paid for being there."

"How much?" Julianne asked Jack indelicately.

Jack rubbed his chin through his beard thoughtfully and looked at Alec considering his options. "Subcontractor wages and union scale for the commercial – I'd say you could probably clear your schedule for three months without feeling a crunch. But would it jeopardize your clientele long-term?" He emphasized clientele, making it clear he referred to her job at Kimball Brothers.

Julianne sat down hard. "And if I don't go?"

"That layout proves you've got what I want. I'd be mighty disappointed to have to go somewhere else now," Hayden pressured.

Jack shook his head. "I can't ask you to do this."

"I'll go," Julianne answered, standing up again.

It was Jack's turn to sit down. "I could probably send Tyler along," he suggested. "He knows his way around a commercial shoot."

"I don't want anyone else, I want you," Ben Hayden boomed. "Don't you want to have an all expenses paid vacation with your wife?"

His emphasis on the word "wife" made Julianne tense into a shrug.

Jack stood up and placed his hands firmly on her shoulders. "When do we leave?"

* * *

"If you wait a couple more weeks we could make it our honeymoon," Steve suggested, resting against the doorframe of her bedroom.

Julianne leaned over the bed and stared into the suitcase. "There won't be a honeymoon. There isn't going to be a wedding."

"You're just upset about Suzanne. If you'd just give it some time . . ."

Julianne wheeled around and faced him with a glare. "I've given you two years. It's over, Steve."

"Maybe this vacation is just what you need," he said quietly. "You'll feel differently when you get back."

With an exasperated sigh, she went back to her packing. "You can't have it all, Steve. Think about it. You don't really want me. If you did, you would have been putting more time into the relationship and not running around at the arcade."

"You are nuts," he grumbled. "You're mine, Julianne. You've always been mine. You can't just say it's over, just like that, and fly off to Mexico. If anyone should be pissed off, it oughtta be me. You just up and quit Kimball Brothers, a perfectly good job, and you expect me to believe this trip to Mexico is actually work?" He grabbed her shoulder, turning Julianne to face him. "You're screwing that guy you had lunch with, aren't you? Is that why you wouldn't let me touch you all this time? You're no better than that sister of yours."

"Stop it!" she shouted. "I'm not screwing anybody else, Steve. And I'm not screwing you, either. Now get out of here and let me pack in peace, will you please?"

He gave her a grim smile of satisfaction. "You'll come back to me."

"Believe whatever you have to," she grumbled, throwing the rest of her clothes from the bed into the suitcase.

Steve reached around her and pulled out a strapless sundress. "You gonna wear this?"

She grabbed it back from him, refolding it and laying it back into the suitcase. "It's hot in Mexico. Can't you just leave?"

"Yeah, but you can't wear a bra with this."

"So?"

"You gonna be around a lot of people or is it just going to be a cozy little job down there in Mexico?"

Julianne closed the suitcase and turned, her hands on her hips. "The things you find provocative always amaze me. It's not like I'd be falling out of the top, and the skirt goes nearly to my ankles."

"They won't be looking at your ankles in that dress."

"Please go," she whined. "I have a lot to do before I leave and I don't want to spend all my time justifying my wardrobe to you."

He stood beside her, the hurt reflected in his eyes. "I love you, Julianne. I don't want you to go."

She shook her head. "It won't work, Steve. You made your choice, now I've made mine."

"But it would be different after we were married."

"It doesn't matter anymore."

"You just think that's what you want because you're still upset. You'll change your mind after you've had some time to cool down."

"Sure," she agreed, pushing past him into the dining room. "Why don't you go on down to the bar and play a few games while I finish getting myself together."

"I'll be here when you get back," he promised.

She waited until he left the apartment before she answered him. "I wish you wouldn't," she whispered to the closed door.

* * *

"What about the job at Kimball Brothers?" Bill asked his sister-in-law.

Julianne carried the cordless phone into the galley kitchen. "I quit."

"They've been very good to you."

"A little too good. Have you heard the term sexual harassment?"

"Not JT?"

"Yes. JT."

"But he has all those kids."

"And he's been married twice."

Bill let out a low whistle and then Julianne heard him take a deep breath. "I'm divorcing Suzanne."

It was the first time he'd actually said the words. Julianne was so surprised she fell into the chair near the phone. "You'll work it out."

"Not this time."

"You shouldn't have Steve to worry about anymore. He's in the reject pile. She loses interest once she's won."

"It's not Steve. He was just a side trip. She's had someone else for a long time now. I have to let her go. It isn't me she wants, and I can't accept a relationship on that basis."

"Are you sure?" Julianne asked.

Bill was quiet for a few minutes, then he asked, "Let me go with you?"

Julianne closed her eyes and smoothed her forehead with one hand. "I couldn't do that, Bill."

"You could get even with her. After all the times she's done it to you - and I want to, Jewel. I should have chosen you in the first place."

"You don't want me, Bill. If you did, you *would* have chosen me in the first place. Besides, maybe I don't want you."

"Ouch."

Julianne smiled affectionately. "You know what I mean. Even after all Suzanne's done to me, I couldn't do that to her. She is my sister after all."

"I could still go with, just to make sure you stay out of trouble."

"I was hired to be a wife."

"Excuse me? So now you're prostituting yourself?"

"He knows I'm engaged. Was engaged. If he had his way we wouldn't be going at all. I don't think he's interested in any kind of relationship."

"But you are."

Bill's ability to see through her unnerved Julianne. "Says who?"

"Who is this guy?"

"The teacher I've been corresponding with online."

"Ohhh. The owl guy?"

"His name's John. I mean Jack Guilder."

"For someone who's not interested in a relationship, he seems to be showing a lot of interest in you so far."

"He's just being polite. Besides, he keeps reminding me that I'm spoken for." Julianne frowned, wishing she had the courage to tell Jack the truth. "It was the client that put us up to this. If it were up to Jack, he wouldn't have even let me into the meeting."

"Mm hmm," Bill hummed. "The unattainable glass princess. He's afraid to touch you for fear the illusion will break."

"You mean if he thought I was available he might not be interested in me?" She bit her bottom lip.

"Maybe he just has principles. Something certain members of your family seem to be lacking."

Julianne laughed. "He lies like a rug. I can't believe anyone who can come up with the stories he can could possibly maintain sexual integrity."

"Every man has his faults. I'll bet Steve never lied to you. Didn't you mention something about trade-offs? What's more important to you?"

Julianne considered his point. She had to admit that Steve never lied to her. Maybe Bill was right, but she chose to reject his theory. "I'm entitled to do as I please."

"Don't overdo it, Julianne." She heard Bill sigh on the other end of the phone. "Right now I'd rather see your face across the dinner table from me than your sister's. And I'll tell you honestly, I'd rather have you lying beside me at night."

"Don't divorce my sister with that expectation in mind."

"I'm not all that bad to look at."

"Some of us do have principles."

"Some advice then," Bill offered. "How many men have you had, Julianne?"

"Why does everyone think the world revolves around sex?"

"Let me rephrase. How many boyfriends?"

Her silence confirmed what he already knew. "Time to come out of your ivory tower. In this day and age it's awful tough for Prince Charming to find you up there. He needs to know you want to be rescued."

"Oh go to hell. I don't believe in fairy tales."

"Sometimes I love you more than her."

"Will you give me a ride to the airport, then?"

Bill laughed. "You know I will."

* * *

Jack took her arm and led her away from where Ben Hayden sat waiting. "You're really coming?" He whispered.

"Should I leave?"

He looked nervously down the terminal. "What did you tell Steve?" He held up her hand. "And where are your rings?"

Julianne's heart was pounding. She hadn't anticipated him trying to stall her out. Bill's words echoed in her memory: "The unattainable glass princess. He's afraid to touch you for fear the illusion will break."

"You don't want to hear the answers to those questions." She pulled away from his grip and looked him over.

In the blue jeans he wore to travel his legs were long and thin. His polo shirt exposed well-developed biceps, a sharp contrast to Steve's thin arms.

"Are you afraid I'll take advantage of you? Me? An engaged woman?"

"Damn it, Julie. Don't tease me."

"I'll make you a promise, John. As soon as the commercial's finished I'll disappear off the face of the earth." She rolled her eyes. "Jeez, I thought we were at least friends."

"We are friends," he said in a low voice, turning first toward her and then away again. "Your fiancé doesn't mind you spending a week with another man?"

She hesitated, trying to decide if she should tell him the engagement was over – the wedding was off. She wondered if her appeal was in being unattainable and if he would shy away if he discovered she was available. "It's not like we're really spending it together, is it?"

He bent down to look in her face. "It's not as if we'll have separate bedrooms, *Darling*. We have a front to keep up."

Julianne bit the insides of her cheeks to keep from smiling. "I hadn't thought of that," she replied coyly. "I'll sleep on the floor if it'll make you more comfortable."

"I'll sleep on the floor," he corrected her, taking her by the arm and escorting her to the terminal. "If we get through this intact, I'll be amazed."

"Dorian seems to think Hayden will see through our little charade. She told me Hayden would realize sooner or later that you weren't ever likely to have a wife. Do you think she could be right?"

Jack relaxed his hold on her. His mouth lifted into a smile beneath the smooth brown beard. "Tell me something, Julie. What would you think of a bachelor over 30 who doesn't regularly keep the company of a woman?"

Julianne stopped in her tracks and stared at him. "Something you forgot to mention on-line at 3 a.m.?"

"People do draw their own conclusions."

"And are 'people' correct?"

He cupped her chin with his hands. "You can make your own assessment. We'll be spending the next week in very close company."

Julianne's heart pounded in her chest. Was he propositioning her or trying to tell her something? It was the first time she considered the trip might be a mistake.

"Mrs. Guilder, how delightful to see you." Ben Hayden rose from his seat and clasped her hands in his. "I was quite surprised when you didn't come together, but then Jack explained to me about his meeting at the office. Let me introduce my wife, Dorothy."

Julianne nodded and extended one of her hands to the plump woman seated beside Ben Hayden. "Mrs. Hayden. It's a pleasure to meet you."

A hand landed on Julianne's shoulder. "Julianne." She turned to face Bill DePalma. Bill held out his hand to Jack. "Good to see you again, Jack."

"Mr. and Mrs. Hayden, this is my brother-in-law, Bill DePalma," Julianne introduced. "He was gracious enough to give me a ride to the airport when Jack had to go into the office."

"Your brother-in-law?" Hayden asked.

"Her sister's husband," Bill explained, taking Ben's outstretched hand. "Julie, I just wanted to wish you a safe trip. And good luck." Bill slapped Jack on the back. "Take care of her, old man. I just wanted to make sure I delivered her safely."

"Thanks, Bill," Jack's brow furrowed.

"We'll have to get together when we all get back home." Bill winked at Jack and turned to walk away. "See you in a week."

"Is your sister as lovely as you?" Mrs. Hayden asked.

With a resigned smile, Julianne told them, "She's the pretty one."

"Somehow I doubt that," Jack whispered to her quietly.

"They're boarding us," Ben announced. "You'll love Acapulco."

* * *

For most of the flight and another hour en route to the hotel Julianne and Jack hardly spoke. The Hayden's carried most of the conversation, telling Julianne and Jack about their three daughters and their families.

When they finally reached the solitude of the hotel room, Jack and Julianne remained silent.

White stuccoed walls opened out onto a veranda that overlooked the hotel pool, the turquoise waters of the Pacific Ocean beyond. From that vantage point, Julianne surveyed the hotels and the beaches where dozens of small huts dotted the sand. The ocean shimmered in the late afternoon sun. A cruise ship loomed large in port.

The humidity seemed to crawl inside her hair, filling it out with frizzled curls that would otherwise lay dormant. The smell of wet sand and algae hung in the air, a beachy scent that Julianne remembered from childhood.

She closed her eyes and pictured her father, running in the sand with her at the Illinois Beach, pulling a kite until it soared over them.

"He thinks you're with your sister?"

"Hmmmm?"

"Steve." Jack opened his suitcase and extracted his shaving kit, laying it on the dresser at the foot of the bed.

She turned lazily to look at him and realized what he said. Julianne reached for her ring finger reflexively to turn the bands that were no longer there. "Isn't it beautiful here?"

"I've seen it before."

"Does that make it less beautiful?"

He stood tall, his hands by his sides as he gave her a mildly reproving look. "How often do you do this sort of thing?"

"What sort of thing?" She sauntered back into the room from the veranda.

He nodded at their surroundings, raising his eyebrows to remind her of the intimacy of their situation.

"Did I miss something?" She lifted her suitcase onto the corner of the bed avoiding his eyes.

They continued to unpack in a silent standoff.

When Julianne looked up, she found Jack staring at her. She put her hands on her hips. "Okay, here it is. I believe in commitment and I believe in fidelity. This," she waved an arm around the close quarters they were to share, "is a business arrangement. Have I misunderstood the purpose of this trip?"

"Why did you come?"

"I didn't think I had a choice." She turned her back to Jack and unpacked the sundress Steve found so shocking from her suitcase.

"There's always a choice."

"Life is a series of trade-offs. Steve doesn't make enough to support me even if I wanted him to. I'll have my degree in a couple more months. Ben Hayden can help me jumpstart my career."

"And when he finds we've been lying to him? You still think he'll stand behind you?"

She threw her toiletry bag on the bed and turned to face Jack, her hands returning to her hips. "And what about you? Look, John, if we're going to make this little act work you're going to have to pretend to like me, whatever your preference may be."

"I'm not very comfortable with this."

"You should have thought of that before you asked me to be your wife over lunch – no, you should have thought of that before you took the plane tickets." She sat on the edge of the bed. "Look. I need the money. We're in too deep to back out. It's a business transaction, John. If we can get through the next seven days together, we'll both come out ahead when we get back to Chicago."

Even as she said it, she felt the disappointment sink in. His discomfort over their predicament made it feel as if rain was predicted for their entire stay. It was so easy when they talked on-line. She never anticipated that he would find her so unappealing in person.

Jack carried his shaving kit into the bathroom. "Why would you say your sister is the pretty one?"

It was uncanny the way he seemed to see into her thoughts. Julianne reached for the sundress and slipped it over her head, discretely removing her blouse and her bra beneath it. "She is. She takes great pains to be."

He turned off the bathroom light and stood just outside the door, one hand still holding the doorjamb. "Where are your rings, Julie?"

"At the jewelers," she repeated. She looked at Jack, her eyes flashing. "When inventing stories, it's best to stay as close to the truth as possible."

"For the record," he added. "I agree with your opinions on fidelity and commitment." He sat down on the opposite side of the bed watching her slip her jeans out from under her skirt.

"Then get off the bed," she told him.

He sprang to his feet. "Julie, I'm trying very hard here." He closed his great eyes and took an exaggerated breath.

"You're a whole lot friendlier online," she pointed out.

"Yeah, but that's different. This is like. . ." he turned away and then back again, struggling for words, "like if I was Catholic and I'd just given a particularly colorful confession to my priest and an hour later he sees me on the street. I feel a little exposed."

She looked across the bed at him. Her heart skipped a beat at the expression in his large eyes, soft and warm. She knew the feeling exactly and missed that intimacy now, but she didn't know how to bridge the gap.

Locked in a stand-off, it was Jack who broke the ice. "This is just an incredibly awkward situation," he paused, then added with a smile, "but it would probably be worse with someone else."

Julianne laughed at the back-handed compliment. "We're in agreement there, too. C'mon. We're in Mexico. Let's just make the most of our free vacation. We might even have fun." She lowered her head while still holding him with her eyes, daring him to argue.

He chuckled uneasily.

Julianne extended a hand. "Friends?"

"You are an amazing woman, Julianne DeAngelo." Jack grasped her hand firmly in both of his.

Smiling, she released his hands and bent down to fasten her sandals. She didn't miss the way his eyes narrowed, his hand smoothing the beard along his jaw. Leaning as she was, he had an unhampered view of her ample cleavage. He licked his lips and turned away.

It was going to be a long week.

Jack rose from the edge of the bed and opened his laptop computer. "I need to check in with the office."

CHAPTER 9 - Mexico

Twenty-four hours had done little to ease the tension. The idea development was going slowly and Hayden nitpicked every detail.

Julianne arched her back and raised her arms over her head in a stretch. "I still don't understand why he wanted to shoot the commercial in Mexico. Wouldn't it have been cheaper in Chicago?"

"For what he wants, yes. But he insisted on Acapulco. You can't argue with the client, especially one with Hayden's backing." Jack walked out of the bathroom toweling his hair. In the mirror, Julianne saw him stop to watch her weave strands of hair into a french braid.

"You know, if you'd prefer, I can get another room," he offered. "That way you can have your privacy when the Haydens aren't around."

Julianne held tightly to a twist of her thick auburn hair so she wouldn't drop the braid. Her nerves were taut after a day of Hayden's micromanaging. "This is your game, John. Whatever you feel comfortable with."

He reached back into the bathroom to hang up his towel. "I'm sorry you lost your job."

"It's better this way," she said while she tied off the bottom of the braid with a hair band. Her eyes strayed to Jack's reflection. He stood behind her, dressed only in his blue jeans. Without his shirt, she admired his well-developed biceps. Her eyes traveled the sparse, wavy line of fine dark brown hair down the center. "You must do a lot of weight training."

He turned away, reaching for a shirt. "Keeps me sane."

Catching sight of her own reflection one last time, Julianne noticed the blush that crept into her cheeks. She'd never appraised a man that way before. "The Haydens will be waiting for us," she reminded him, clearing her throat.

As if on cue, there was a knock on the door. Jack walked across and opened it, still buttoning his white linen shirt down from the banded collar.

"Hey, we got the room right next to yours," Ben Hayden announced. "Thought I'd pick you up on the way downstairs." He walked into the room, looking around. He smiled at Julianne. "My hunches are rarely wrong," he laughed. "I think you're going to make me a lot of money, young lady. Both on and off the camera. Hey, what's with the computer?"

"Portable office," Julianne explained.

"Business is business, but it's time for a little relaxation," Hayden scolded.

Julianne rose from her chair at the dressing table, the tight braid keeping her humidified hair under tight control. "It's happy hour."

* * *

The warm night air swirled through the open corridor, gently nudging Julianne's braid across her back. Below in the open-air hotel restaurant, mariachis strummed guitars, their voices carrying with strains of Mexican folk songs.

Julianne smiled, enjoying the caress of the wind like a lover's warm breath on her neck. She imagined it was Jack standing behind her, his arms encircling her and for the first time in months she felt completely relaxed.

The blare of a ship's horn in the harbor brought her back to her purpose and she turned to unlock the hotel room door. Jack sat before his laptop computer, a pencil perched against his chin as he stared at the screen in search of inspiration.

It must have been the vacation atmosphere that made her imagine him waiting for her, smiling to greet her, taking her into his arms. Julianne quickly shook the image away. Jack had established very defined personal boundaries. There was no room for her girlish fantasies. They had a job to do.

"I had an idea," she announced, closing the door behind her.

His round eyes trained on her face. Was he deliberately avoiding the short beach wrap she wore over her bathing suit?

The thought inspired a hint of a smile, but Julianne had other things on her mind. She hurried across the room to where he sat and looked over his shoulder at the screen saver playing across the monitor, then she backed up to sit on the edge of the bed. Breathless with the excitement of creativity, she waved her hands up to present the picture in her mind. "What about Mexico City? We could shoot in the castle of Max and Carlotta. Chapultapec Palace. 'In Hayden Casualwear, a woman is queen of the castle.'"

Traces of a smile turned up the corners of John's moustache. "You know, that's not half bad. I'll pitch it to Ben tomorrow."

Julianne reached for her sketch pad and began outlining the setting. "I was thinking something like this . . . "

Jack brought the computer screen back to life. "Queen of the castle," he repeated as his fingers found the letters on the keyboard. He pulled pictures into the thought with the click of a mouse. "We'd have to get authorization," he murmured, "but I think we could pull it off. . ."

Setting down her pencil and pulling her legs up beneath her, Julianne cocked her head and watched the master at work. "Why am I here?"

"Hmmm?" he turned an ear almost nonchalantly, busily expanding his ideas into the program.

"Why did Ben Hayden want me?"

"Ben Hayden?"

"Yeah. Why am I shooting this commercial? Beside the fact that I'm talented and beautiful," she said flippantly.

Jack raised his eyes to a point on the wall above the computer before turning to face Julianne. "Cheap labor?" he suggested.

"He's paying me twice though. Once as a model and once as a consultant. Where's the economy?"

Jack leaned back, pulled his hands together and then pushed them back to crack his knuckles. "You made a good presentation. He's only paying you scale as a model. Don't get used to it. Perkins & Stone was not built around outside consultants and freelance models. Ben Hayden has deep pockets and I intend to grossly overbill him, even though he believes that by using an unknown model and independent contractor he should be saving money. He'll play by the rules in the future."

"Will you hire me?"

"No."

The pout was automatic. She couldn't suppress her frustration. Laying the sketch pad beside her on the bed, Julianne turned away.

"I don't believe in inflating people's egos, Julianne," he continued gently. "In this business they're overinflated far too often. So listen to me now, because I'm only going to say it once. You have remarkable instinct and an extremely creative mind. The things you did to improve the shoot today some of the senior staff at P&S would never dream of. You're a natural. Add to that the fact that you're very photogenic. The camera likes you. Ben Hayden's going to pay for the talent he's uncovered."

"But you won't?"

He rubbed his forehead, exhaling a deep sigh. "Julianne . . . maybe under different circumstances . . ." His beard took on a cinnamon tinge from the heightened color showing on his cheeks. "You don't have your degree yet."

"I could intern."

"Doesn't this feel at all uncomfortable to you?"

"I'm only asking you for a job."

Jack's chin lowered to his chest. He closed his eyes and with another sigh, he looked back at Julianne. "I feel guilty about the whole fiancé thing, Julianne. Don't you wonder what he must be thinking?" He pulled his hand through his hair. "Maybe after you finish with your degree. After things have a chance to settle down a little again. I feel like we're in this whirlwind, Julianne. I don't want to add more complications to either one of our lives."

"But . . . " as she began her appeal, Jack rose to his feet.

"Look. We have a lot of work to do. How about we go over this palace idea."

Julianne held her argument, wondering when she would be able to tell him there was no more fiancé. She swallowed her disappointment and re-channeled her energy into the presentation she dreamed up while floating around the swimming pool an hour earlier. She had to keep focused.

"I pictured a stroll through the passages where they have those big columns, you know, a leisurely walk through the palace, maybe a book or an apple in hand . . ."

"I've never been inside the palace."

Julianne sat back down on one of her legs, caught up in the excitement of the idea once more. "Oh, you have to see it. Even if we don't get the shoot."

Jack lifted his laptop from the dresser and pulled it over to the bed. "Show me what you have in mind."

"It sort of looks like this." Taking the computer on her lap, she pulled in pictures to complete what he started and added moving graphics to represent the model. "And then there are the steps . . ." Jack watched while she turned the gleam in her eyes into a miniature screen show.

* * *

Even if there was no future with Jack Guilder, Julianne desperately needed a job. She meant to prove to him that he needed her at Perkins & Stone, hoping to save herself the job search after graduation. Neither of them slept much, the two of them brainstorming every night until the early hours of the morning - until she succumbed to her body's demand for rest.

She would collapse on the bed while he retired to a chair in the corner of the room, his computer on an end table pulled up in front of him. Too exhausted herself from the work she had done during the day, she didn't know if he slept at all. Once or twice she had woken with a start to find his large round eyes fixed on her from his vantage point across the room, reflecting whatever light remained.

It was enough to unnerve most people, but there was nothing threatening in the way he watched her; rather, she felt he watched over her, protecting her like the gargoyles protected buildings - *like a gryphon.*

* * *

They were six days into the campaign. While she waited to begin the shoot, Julianne pulled the earrings out of her pocket and put them on. She found them at the market the day before and bought them on a whim. When they left Mexico, her gryphon would more than likely disappear from her life, but she would keep the earrings as a memento.

She indulged herself in the compliments he'd offered her when she woke that morning, even if his words were merely sleep-deprived ramblings. "The way the sun lights up your hair is remarkable," he'd told her. "Red and blond and brunette, I've never seen so many different natural shades on one head of hair before." Memories of his deep, all-night voice warmed her through in the chilly stone fortress.

Julianne wrapped her arms around herself, smiling. Then, with a deep breath, she shook her head to clear it. *"The man's exhausted,"* she reminded herself. *"It's just delirium."*

Bright floodlights startled the palace with their brilliance, signaling Julianne to the stage that awaited her.

The experience was surreal. There was no Suzanne to steal her spotlight, no competition to make her feel second best. For this one week, she would indulge the fantasy of beauty before returning to the life she was more comfortable with.

It was a game. Julianne walked blindly to her starting cue, unable to see the cameras or the directors behind the lights. Orders echoed around the palace and then she heard "Action" shouted from the floor below. With a deep breath, Julianne began her stroll down the stairs and through the corridor, reciting her lines to the grip that followed her. She rounded the last column, casually leaning around it while she flirted with the camera.

"Cut!" the director shouted, appearing in front of the lights as he advanced up the staircase. "What are those earrings?" He pulled back her hair. "What have you got in your ears?"

The cool palace suddenly seemed very warm. She put a hand to the side of her face and whispered. "They're gryphons." She could feel the heat of embarrassment and wondered if her make-up would hide the color in her cheeks.

"What's the problem?" Ben Hayden's voice boomed out.

"She's wearing earrings!" the director shouted back, clearly annoyed.

"So?"

"Take them out!" he ordered Julianne, scurrying back down the steps.

Julianne walked back to where the shot began, removing the offending jewelry as she went.

"What's wrong with earrings?" she heard Ben Hayden ask.

"They're a distraction. They disrupt aesthetic appearance," Jack explained.

"God, they're awful," the director complained. "Ugly, gaudy looking monsters, hanging from her ears."

"Monsters?" Jack repeated.

The director made a noise of disgust deep in his throat. "How did she get on the set wearing those dreadful things?"

"They're not monsters," Julianne said quietly. "They're gryphons."

"Whatever! They spoiled the take. Now let's try it again."

Mortified, she bowed her head, took several deep breaths and then straightened her shoulders. She nodded to the grip that she was ready to go again. The director watched from below, in front of the wall of lights this time. With a wave of his hand, he signaled her to start again. The palace was silent now except for Julianne's voice, reciting the script they had written last night.

Again, she leaned playfully around the column, grinning as she swung her hair behind her. The best way to sell Hayden's sweats was to hide them. She hoped he didn't realize her ploy.

Jack appeared beside the director with a smile on his face. Would they make her do it again?

"Well?" Jack asked quietly. The crew watched the director in anticipation.

The man in charge leaned over toward Jack and spoke in hushed tones.

"We can always do it again," Jack replied in a low voice.

"One more time," the director bellowed.

"What was wrong with that one?" Hayden objected.

"Just to be sure," Jack reassured him. "Easier to do it now than have to throw it away or start over later."

Ben Hayden shrugged. "I don't mind. I could watch your wife model my clothes all day. She's a lovely woman, Jack."

"Agreed."

"Quiet!" came the command, and then the extended arm pointed upstairs to start again.

It was like Halloween, dressing up and playing make believe. Julianne sauntered the hallway one more time. When all was said and done, the commercial would probably end up on the cutting room floor in favor of the professional model, but she was having fun with the part while it was hers.

"That's a wrap!" the director shouted.

Jack walked out from behind the glare of lights toward the star and wrapped her in a hug. "That was great, honey."

She knew the hug was for Hayden's benefit. Julianne shied away, reaching for a towel to pat her forehead.

Jack raised an eyebrow. "Monsters?"

"They're not monsters," she insisted, feeling the warmth flush in her cheeks once more. "I only wore them for good luck. I didn't think anyone would see them under my hair."

"You can't tilt your head if you're going to wear danglers," he told her.

"I'll remember that in the future."

"I meant to tell you, I talked to Alec this morning. I won't be flying back with you tomorrow. I have to wrap things up with the model's shoot and then I have to go to New York."

So this was the end of the charade. Julianne smiled at Ben Hayden and curled an arm around Jack's waist. "Oh?"

"Alec told me to assure you there would be a car waiting for you at O'Hare when you land."

"Well, at least we have one more night," she replied cheerfully. "What's on the agenda tonight, Mr. Hayden?"

"I think you two deserve some time alone," he said. "Why don't you go for a swim, or just hide yourselves away in your room." He slapped Jack on the back soundly. "My instincts have rarely proven me wrong. Best damn campaign I've seen yet. That wife of yours is a treasure."

"You wanted a woman's touch. I think you're getting your money's worth."

"Just a little prejudiced on her account?" Hayden took Julianne's hands into his puffy paws. "I knew you wouldn't let me down, little lady." He gave her a wink, kissed her cheek and walked away.

Julianne needed to cool off and regroup her emotions. She watched Hayden exit the castle. "Actually, a swim sounds good."

"You go ahead. I'm going to watch the model's shoot."

"I wanted to thank you. I don't guess I'll be seeing you again after we get back to Chicago."

Jack smiled and put an arm across her shoulders, hugging her to him sideways. "You never know. And I should be thanking you. You made me a lot of money here and I promise you'll get your share. With what you've earned, you can take your time finding a job, Julianne. After you've finished school."

She bit her lip to avoid asking him one more time to reconsider hiring her. Instead, she wriggled out from under his arm. Julianne walked away from him backward with a quick wave. "See ya later."

Intimate Distance

* * *

Thoughts of Jack spending their last night in Mexico with the model shooting her commercial bombarded Julianne. She fell into a restless sleep. In her dreams, the gryphon earrings flew over the Pacific Ocean, circling menacingly and looking more like dragons than the lion/eagles they were.

From across the Gulf, her father's voice spoke to her reassuringly. "You knew they wouldn't be the same," he said.

"They're only earrings," she replied, still ducking beneath the swooping monsters. "Why are they so mad?"

Frightened, Julianne curled her toes into the sand on the beach beneath the flapping of great black wings shuttering the moonlight. "Make them stop, Daddy."

The Gulf breeze blew her hair over her face, carrying the gryphons off across the horizon. In her dream, Julianne dropped to the beach and curled her knees up tight against her chest.

The wind changed directions to caress her hot forehead, pushing her hair back over her shoulders.

Gentle waves rippled along the shoreline, occasionally rolling high into a white cap. Julianne rolled onto her side, curled up tight and closed her eyes. The sand was smooth against her cheek, becoming the sheets of her bed. She heard the rush of wings behind her, or maybe it was just the surf. Strong, velvet wings wrapped gently around her. Julianne straightened one leg and drifted into peaceful dreamlessness.

CHAPTER 10

It was raining when the plane landed at O'Hare International Airport; 100 percent humidity without the benefit of a sandy beach and a warm sun.

October in Chicago signaled an end to the hot days and nights of summer; the cool rain steamed from the pavement and washed away any remains of warmth and comfort.

Julianne considered the way a mood could reflect the weather, feeling more than a little bit rainy inside herself. It didn't matter that she carried the mood all the way home from Mexico.

She passed easily through customs, carrying one suitcase and a shoulder bag through the terminal. She repeated the limousine number the dispatcher gave her and made her way outside in search of the driver Perkins & Stone sent to deliver her home.

Wind carried the rain across the lanes of traffic, misting the travelers who waited for their rides. She checked each limousine for its identification and its license plate while she stood in her assigned spot. Beside her another couple from her flight found their ride and packed themselves into the town car and out of the semi-sheltered rain.

Anxious to get home to her own bed and a good night's sleep, Julianne bounced on the balls of her feet, warding off the chilly breeze that stirred the humid air.

A black limousine approached bearing the correct designation. Julianne leaned over, squinting to read the license plate while she chanted the number she was given. When she realized that the two matched, she waved to the driver.

The vehicle pulled up to the curb and the driver stood in the street across from her. "Miss DeAngelo?"

She nodded, still bouncing on the balls of her feet to ward off the wind. The driver pushed the trunk release button and walked over to the curb. He opened the rear door for her and picked up her suitcase.

"Welcome back, Miss DeAngelo." Alec Stone was sitting in the car, his salt and pepper hair outlined in blurs of neon that reflected against the rain splattered window behind him.

Julianne hesitated before climbing into the car. "Mr. Stone."

"I hope you don't mind, I thought I'd ride back with you. Save the firm some money, you know, two for the price of one."

Exhausted, Julianne ducked into the plush black interior. It was too late to find another way home. "I hope it's not too much out of your way."

"Not at all." He motioned toward the bar in front of him with a glass in his hand. "Would you like something to drink?"

"Thank you, but I had a Coke on the plane."

The driver took his place behind the wheel and the car pulled away.

Alec sat back in his seat and sipped his drink. "I also wanted a chance to talk with you." He looked over the top of his glass. "You did a creditable job on your commercial. You should be proud."

"Thank you." She pushed her shoulders back, and closed her eyes, unfolding her long legs, stiff from the restricted space during the long flight back.

Alec swirled his drink, ice clinking against the sides of the glass before he set it down. "I expect you'll have some considerable success as a commercial model."

Julianne's eyes narrowed. "Why would you expect that?"

"You were quite good, in front of the camera as well as behind. Any director would want to offer you more work."

"You think so?" She pushed herself back into the corner of her seat, half facing Alec Stone. "Especially when a man such as yourself suggests it?"

Alec chuckled. "Are you always so suspicious?"

"Did the director also tell you what my answer was?"

"Julianne, you were quite good. I would be more surprised if he hadn't offered you more work. It has nothing to do with me. You are a woman of many hidden talents, I'll wager. The performance you gave at Hayden's presentation by itself was a prime example of your acting abilities."

"I'm not interested in becoming a commercial model. I don't have the discipline or the constitution for it."

"You surprise me. Most women would jump at the chance to be beautiful before the world."

Julianne turned to face Alec. "What is it you want from me, Mr. Stone?"

"Are you always so direct?"

"Why not?"

Alec stared at the back of the driver's head, a look of amusement in his smile. "What makes you think I want something?"

"Is it just coincidence that Perkins & Stone sends a limo to pick me up at the airport, and you just happen to be in it, while Jack gets sent off to New York?"

Alec sniffed out a sound of amusement. "Intelligent, perceptive." He turned to face Julianne, saluting her with his drink. "Have you told Jack you broke off the engagement?"

Julianne's hands rolled into fists and then released, stretching her fingers again. "How do you know about that?"

"He asked me to do a background check on you."

"That isn't public knowledge."

Alec didn't take his eyes off Julianne, making her feel like prey. "I have my sources. Are you going to tell him?"

"It isn't important."

"It is to him."

The adrenaline rushed to numb her brain from the anger that was mounting. "A background check? He doesn't trust me?"

"More like he wanted to make sure your outlook for the future was promising."

She snorted. "If he was worried about my future he'd give me a job." She leaned forward, reaching for a bottle of water from the bar. "So you told him that I'm a free agent?"

"Not yet. I was curious about you - what your plans are."

"So you delayed Jack's return in order to interrogate me more thoroughly."

His smile turned up one corner of his mouth. "Something like that." Alec continued to make circles with his glass. "What *do* you want, Miss DeAngelo?"

"I want to use my degree," she answered immediately, turning full face toward him. "I want a job at Perkins & Stone, or another advertising firm."

"It's yours."

Julianne sat in stunned silence. "Just like that?"

"Julianne, you've proven your talent. You developed the layout, you made the presentation. You wrote the commercial and starred in it. You've taken this account from inception all the way through. Do you know how many people have done that? It's unheard of in the industry. And the changes you've adopted along the way show a lot of creativity."

A rush of pride distracted her. "You're using my take?"

Alec nodded slowly. "It was so much better, Julianne."

She couldn't suppress the smile. The commercial was good. And it was hers. And then she remembered the job offer. "I asked Jack for a job," she told him.

Alec continued to nod, watching the ice diluting his drink. "I'm guessing he turned you down."

The cold hand of reality brought her back to the conversation. "So this is where you rescind your offer?"

"Tell me about Jack," Alec coaxed. "You've just spent a week pretending to be his wife. Tell me what you know about your husband."

"What can I tell you? You're his godfather. There probably isn't anyone who knows him better."

"You converse with him on-line. Behind the security of a modem people can sometimes be more open than they could be face to face." He squinted, studying her more closely. "Will you tell him about your wedding plans?"

"He's bound to find out sooner or later."

Alec nodded and downed the last of his drink. "Then let it be later." He set the glass down deliberately and then turned back to face Julianne. "Why did you agree to pose as his wife?"

Julianne shrugged her shoulders. "He asked."

"You could have said no."

"I was curious."

"I understand you were ill that day."

Fresh tears stung the corners of her eyes. She put the bottle of water in a cup holder beside her seat. "So what about the job?"

"Isn't that one of the reasons you went to lunch with Jack?"

Julianne turned to look out the window again. It had been her excuse, but not the primary motivation. It wasn't until after that meeting the she realized she would need the job sooner than she'd expected. She wondered what kind of reference Kimball Brothers had given Alec. "And exactly what will be expected of me?" she asked warily.

"Even after a week with him I'll bet you don't know him any better than you did when you left. Am I right?"

Julianne massaged her forehead, tired and unsure about Alec's direction. "You know, it's been a long flight, and maybe Perkins & Stone isn't the right career choice. If I'm so brilliant I'm sure other agencies will take a look at what I have to offer."

Alec rubbed his mouth and chin with one hand, pulling his fingers down along his jaw line. "When Jack's parents died, I saw to it that he finished college and set him up in business. I also saw him build up a wall around himself that no one could penetrate. You are the first glimmer of light I have seen in his eyes in ten years, Julianne DeAngelo." Alec reached across and took Julianne's hand.

Julianne pulled back, still suspicious. "That's not a good enough reason to give me a job."

Alec smiled and settled back into his seat. "I run Perkins & Stone."

Julianne folded her arms across her chest, watching Alec and still guessing at his motives. "I suppose in my background check you had occasion to talk with John Thomas."

"He had some very interesting things to say about you."

She couldn't suppress the shudder of apprehension. "I'm sure he did."

Alec cocked an eyebrow.

"I don't know what he told you, but I have no interest in putting in creative overtime, Mr. Stone."

"I'm not asking you to."

The car pulled to a stop in front of Julianne's apartment building. Alec looked wistfully out the window. "Here already?" He leaned toward Julianne. "I think you and Jack would work well together. Given the opportunity, I think he will come to see that as well."

"Exactly what kind of work do you have in mind?"

"Advertising, Julianne. I want you on my staff before some other firm lures you away with a bigger and better offer." He raised his eyebrows. "And, from a personal standpoint, I want to see how Jack deals with you. If he gives you any trouble, makes you uncomfortable the way your last boss did, suggests anything you find distasteful, I want to be the first to hear about it. And I want to hear about it from you." He sat back again. "But I think you know he wouldn't do that to you." He chuckled half to himself. "Although he just might work you so hard you'll wish you hadn't taken the job."

"You don't think he's going to object to this?"

"Of course he'll object, but he'll come to see things my way."

Julianne's exhausted mind raced to catch up with the conversation. She put her hand to the door handle, her eyes following the chauffeur as he walked around the car to the trunk. "And if he decides to fire me?"

Alec shrugged. "Jack will be upset initially, but he will have to go through me to let you go, Julianne. Even he must realize that you would be a valuable asset to our firm, or a fierce rival. I prefer to think of you as an ally."

Julianne stepped out of the limousine and put a hand on the roof to lean back in. "I just spent a week sleeping in the same room with Jack at a beautiful resort in a tropical paradise. You haven't once intimated that he might have been any less than a gentleman, in fact you seem positive that I don't know him any better than when we left Chicago. Wouldn't that indicate to you that he doesn't like me, that we might not work well together in an everyday situation?"

Alec leaned across the seat. "As you've pointed out, there probably isn't anyone that knows him better than I do. Whether he likes you or not, you two put together one of the finest ad campaigns I've had the privilege to put my name on. You quite obviously work well together." He raised his glass to her. "And I would think it should prove to you that the same thing that happened to you at Kimball Brothers will not happen to you at Perkins & Stone."

The cold October wind caught up her hair sending a chill down her spine as much from the confirmation of her reference from JT as from the weather. She wrapped her arms around herself and nodded at Alec Stone. "Thank you."

"Don't thank me," he laughed. "You deserve the job, Julianne."

"No," she corrected him. "Thank you for not believing the worst."

CHAPTER 11

Julianne was still trying to decide if she should be happy or skeptical about her new job offer when she walked into her apartment. But all thoughts were immediately chased away by the intruders waiting inside.

"So where's Bill?" Suzanne stood in Julianne's dining room with her hands on her hips.

Julianne dropped her suitcases and took a deep breath. "What are you doing here?" Seeing the two of them together made her skin crawl.

"Have a good business trip?" Steve asked sarcastically.

Julianne looked from one to the other, surrounded in her own home.

"Was it worth it?" Suzanne demanded.

"Neither one of you are supposed to be here."

"My name's still on the lease," Steve reminded her.

"You agreed to move out," Julianne said.

"Changed my mind."

"Is this how you take your revenge?" Suzanne whined.

Julianne winced at the tone in her sister's voice. "What are you talking about?"

"Who's the injured party now?" Steve sneered.

Julianne walked past her sister into the living room, pushing Steve out of her way. "I've had a long trip and I'm too tired to make sense of this conversation." She dropped down on the sofa. "If you want to explain, I'd be glad to listen, but if you're going to stand there with that self-righteous indignation on your face, you might as well leave. I'm not in the mood for games from either of you."

"Tell me," Steve began, trailing behind her, "where did you go?"

Julianne rubbed her temples, fighting the fatigue from the trip and irritated by the invasion. She repeated what they already knew. "I shot a commercial in Mexico."

"With Bill?"

Understanding dawned. Julianne couldn't keep the smile from her face when she asked, "Where is Bill?"

Suzanne took a stance directly in front of her sister. "Didn't just drive you to the airport, now did he?"

He had finally taken action against his wife. "Are you telling me he didn't come home?"

"You know he didn't," Suzanne said.

"You shot a commercial?" Steve asked derisively.

Julianne's patience threshold had evaporated. She pushed herself to her feet and pointed toward the door. "It's time for the two of you to leave."

"And you just thought you'd invite my husband along for the ride?" Suzanne asked, matching Julianne's stance.

"I haven't seen Bill since I left O'Hare a week ago," Julianne snapped, "although I'm surprised you noticed he was gone."

"He must have told you where he was going if he didn't go with you," Suzanne insisted. "He tells you everything. You'd think you were married to him instead of me."

"Says something, doesn't it?"

"Juliaaaaanne . . ." Suzanne moaned.

Julianne turned on Steve. "And if you want to move back in, I'm moving out."

"Not good enough for you anymore?" He sneered.

"You don't want to be married, I'd spoil all your fun."

"C'mon, you've had plenty of time to get it out of your system. You're not really calling off the wedding."

Suzanne huffed and walked out of the living room.

"I've always appreciated your honesty," Julianne told Steve with more patience than she thought she had left.

He straightened. "Then everything's okay?"

"How long has it been since we actually had a conversation? And look how many other women you've dated since we got engaged. There isn't anything left."

"But I love you, Julianne."

"That's not enough, is it, Steve?"

"Tell me about the commercial. What's it for?"

Julianne rolled her eyes, exasperated by his attempts to distract her from the issue. "Do you really care?"

"How will I know it's yours if you don't tell me what it's for?"

"You'll know."

"So help me, Julianne," Suzanne growled, storming back into the living room with her car keys in hand, "if Bill's home when I get there, I'll kill you both. You expect me to believe you went to Mexico to make some commercial? You?"

Julianne bit the insides of her cheeks to hold back the return insult. "In case it really makes any difference, you can believe it when you see the proof."

"What proof? It's not like they put credits on a commercial."

"Look you guys, I'm really tired. Can you go somewhere else to fight or worry or whatever it is you two are doing together these days?"

"What's that supposed to mean?" Suzanne fumed.

Julianne got up off the couch. "If you aren't leaving, then I am." She marched past her accusers, their mouths hanging open, and slammed the door closed for emphasis.

* * *

Julianne shuddered, hardly able to look at the pictures of Suzanne that adorned her mother's shelves. Home didn't feel any more comfortable than her apartment. She needed to rethink her options.

She trailed her mother into the kitchen, contemplating if she should broach moving back in.

Barbara DeAngelo poured Julianne a cup of coffee. "I suppose you know Bill left your sister."

"So I've heard."

"What's going on, Julianne?" Her mother covered Julianne's hand to get her undivided attention.

"You'd never believe me."

"But you know." Her mother's eyes were accusing, her face sternly set. "Your relationship with Bill has been more than just friendly."

Julianne felt the anger rise with yet another indictment. "Yes, mother, you're right. We've become very good friends as a result of a common concern, namely unfaithful mates."

Barbara stepped back. "It's true, then? You've been sleeping with Bill?"

"Is that what Suzanne told you?" Julianne's nostrils flared, incensed at being put in the second-best position once more. Suzanne might be prettier, but she didn't possess half of Julianne's intelligence and common sense. "Maybe it's time to tell you the truth, mother. I've been trying to protect the both of you far too long."

Barbara's eyes opened wide, surprised at the intensity of her younger daughter's words. "Julianne!"

"You wanted to know," Julianne reminded her. "I put up with a lot from Steve Montgomery, but chasing after my sister was one step too far."

"You can't be serious."

"I wish it *was* all just a joke."

"Did you catch them . . .?"

Julianne looked to the ceiling of her mother's kitchen searching for words of explanation. "I saw them having lunch together." She sat down hard into a chair at the round table, stirred cream into her hot coffee and fought to keep her emotions in check.

Barbara straightened her blouse and walked back to the table taking a seat beside Julianne. "That seems innocent enough. Which one of you should I believe?"

Julianne waved a hand through the air. "Take your choice, mom. I really don't care anymore."

"And Bill?"

Julianne leaned over the table. "You know what, mom? Bill did proposition me. But I had the good sense to respect my sister's feelings. I can't say I blame him after all she's put him through, but at least I respect that last boundary of good taste." She sat back and sipped at her coffee, closing her eyes and inhaling the warmth. Her homecoming wasn't quite what she'd hoped for.

"Was he in Mexico with you?"

"No, Mom." She considered the improbability of her mother believing the truth of her situation in Acapulco. "I spent the week pretending to be another man's wife." She began to laugh, tears streaming down her face in a flood of mixed emotions. "But that's a whole other story that you'd never believe."

"Try me." Mrs. DeAngelo crossed her arms and leaned on the kitchen table. "Oh, Julianne." Her mother reached across for Julianne.

Julianne shook her head, rebuffing her mother's attempt at comfort. She knew the consolation her mother offered would be cold.

"Tell me?" her mother coaxed.

Unable to hold it inside any longer, Julianne began to relate the events of the past several weeks.

"You went to lunch with a strange man?" Barbara extracted from her story. "Some man you hardly know? Julianne, he could have been a serial killer."

Julianne snorted. How like her mother to look for the flaw in her character. "Do you want to know or not?"

"I can't help but worry."

"I'd met him before. I'm not that stupid."

"I know you're not stupid."

Julianne took another sip of her coffee. "He asked me to help him out. The client is a family-oriented man and John thought a wife would add credibility to his presentation. Things weren't going so well at Kimball Brothers. It seemed like a good opportunity to get my foot in the door."

"That's not like you at all."

Julianne nodded. "Well John wasn't a total stranger, I mean we've been corresponding for the past six months, and the client liked me, so I worked on his campaign."

"So you spent a week in Mexico with a perfect stranger?" Her mother asked dumbfounded. "And I'm not supposed to worry about you?"

"Well he's not a perfect stranger."

"I'm sure he isn't now."

Julianne bristled. "He was a gentleman, mother. Never laid a hand on me."

"I find that hard to believe."

"In light of everything else I've told you, why would I lie about that?"

"So you're the innocent bystander in all this? You throw over the only man you've dated for the last two years - the man you were planning to marry - for someone you hardly know? You knew that Bill was planning to leave Suzanne and you said nothing to your sister, and you've done nothing wrong. Is that about it?"

It always came back to Suzanne. Julianne rose from her seat abruptly. "I didn't throw Steve over for John. I thought maybe I could come home for a little peace and quiet, for a little understanding. My sister and my former fiancé have taken over my apartment and I'm tired. I should have known you would side with Suzanne." She put the half-full cup into the kitchen sink and turned to leave. "All right then. Make me the villain if it makes you feel better. I need to find a place to stay."

"Julianne, don't go," her mother protested following Julianne back into the living room.

"Forget it, Mother. I'll be fine. And as for Suzanne, Bill warned her a dozen times before he left. She acts like a child. What's he supposed to do? Ground her?" She grabbed for her purse and headed for the door. "She told you Bill was sterile. Did you ever stop to think that maybe it was her way of telling you she wasn't ready to have children? She's certainly had dozens of other donors."

"Why haven't you told me any of this before?" her mother asked quietly.

Julianne bowed her head and turned slowly to look at the older woman standing before her, ashamed at her outburst. She let out a long, slow breath. "I didn't want to upset you. Or maybe I didn't want to upset myself. It's very difficult for you to see Suzanne's faults, Mother. And I didn't think Bill would really leave her."

Barbara made one more half-hearted attempt to reach out for her daughter, but Julianne had outgrown her need for false reassurances. "I gotta go, Mom."

* * *

Julianne unlocked her apartment cautiously, making sure it was empty. She peaked in, calling on whatever strength she might have left to help her face any surprises that might still lay in wait to ambush her.

Once inside, Julianne let out a sigh of relief and hurried to her bedroom. Pulling out another suitcase, she packed as many of her remaining clothes as would fit and rushed back to gather her still unpacked luggage from Mexico from the dining room.

With a cursory glance over her shoulder, Julianne saw her laptop computer still closed tight on the desk. The comfort of finding his name on a computer screen beckoned to her. Would he still be there?

She hesitated a moment, then left her luggage and approached the computer. She opened it slowly as she sat down in front of it, bringing it to life with the touch of a finger.

There was a safety in their on-line relationship, an intimate distance. She had been a week without her computer. She hadn't needed it.

Julianne felt her heart rise in her throat, wondering if their friendship would survive. Losing JGGuilder would be the final blow in a day already filled with disaster. Her fingers worked feverishly to open programs and connect to the on-line service. After all the nights they spent chatting across phone lines, she wanted desperately to hear from him now.

One week. He had been solicitous and affectionate in the presence of Ben Hayden, but never imposing when they were alone. She knew the emotional wall Alec Stone referred to quite well. Was she really the glimmer that Alec saw in Jack's eyes?

Her fingers hovered over the keyboard, afraid her mailbox would be empty.

He suggested he was gay. Going into the trip she hadn't believed it from what she knew of him on-line. She'd seen him surveying her assets when she wore the sundress Steve found so scandalous. Yet in seven days together, Jack never made a pass at her.

The computer chimed an alert to her. She could only stare at the dialog box on the screen from JGGuilder, her heart pounding. "Julianne."

Relief, doubt, anger, anxiety. They all crowded around her as she stared at her name in the small box. She hesitated, unsure of the evolution of their relationship.

The screen chimed again with another pop-up message. "We need to talk."

Talk. Julianne reached into her pocket retrieving a piece of paper she picked up from the Mexican hotel. The hidden earrings fell out in the process. Clumsily, she reached for them and set them beside the computer before putting her shaking fingers to the keyboard once more.

"Are you in the room?" She sent her reply and waited for him to respond.

"Yes."

She didn't want to chat anymore. She wanted to hear his voice. "Telephone," she typed. "I'm calling you."

Her eyes lingered a moment on the statue of the gryphon before her cold fingers pressed each number on the cordless telephone as she read them from the folded piece of stationery. "Cinco, Uno, Dos," she told the hotel operator.

The earrings stared back at her from the desk. Were they really monsters? She brushed them into the waste basket as if they were bugs.

Julianne closed her eyes when he picked up the phone, envisioning his angular face, the bristles of his beard, his warm, brown eyes. He didn't speak right away as if testing the weight of their connection. "Julie?" he finally asked.

His voice raised goose bumps on her skin and sent a lump to her throat. Julianne took a deep breath. "It's a lot warmer there than it is here."

"I think I'd rather be there."

"What's on your mind?"

"You." The word struck a corresponding chord inside her. She wanted to throw her arms around him and hide in his strength. She wanted to feel the wings of the gryphon around her, protecting her.

"John, there's something I ought to tell you." It was a day for confessing, for telling all. There was nothing left to lose. She would tell him about the broken engagement. She didn't want to be unobtainable, as Bill had suggested. She decided she'd rather mourn all her losses at the same time.

"He threw you out, didn't he?"

Tears welled in her eyes. "What?"

"If it were me, I don't think I'd appreciate having my future wife spending a week sleeping in another man's bed."

Julianne laughed through the tears. "Actually, he moved back in."

It was his turn to ask. "What?"

Tell him now, she thought, before it goes any farther. "I called it off."

"The wedding?"

She sat silently, afraid to speak.

"I'm confused. You said he moved back in?"

"So I have to move out. Before I left he agreed to let me finish out the lease on my own, but he decided to move back in." She held onto the phone as if it were a lifeline, wrapping both hands around it, wanting to feel his solidity.

She heard his breath, several sharp intakes as if he was preparing to speak and then thought better of it. "Where are you going?" he finally asked.

"I'll find some place." Her attention wandered to the statue leaning over the shelf in front of her.

"Where's your family?"

"Tried that. Won't work."

"I have to go to New York." Julianne could hear him take another deep breath. "I won't be back for another week." It seemed for a moment the line went dead, and then he spoke again. "You can stay at my place."

Her heart leapt at the thought, and then she reigned herself back in when it registered that he was going to be in New York. "Aren't you afraid I might rob you blind? You hardly know me."

"It's a secured building. They wouldn't let you take anything out."

Julianne laughed in spite of herself. "I don't even know where you live."

"In the city. I'll call ahead and have them let you in. There's an extra key in the kitchen."

"I couldn't, Jack. It would be such an imposition."

He was quiet for a moment, and then his voice returned softly. "I like it better when you call me John."

He liked it. He liked her.

She considered his invitation realizing she didn't have anywhere else to go. "I don't know if I could find a place in a week's time. I need to show income and I haven't started my new job yet. I couldn't impose on you like that."

It was his turn to laugh. "You found a job already?"

She felt a twinge of guilt and was suddenly afraid of fracturing their fragile relationship. "I'll tell you about it when you get back."

"Julianne, you can stay as long as you like. I have three bedrooms. There's plenty of room and I'm hardly there."

"I'll pay you rent until I can find something else," she offered.

"I'll call and tell them you're coming."

"Still friends?"

"Don't usually open my home to my enemies."

"Why *are* you doing this?"

"I kinda got you into this mess."

"And I'm collecting my paycheck for it. As I recall it was my choice." Julianne looked to the window behind her at the darkness that settled across Schaumburg. "It all works out in the end, doesn't it?" she asked uncertainly.

"What do you mean?"

"What could be worse than marrying the wrong man?"

"You're right, you know."

"I know I'm right."

"I mean about the telephone. I much prefer hearing your voice to reading one line of type at a time."

She basked in the warmth of his words. "And maybe I'm not so bad to look at either?"

"Fishing for a compliment?"

Julianne bit her lip, wishing he would throw her a line.

"Would you be starring in your own commercial if you weren't at least minimally attractive?"

"I'm perfectly comfortable with my appearance."

"As well you should be."

"So why aren't you?" she challenged.

She heard him catch his breath before he deflected the question. "I have to go."

The line went dead and Julianne immediately cursed her insecurity. Then she realized she hadn't gotten his address.

Fresh tears streamed down her cheeks with her latest failure. She stared at the computer in front of her that still flashed three downloaded messages from her on-line session, none of which was from JGGuilder. With one last hope, she sent out to pick up her messages again and walked out of the spare bedroom while the computer executed the automated process.

Her heart skipped a beat at the sight of Steve standing in the dining room, keys in hand. "You can still live here, too, you know," he offered.

"Not a chance," she said, wiping her face with a sleeve.

"It's not like we're ever here at the same time, except for a couple of hours when I'm sleeping and you're on that damn computer."

"I'm on that damn computer so I don't have to go to bed. And you know what? I'm tired."

"This isn't the homecoming I planned, but then Bill left Suzanne and she was so upset. . ."

"Just couldn't say no," Julianne finished bitterly.

"I don't care about Suzanne," he said firmly, advancing and taking Julianne by the shoulders. "You're the one I want, Julianne."

"What's the matter? Slim pickin's at the arcade tonight?"

"That's not fair."

"No, it's not." She turned her back on him and walked back to the computer.

The message was there, short and sweet. She printed out the address and began to gather her luggage. "I'll be back for the rest of my stuff tomorrow."

"What are you taking?" he demanded.

"The wedding gifts are going back to the people who sent them. The things I brought with me are going with me."

"And the things we bought together?"

Julianne stopped and turned to look over her shoulder as she opened the door. "I don't want them."

"You can't go, Julianne."

"Watch me."

He rushed toward the door as she walked through. "We belong together. You can't just leave me."

She continued silently down the corridor, juggling her suitcases.

"You belong to me, Julianne," he shouted.

She stopped, deliberately turning to look at him. "I belong to myself."

* * *

"My name's Tommy," the doorman told her, carrying her bags down the hallway with a ring of keys hanging from his wrist. "Mr. Guilder said you knew where an extra key was after I let you in."

"Yes, he told me," Julianne reassured him. Tommy looked more like an organ grinder's monkey in his pillbox cap and braided uniform than a doorman, but he obviously knew his job, as well as the tenants of the building. He took several furtive glances in Julianne's direction.

"Mr. Guilder don't usually have too many visitors," the bellman said. "Come ta think of it, I can't say as I've seen anyone visit him in the eight months I been workin' here beside Mr. Stone. You family?"

"No," she answered politely. "Just a friend."

The doorman seemed disappointed. "Yeah, guess I shoulda figured. Keeps pretty much to himself." He stopped in front of a door and dropped the ring of keys to his hand, setting Julianne's luggage down as he unlocked the condo. He pushed the door open for Julianne and switched on a light before picking up her bags again.

Her mouth dropped open as she took in the size of the great room. A staircase marked the center of the main floor leading to a loft overhead. At the top, a narrow landing was cluttered with office equipment.

"If ya need anything, just pick up the phone and call downstairs," Tommy offered, pointing to a telephone mounted on a metal girder that rose up beside the staircase.

"Thank you," Julianne said, overwhelmed by her surroundings. She turned to see the doorman out, but he was already closing the door, returning to his post.

Julianne took another step into the great room, her footsteps echoing off the hardwood floor to the cathedral ceiling overhead. To her right there was an area rug that marked off the boundaries of a living room. A futon sofa was turned away from the front door facing an entertainment center. Bookshelves lined the front wall.

Across the room to her left was a small desk angled into the corner beside tall windows in the brick wall.

Toward the back of the room there was an Amish dining set in front of a partial wall that marked the kitchen. Opposite the kitchen and behind the living area, a door was shut, closing off the last quarter of the downstairs area.

Julianne pushed the door open, discovering the first of Jack's advertised three bedrooms. The double bed was mounted on a metal frame, no headboard or footboard. A pillow lay on top of a blanket, neatly folded at the foot. Along one wall there was a long, six-drawer dresser that looked as if it had been purchased at a rummage sale. Traces of white paint peeked through the refinished oak surface.

Julianne pulled out the closest drawer to discover the bed linens. The scent of a cedar sachet wafted up to greet her. In spite of herself, Julianne smiled. No man paid that much attention to details.

Spurred on by the adventure of exploring her new surroundings, Julianne walked back out to the staircase. With one hand on the wrought iron railing, she propelled herself up.

At the top, she stopped before the tables that supported Jack's home office, screen savers chased around two monitors that appeared to be network servers. Beside the computers sat an array of peripherals. Across from the wrought iron railing that ran the length of the loft were two doors. The other two bedrooms.

Julianne decided to work her way back to the staircase. When she opened the door to the second bedroom, she wrinkled her nose, recognizing the stale smell of perspiration in the make-shift gym. Jack's weight bench and barbells rested on a mat in the center of the room. Against the farthest wall he had a stationary bike parked beside a stereo with headphones. A television was mounted on the wall overhead.

She stood in the doorway for several minutes, recalling the sight of Jack standing in the Mexican hotel room without a shirt. While not overdeveloped, his torso was well sculpted. It wasn't difficult to imagine him in this room, pumping up, blood coursing through his muscles. . .

Julianne closed the door quickly and exhaled, her heart pounding. After spending a week sleeping less than three feet away from him without so much as a second thought, she scolded herself for turning him into a pin-up.

She reached for the next doorknob and, again, stopped just inside.

This was his inner sanctum. The room made her feel a voyeur, intruding on his privacy, yet her eyes lingered a moment longer on his bed. *That's where he sleeps.* She felt her heart skip a beat, remembering him slumped in the chair across the room from her. *If he sleeps.*

She surveyed the four-poster bed covered by a navy blue coverlet. Aside from a few pictures adorning the top of a long dresser and some toiletries on a tray on the tallboy, there was nothing out of place. Not even a speck of dust to mar the smooth finish. She saw a bathroom at the other end of the room and knew without checking that it, too, would be spotless.

Taking another step into the room, she picked up one of the pictures on the dresser. A family of three stood on a dock with a fishing boat behind them. Jack, a few inches shorter and several years younger, wore a captain's hat and smiled broadly back at her.

Julianne set the picture back on the dresser and turned to leave when she saw the coat of arms on the wall beside the door.

It was in no way unusual - a banner across the top proclaiming the name Guilder. It was the winged lion on the shield that made her heart skip a beat - a gryphon.

CHAPTER 12

Jack burst through the glass doors of the 42nd floor with an angry shove. He ignored the greetings from the staff he passed, stalking toward his office like a missile seeking its target.

"Julianne!" he barked without looking at her, "I want to see you." He stormed into his office and dropped his briefcase onto his desk with a crash.

Julianne offered a timid smile. "Welcome back."

"Close the door," he ordered.

Stepping inside, Julianne took a seat on the opposite side of his mahogany desk. Jack stood at the window staring down at the city below.

"Why didn't you tell me?" he fumed.

"Because you turned me down."

"So you went over me?" He turned abruptly and slapped the desk.

Julianne flinched. "I didn't go over you. Alec met me at the airport and offered me a job."

"And you accepted. Even after I told you no."

"I needed a job," she argued, leaning forward. "I didn't ask him, John. He offered it to me."

"Alec," he said half to himself. "What right does he have to meddle in my life?"

Julianne tensed, straightening in her chair. "There's no good reason why I shouldn't have this job. If you don't think I can do it then fire me."

"I can't." He turned his head away and pursed his lips. "I don't have the authority."

She rose to her feet, meeting his anger. "But you would, wouldn't you? Even after I saved your butt in that presentation with Ben Hayden."

The muscles in his jaw clenched. She sensed he wanted to say something but was deliberately holding back. After several moments, he looked away from the challenge in her eyes.

Frustrated once more by his attitude, Julianne reached for the door. "Live with it." She turned on her heel and stormed out of his office, leaving him with his ringing telephone.

Julianne laid her hands flat on her desk, taking deep breaths to control her anger.

"What did you do to piss him off?" Bev asked from the cube beside her.

Julianne gave way to a sarcastic smile. "I exist." Her phone rang, and Julianne gave an apologetic smile to Bev before she answered it.

"Alec wants to see you in his office right away," a woman told her. "Ben Hayden is here and he's not happy."

Julianne took a deep breath and grabbed a handful of her hair around her neck, leaning her head back. Jack was staring at her from his office. He shook his head and walked out to meet her. "Shall we?"

"After you."

* * *

". . . Don't like being taken advantage of this way . . . misrepresentation . . . fraudulent basis for getting me to sign the contract." The words floated clearly through the open door of Alec Stone's large office on the 43rd floor.

"Sounds like the game's up," Jack whispered, putting a hand to Julianne's back and directing her into the lion's den.

"Is this how you folks do business? I expect integrity from the firms I work with."

"You got one of the best damn advertising campaigns we've ever done," Alec argued.

"That don't mean spit to me if I can't trust the people I'm working with. There are plenty of other firms in this city who would be glad to have my business."

"What . . .?" Jack began.

"And you, Guilder," Hayden interrupted, "I thought your wife didn't work here. Is there something else that you haven't told me?" He shook a finger at Julianne. "What kind of people are you?"

Jack rubbed his forehead and walked around the smoked glass and chrome desk until he stood beside Alec.

"Alec brought me in when I got back from Mexico," Julianne said. "Prior to that I didn't work in the office."

"Are you sure you two are married? Where is your wedding ring, young lady?"

Julianne twisted her fingers around the empty space where her ring used to be. "At the jeweler. What's the problem Mr. Hayden?"

"Stone, here, won't clear space for another commercial. I'm paying you people good money . . ."

Jack's temper still piqued, he jumped in before the client could continue his tirade. "Ben, we've just cleared the decks for you. We created a damn good advertising campaign for you. That promotion should hit the markets as early as next week. You should know things don't normally happen that fast. I think we've delivered what we promised. There isn't a need . . ."

"I'll decide what there's a need for," Hayden puffed. "I want to strike while the iron's hot. I want a media blitz. More commercials, more ads, more radio spots."

"If you'll just give us a little time," Alec pleaded.

"Just because you've signed me to a contract doesn't mean you can push me to the back burner," Hayden sputtered while his face turned a deeper shade of red.

"I think we've proven our commitment to you," Jack repeated in a voice that was much too calm. His eyes squinted and he crossed his arms across his chest.

"Maybe you could assign the little lady to me," Hayden suggested. "Since she's just come on board, that is. Let me keep her busy. She can't have a full schedule yet."

Julianne let out a grunt of frustration. "Mr. Hayden, I would love to help you out, but I do have a full schedule at the moment." Visions of her degree flying out the window with only six weeks to go coupled with the adjustment to her new job frightened her.

"To be fair," Jack said in a deep, resonant voice, "we did drop everything at your request once. You are very important to us and I think we've proven that. However, we do have other clients that require our attention. Maybe if you can give Julianne a couple weeks to transition in, we can dedicate her to your account, but you have to allow her to finish what's on her plate."

Julianne's eyes popped open and her jaw dropped. It was a death sentence. Once Hayden's account was gone, he would get his way and push her out of Perkins & Stone. Without any other clients, she would be dispensable. "John . . ."

Hayden stopped huffing and a slow smile spread across his face. "Well now I think that would suit me just fine."

Julianne pursed her lips, afraid to say anything else although the tears began to sting at the back of her eyes.

"I want a new commercial playing no later than Super Bowl Sunday," Hayden dictated. "Whatever time frame we need to make that happen, I will live with. I also want to see the rest of it in motion. I'll give you time, but I want attention during that time."

"Naturally," Alec agreed. "We won't just hang you up. We'll get started on your next campaign as long as you understand it probably won't unfold quite as quickly as what you've got now."

Hayden held out his hand to seal the deal with Alec and saluted Jack. "I want weekly reports. At a minimum."

"Done," Alec promised.

"Looking forward to more of your ideas, Julianne." Hayden winked at her and walked briskly out of the office.

Julianne collapsed into one of Alec's chrome and leather guest chairs cradling her face in her hands.

"Didn't see that one coming," Jack whispered.

"Julianne?" Alec asked, leaning solicitously across the desk.

She raised her head, glaring, not sure what to say or who to attack first.

Alec made a tent with his fingers in front of his face. "Jack, why don't you give us a moment?"

It was Jack's turn to drop his jaw. "Excuse me?" He asked, his eyebrows raised.

"You'll just have to trust me, son."

"Trust you? I know I'm in trouble when you call me son."

Alec gave way to a little smile. "Julianne doesn't seem quite pleased with this arrangement. Will you allow me to convey the importance of this situation to her?"

"You do want me to finish my degree, don't you?" she asked pointedly. "Hayden doesn't seem the type to be content with 40 hours a week."

"Jack?" Alec asked again, nodding toward the door.

The scowl firmly set, Jack straightened. "You're pushing my limits, Alec."

Alec took a deep breath. "Maybe your limits need to be pushed. Now get out of here."

Jack considered for a moment, narrowing his eyes once more. He looked from Julianne to Alec and back again. "Why don't I trust you?" He asked Alec. "Oh yeah, it's because you've already gone behind my back."

"Maybe you shouldn't let your personal life interfere with business," she suggested.

Jack raised a hand into the air. "Exactly my point."

"She is your wife," Alec reminded him. "At least for the next year."

Jack rolled his eyes, throwing both hands into the air. "How did I get myself into this?" He stormed out of the office.

Alec followed behind him and pushed the door closed. Calmly returning to his seat behind the desk, he again made a tent with his fingers. "Is it just about finishing school?"

Julianne looked for a neutral point on the wall to focus the emotions that were rebounding inside her brain. "I'm in the home stretch. I need to finish."

"You knew that coming into the job. What's really bothering you?"

She bit her lower lip. "Is Hayden safe?"

Alec raised his eyebrows. "Safe?"

Julianne stared directly at Alec. "Safe. I'm a little gun shy right now, Alec. Safe."

"You met his wife."

"He wants me personally. To be at his beck and call."

"I wouldn't read any more into it than that. You could just as easily have been a man that he requested."

"And when his contract is terminated?"

Alec chuckled. "You're thinking Jack has found a way to circumvent me. If you only work for one client, we won't need you when he's gone? Is that it?"

The tears threatened a little closer. "Something like that."

Alec leaned across his desk. "I didn't hire you as Ben Hayden's personal ad rep, but if that's what he wants, that's what he'll get. You bring more to the table than that and you'll probably hate me for all the other things I'll be throwing at you before he leaves our firm." Alec leaned back again. "And Julianne, if I were you, I'd file a complaint with the HR department of that company you came from. At the very least it will give you peace of mind."

She relaxed, the anger dissipating, and yet the future suddenly seemed overwhelming. "Why are you doing all this?" she asked simply, a catch in her throat.

Smiling, Alec swung his chair around to look out his window at the city beyond. "Your future is up to you Julianne. Make of it what you will." He turned his head, addressing her over his shoulder. "Maybe I'm your fairy godfather. Then again, I might be your worst nightmare. I want to see what you're made of."

CHAPTER 13

Julianne tapped her fingers on her briefcase, looked out the window, watched the people bustling through the street. Then she fiddled with her watch, examined her fingernails, tapped her foot. For the ten-minute ride back to the condo, she refused to speak a word. Although he'd made a few attempts at conversation, the most direct response Jack got from Julianne was an undisguised glare.

The cabbie watched them in the rearview mirror. The silence was much louder than the words they should be speaking. Jack covered a chuckle with a cough as the taxi pulled up to their stop, inflaming Julianne's ire even further.

Julianne jumped out of the cab first, leaving Jack to pay the driver. When he walked into the condo moments after her, she threw her briefcase and keys on the desk. She wasn't going any further for the time being.

"You're just going to sit there and smile?" Julianne put her hands to her hips, glaring at him.

"Just waiting for you to open the conversation. I've been trying since we left the office."

"I suppose I should thank you for at least giving me leeway to finish school."

Jack held out a hand in supplication. "It seemed the easiest solution at the time."

Julianne threw her hands up and looked to the beamed ceiling overhead. "What about the truth?"

He winced and scratched his beard. "Well I suppose that's my fault, since I started off with Hayden in a lie. You know how that goes, one lie leads to another until you have trouble finding out where you left the truth. And," he pointed out, "you played along."

"I can't talk about this now. I need some time to think."

Jack raised his eyebrows, and Julianne suddenly felt foolish. Did she expect him to leave his own home? One hand went to her forehead and she closed her eyes. "I haven't had time to look for a place. I'll move into one of those extended-stay hotels."

"I'm not going to kick you out. There's plenty of room for both of us. And it will work to our advantage with Hayden if we're at least living in the same place."

"Then let's decide right now how much you want me to pay in rent."

"Consider it a favor from a friend."

She put her hands to her hips. "I don't want anyone taking care of me. I can take care of myself. I'm not some helpless, homeless waif. I appreciate what you've done for me but it was meant to be a temporary solution. I don't want to owe you anything."

"That's why I didn't want to hire you," he told her. "I didn't want you to feel I'd done you any favors. I should probably have leveled with Hayden from the start and told him you were an outside contractor. I was trying to play an angle."

Julianne tilted her head back, eyes closed. "I'll share some of the responsibility, but I think we've gone a little overboard in this charade. If I'm working that closely with him, don't you think he's going to figure out pretty quickly that we aren't really married? After his little tirade today I can only imagine his reaction to that. Or maybe that's what you're counting on. You think it'll just be my head he wants when that happens?"

"I might point out that my head is on the chopping block right next to yours. Alec has done a lot for me but he won't let me jeopardize the firm. And nepotism doesn't look too good on a resume, but let's look at this from your position."

"I don't have any position," she interrupted. "I'm here because you guys put me here. I have no name in the business. I don't even have my degree yet. I don't need you as a reference."

"On the matter of references," he said, pointing his finger at her, "do you know what kind of reference you're getting from Kimball Brothers?"

The sting of his remark produced tears immediately. Instinctively, Jack reached for her, cupping her head with one hand. Julianne fluttered her eyelashes, trying to prevent the tears from falling. "Reference checks go through the human resources department," she told him.

"You need to file a complaint against that guy."

"I don't need to use Kimball Brothers."

"You don't have any other employment history."

A tear trailed down Julianne's cheek and Jack gently brushed it away with his thumb.

"Why can't we just tell Hayden the truth?" she asked again.

Jack pulled his hand back. "He'd probably fire the firm and the firm would fire us."

Julianne grimaced and wiped at her eyes. "How did we get here?"

Shrugging his shoulders, his face took on an impish grin. "In a cab?"

Julianne couldn't suppress the responding smile.

"Look, it's a short-term solution." Squeezing her hands gently, Jack continued. "Hayden's contract is for one year. You staying here would be a sensible solution. You're closer to school and it will look better from Hayden's standpoint."

"You make it sound so casual."

With one hand, Jack waved around the condo. "In return, I give you a place to stay, rent free. You get your foot in the door with the advertising world making a decent salary that you can tuck away for later, and we get to continue our friendship – we are still friends, aren't we?"

She wouldn't meet his eyes, afraid he'd see her feelings written there. "Like Mexico," she said quietly.

"We do make a good team. Beside, I'm not here that much. You know how often I travel."

She shook her head, trying to think rationally. She didn't want to make another mistake. His arguments made sense. And she wanted to stay, but would she be buying into the fantasy they'd created? When she finally met his eyes, Julianne smirked. "I must be insane."

"We both stand to benefit from this," he pointed out, still trying to convince her.

"I won't let you put me in this position again," she told him. "Don't expect me to play along with any more of your schemes. And I *will* pay you rent."

She leaned back into the sofa and closed her eyes, still shaking her head and wondering if she would regret her decision.

"Uh, Julianne," he began, smoothing his beard, "there's probably one more thing we ought to cover. Did anyone mention the radio voiceovers?"

She opened her eyes briefly. "Voiceovers?"

Jack nodded, running his hand through his hair. "And we put together a press conference in the studio to start running the Hayden campaign. That media blitz he wanted." The pained expression on his face gave her the sense there was more he wasn't telling her.

"And?" she prompted.

"You know how a PR department can be," he began, laughing nervously. "Since Hayden's so high on you they want to promote your hand in all this."

Julianne stiffened, wondering why she hadn't already heard about the press conference. "Do you have a press kit?" she asked, "Something I can look over? Or do you plan to ambush me?"

With a cautious smile, Jack reached into his briefcase and pulled out the book. "There's probably one waiting for you in the office, but here's mine if you want to look it over. You need to know that I didn't have any part in putting this together," he prefaced.

"Why doesn't that comfort me?" She opened the materials and began reading the bio Perkins & Stone manufactured for her. It was a house of cards, waiting for that vibration that would send it all falling to the ground. The whole charade would be exposed if they fed their weak story to the press.

Finally, she closed the book and set it on her legs. "Can't they verify this information? We'll be dog food before the end of the day." She shook her head and looked toward the ceiling. "Just a simple lunch," she muttered.

"Well the part about your degree is perhaps a bit premature, but it isn't likely they'll check too deeply. Right now it's just a client promotion."

"How long before we become the center of attention?" She leaned forward, pushing the book to the edge of her knees. "I don't really relish the idea of living my life in the spotlight. All of this falls to pieces under any kind of scrutiny."

"Let's not look that far ahead," he suggested. "For now the focus is Hayden Casualwear and we're just the gimmick." He frowned and rephrased his thought. "You're the gimmick. The unknown model that Hayden hand-picked. The diamond in the rough."

"The wife of one of the leading ad men in Chicago. Doesn't that diminish my role?"

"That's part of the whole angle. You're the secret weapon, the shining star that's been kept under wraps."

"Being thrust front and center into the spotlight. It will all melt away under that kind of heat."

Jack shook his head. "You can decline all further interviews at your leisure. The PR department just thought it would be a great angle to get the commercial out there. It is an incredible commercial, you know."

Julianne grimaced and looked away from him. "My mother is going to flip out."

"Give her the heads up. That way she can't be caught off guard."

Julianne laughed and felt the tears stinging in her eyes again. She shook her head. "You don't understand."

"She'll have all her friends tuning in to see you on TV. Mothers love to brag about their daughters."

"Yeah, but I'm not the right daughter."

"What do you mean?"

She wiped back a tear that escaped and gave a little laugh. "I'm not the pretty one. It should have been Suzanne."

"Suzanne?"

"My sister."

Jack shook his head, missing her point. "What does your sister have to do with this?"

Julianne pulled back and closed her eyes once more. She shuddered and wrapped her arms around herself.

"Are you cold?"

She shook her head. "No." Her mother couldn't know the truth. Barbara DeAngelo would take the first opportunity to discredit her as retribution for trying to be prettier than Suzanne. "My mother's part of the audience on this one."

"But . . ."

Holding a finger up to stop him, Julianne continued to shake her head. "No. She doesn't need to know the details."

Jack nodded agreement, his eyebrows wrinkled into confusion.

It was time to run interference. If Jack wanted to play with dynamite, he had to help her douse one of the fuses. "You're going with me. Let's go see her now," she suggested, rising from the sofa.

"Going . . . I thought you said she was part of the audience?"

"You wanted a wife, let's see you deal with the mother-in-law. Put on your hip waders, it's going to get pretty deep."

* * *

Julianne's long fingers clenched and unclenched around the steering wheel. "She'll never believe it," she said half to herself for the third time in 10 miles. She checked the rearview mirror and exited the tollway, reducing her speed.

She slowed in front of the brick ranch, studying it as if it were haunted.

"This is it?" Jack asked, leaning forward to look past her out the driver's window.

Through the front picture window they could see a woman rising from a chair to look out. Julianne turned the car into the driveway and shifted into park. Leaning her head on the steering wheel, her auburn hair draped her hands. "I think I'm going to be sick."

Jack opened the car door and stepped out. "Well you won't want to throw up in the car." He walked around to the driver's door and opened it for her.

"You're all heart, John Guilder."

He smiled, holding out a hand for her. "How was I supposed to know you could sling shit as well as I could? Do you always lie to your mother?"

"There are things I don't tell her, but I never lie to my mother. That's why you're going to tell her." He needed to understand just how dangerous her mother could be to their secret. Julianne took hold of his arms, demanding his attention. "Listen up. If I was Suzanne, my mother would remain quietly unconfirming of any and all rumors, but because it's me, she would go out of her way to make sure the whole fairy tale is exposed."

"I don't get it. Why?"

"You don't have brothers and sisters. You wouldn't understand."

"So explain it to me."

Julianne wove her hands into her hair. "It's like it's a competition, but there are no rules and no prize."

Jack furrowed his brow and Julianne took a deep breath. "Okay, let me go back to where it started. We were in grade school at a science fair and one of the teacher's husbands came up to us. He made a comment about how much we resembled each other: sisters, you know. Then he took his comment one step beyond appropriate and said, 'except of course one of you is prettier.' Well he didn't elaborate and I didn't really care, but to Suzanne, it was imperative that she be the prettier one. And, in truth, I believe she is. But that doesn't matter to me. On the other hand, it became an obsession for her.

"Suzanne came home and told my mother what this man said to us. My father was floored and my mother beamed. My father felt he needed to protect me, even after I assured him my self-worth didn't revolve around my appearance. But my mother fed Suzanne's insecurities by pushing her to be more beautiful. Both Suzanne and my mother resented my father trying to protect my feelings when it was clear to them that Suzanne had so much more going for her." Julianne shook her head. "I actually feel sorry for Suzanne sometimes. So much pressure. I just get to be me. That's so much easier."

"You really think your mom would rat you out?"

"In the blink of an eye. Battle lines were drawn that day. It's her defense mechanism to protect Suzanne."

"We could always leave and let her find out with the rest of the world."

"Too late for that now." Julianne nodded toward the front door where her mother watched their progress up the front walk.

Barbara DeAngelo's dark hair was freshly colored and permed into tight curls. Julianne recognized the Hayden Casualwear her mother wore. The blue knit sweatshirt was embroidered with big, bold flowers.

"Mom, I'd like you to meet John Guilder. John, my mother, Barbara DeAngelo."

Barbara pushed the door open further. "Pleased to meet you. Won't you come in?"

While Julianne ducked inside, Jack extended a hand. "It's a pleasure to meet you, Mrs. DeAngelo. Julianne's told me a lot about you."

Barbara shook his hand and stepped back to let him pass. "I'm always glad to meet Julianne's friends."

They walked into the living room where Barbara offered her guest a seat. "Would you like something to drink? I always have a pot of coffee on."

"I think a glass of water would do the trick." Jack took a seat on a gold brocade loveseat.

"I'll get it," Julianne offered, wishing there was some way to avoid this situation.

"Thank you," her mother replied, sitting opposite Jack in a matching easy chair. "Do you work with Julianne?"

"I do now," he said, laughing. "Actually, we've known each other for quite a while now."

When Julianne returned, she saw Jack look at the wall of built-in bookshelves behind her mother's head. Along with knickknacks and photo albums, dozens of pictures of Suzanne smiled back at him. "Are these pictures of you?" Jack asked Barbara solicitously.

Barbara smiled and laughed. "No, no. That's my Suzanne. People do say she looks like me, though. Such a lovely girl."

Julianne saw the realization strike Jack in that moment when he turned sharply to look at his proposed bride. "I don't see any of Julianne?"

Barbara pursed her lips. "She was a little more shy in front of a camera, not quite as photogenic, I suppose."

The change in Jack's face was obvious to Julianne, but his expressions quickly became cloaked. "I understand Julianne's father has passed on," he proceeded, "and so there's something I'd like to ask you."

Julianne's mother sat forward in her seat, folding her hands between her knees. "I'm not sure what it is I could do for you, but I'm willing to listen."

It was the moment she was dreading. Julianne set the glass of water down in front of Jack, spilling some onto the highly polished coffee table.

"I'll get a paper towel," she told them, hurrying back to the kitchen. How was she going to be able to look at her mother while Jack presented their story?

"I can't imagine what's gotten into her," Barbara said.

Jack cleared his throat. "Actually I suppose it's too late to ask the question, we've come to share some news."

Sneaking back into the room, Julianne kept her head down while her mother sat back into the cushions of the easy chair. "What did you say your name was?"

Jack gave her the smile he reserved for clients, smoothing his beard with one hand. "Jack Guilder, ma'am."

With trembling hands, Julianne wiped at the spilled water. Jack leaned forward a moment, as if he wanted to help, but then sat back in his seat.

He took a deep breath and plunged ahead. "She swept me off my feet. I apologize for not asking you ahead of time, but I just knew I couldn't live without her. Mrs. DeAngelo, when Julianne agreed to marry me I didn't want to wait another minute."

"Is this a joke?" Barbara asked.

Julianne sat on her heels and turned to her mother. "Why don't you just hear him out, Mom."

"You wanted to ask my permission?" Barbara asked Jack.

"I don't have any family of my own," he explained with his best "poor me" expression. "I was hoping to have your blessing in spite of our impulsive decision. It would mean a lot to me."

"Are you pregnant?" she asked Julianne directly.

Julianne felt the indignation rising in her cheeks once more. "No." Julianne brushed her hair to her back.

Barbara shook her head in disbelief. "But the wedding. I haven't even canceled your wedding plans to Steve yet." Her eyes opened wide when the thought occurred to her. "What about Steve?" Barbara looked at Julianne and whispered loudly, "Does he know about that?"

"Yes," Jack spoke up. "We have no secrets."

"A few secrets might not be a bad thing," Barbara commented. "This is what you want Julianne?"

Julianne leaned her head against a wall, wadding up the paper towel inside a fist. "This is where you congratulate me," she prompted her mother.

"What about this man you went to Mexico with?"

"That would be me," Jack replied.

"You're the man she's been talking to on-line?"

Jack looked at Julianne and she wished she could melt into the wall. "Yes," he said.

"Not quite the serial killer you imagined?" Julianne asked.

Jack raised his eyebrows, and gave in to a smile.

It was Barbara's turn to be discomfited. She pursed her lips and reached for her cup of coffee. "You seem like a very nice gentleman," she said discretely.

Julianne threw the paper towel into a corner wastebasket. It was one thing for her mother to be rude to her, but quite another to be rude to company. "He is a very nice gentleman, Ma."

Barbara shrugged her shoulders. "As long as you're happy."

Jack rose from the couch and put his hands to Julianne's shoulders. "You're going to be so proud of her. You should see the commercial she made."

"You mean you really did that?" Barbara asked Julianne.

"She was incredible," Jack said. "It was hers from conception to realization. She's a beautiful model."

"Model?" Barbara asked, raising one eyebrow. "Now I know you two are pulling my leg."

Julianne felt Jack's hands tighten on her shoulders. Acknowledging his response, Julianne touched one of his hands with hers. It was no less than she expected from her mother.

"You don't have to believe us, Mom. You'll see it on TV." Julianne looked up at Jack, her fists clenched at her sides. She could see the muscles in his jaw rippling the hairs of his beard like a cat circling a mouse. Locking his eyes with hers, she needed him to see there was no point in attacking.

"You two don't exactly seem the happy couple," Barbara observed.

"I spoiled Julianne's surprise. She didn't want to tell you about the commercial until it ran. She's a little unhappy with me. I knew you'd want to hear all about it though." Jack turned away from Julianne's glare back to Barbara.

Julianne whispered in an almost inaudible voice. "She'll never believe this, John. Us."

Jack took hold of Julianne's shoulders and leaned his forehead against hers. "We stretched that rope when we were in Mexico. Didn't it make our friendship stronger? We did graduate from the computer to the telephone."

"You're so sure of yourself, aren't you?" Her attention was completely focused on Jack, lost in the dark brown of his eyes. He put a hand to cradle the side of her face, and Julianne closed her eyes.

"Will you two quit whispering," Barbara interrupted. "It's not polite."

"You'll be less anxious once the commercial is running," Jack said to Julianne loud enough for Barbara to hear.

Barbara smiled, crossing her legs. "Well now I'm curious to see Julianne's work."

"It's for Hayden Casualwear," Julianne said before she turned her attention away from Jack. She flexed her hands and turned away.

"Why don't you both stay for dinner so I can get better acquainted with your young man, Julianne," Barbara invited.

Julianne leaned back toward Jack on the tips of her toes. "We can't stay for dinner," she pleaded in an urgent whisper.

"Is she always this nervous?" Jack asked, laughing to cover Julianne's anxiety. Jack put an arm across Julianne's shoulders. "I've been gone for two weeks, just flew in from New York. I haven't even been home yet. We really should go."

Julianne took long strides toward the door. "Are you coming, then?" Julianne prodded.

"Mrs. DeAngelo, it was an honor to meet you. Let me get settled back in and I'll take you both out for dinner."

"I'd like that. Please call me Barbara."

Julianne was out the door and walking toward the car. She rested both hands on the roof, looking ruefully back at her mother. "I'll call you," she promised.

"I don't even know where you live," Barbara called after her daughter.

Jack stopped and pulled out a business card, quickly penning his phone number and address. He hesitated before giving it to her, looking to Julianne for approval.

Julianne nodded. "Don't give that to Suzanne," Julianne warned her mother.

"We'll be in touch, Barbara," Jack promised.

Julianne climbed into the car and gunned the engine. Jack hurried down the walk, taking his place in the passenger seat of Julianne's small car. "Are you all right?"

"Try living my life for the past month and see how it affects you."

"Seems as though I have."

"You only know the half of it." She backed down the driveway and steered the car back toward the city.

* * *

The doorman had delivered Jack's suitcases to where they remained, just inside the door. Jack grabbed both bags and carried them up the staircase, disappearing into the inner sanctum of his bedroom.

Julianne sat at her desk in the corner of the first-floor great room and closed her eyes, taking deep breaths. Her eyes filled with tears feeling the effect of the emotional elevator she had been riding all day. She leaned on the desk and rested her head in her hands.

All those nights they had chatted on-line, all the conversations they had shared. The week in Mexico learning to be comfortable in each other's company. She was in love with Jack Guilder, but it was all a game to him.

A knock on the front door startled her. "What now?" she sighed, rising to answer.

Alec Stone stood in the hallway, a self-satisfied smile on his face. "I assume he's told you about the press conference tomorrow," he said, stepping past her into the condo. Alec pointed upstairs, raising his eyebrows in question.

Julianne nodded and closed the door behind him.

From behind his back, Alec produced a bottle of champagne. "A present," he offered.

"What are we celebrating?"

"The wedding, of course."

"I'm so glad you're happy." She walked back over to her computer to read the e-mail message her brother-in-law sent.

"Aren't you at all excited?"

"Delirious," she replied, not bothering to face him.

"And you were worried you wouldn't get along."

"Baring your soul to someone through a computer isn't nearly the same as sitting in the same room with him. Or her." She cast a glance up the stairway.

"Isn't it better to have him here in front of you instead of somewhere on the other end of a computer?"

Julianne stood eye to eye with Alec Stone. "That's the beauty of it, Alec. That distance provided safety. No expectations. No disappointments. He likes me better at a distance."

"Your wall's just as thick as his, isn't it?" Alec observed, shifting his gaze from one to the other of her eyes in disbelief. "You would have walked right into that meeting if you hadn't been invited."

The tears rolled silently down her cheeks. "A perfect match."

Alec set down the bottle of champagne and wrapped his arms around Julianne, holding her tightly. "Not quite the thing fairy tales are made of, now is it?" The hot wool of his suit coat burned her nostrils, beneath it the faint scent of Old Spice.

Julianne accepted his embrace. "When this is over," she snuffled, "I want you to promise me something."

Alec smoothed her hair tenderly. "If I can."

"Send me away from here. Send me to New York or L.A. or somewhere I don't have to run into him every day."

"Is it really so hard?"

Julianne pushed away from Alec. "Now I know why he didn't want to hire me. He hates me, Alec."

"Have you found what I was looking for?" Jack called from the railing overhead.

Alec tweaked her chin and looked reluctantly away from Julianne. "Yes, I have them. Do you want a glass of champagne?" he asked, turning to look up at his godson. "Would be a shame to let it go to waste."

"Been a long day. How about if we do a dinner tomorrow night. Julie, we can invite your mom over and we'll all drink a toast then."

Ignoring him, Julianne walked to the rear of the condo and retreated behind the bedroom door under the loft where she had taken up residence.

CHAPTER 14

Although she tried to think of it as the start of just another workweek, Julianne couldn't fight the feeling that this particular Monday would be the beginning of the longest week of her life. She hoped the job would preoccupy her thoughts when she took her place in her cubicle. Julianne checked her watch noting that Bev, the woman she shared space with, was already at her desk.

"How was your weekend?" Bev greeted.

"Don't ask. How about yours?"

"Great. We saw that new movie, you know the one with Mel Gibson."

"How was it?"

"You've gotta see it."

"Hey Julie," Tyler Stern peeked over the half wall that separated their workspaces. "Some of us are going up to Wisconsin for a concert next weekend. Wanna go?"

Dorian Lannon walked by the quad and dropped a large envelope on Julianne's desk. "She can't go, she's going to be out of town."

Julianne smiled at Tyler apologetically. "Maybe next time."

She picked up the packet and found her copy of the press kit Jack showed her. Also included was a schedule for the next month that had Julianne attending an awards banquet, flying to Houston to spend three days with Ben Hayden and a trip to New York for a presentation she knew nothing about. With a sigh, Julianne leaned her head in her hands.

"You seem a little quiet today," Bev observed. "What happened Friday? They didn't fire you, did they?"

Julianne laughed. "No. They didn't fire me."

Tyler walked around the quad, and stood behind Bev and Julianne. He nodded toward Jack's office. "I've never seen him so upset. He's liable to make your life a living hell. He can be a real slave driver when he wants to be."

Julianne shrugged her shoulders and turned back to her computer. "He hardly speaks to me."

"He doesn't talk to anyone," Bev confided. "A real loner."

"How do you know him?" Tyler prodded.

It was still hard for Julianne to forget the catty women at Kimball Brothers, always looking for gossip. "I don't want to talk about it right now," Julianne said. She reminded herself these were different people, a different company, a different position, but she couldn't shake off the intrusive nature of the questions.

"I heard Ben Hayden chewed his ass out. Didn't you help make that presentation?"

"Yes," she answered shortly.

"And I heard Ron Perkins has been asking about you."

Julianne flinched, wondering about the other senior partner of the firm. Maybe Jack couldn't fire her, but Ron Perkins could. "Can we just let it drop?"

"What did you have to do to keep Hayden's Casualwear?"

Julianne pursed her lips and turned to face Tyler once more. All the petty remarks about Megan, who had been promoted into the position they'd offered her at Kimball Brothers, crowded to the forefront. "Look, Tyler, I don't want to talk about this right now."

Tyler held up his hands in truce and retreated to his side of the quad. "Excuse me."

Julianne hung her head and pushed away from her desk. She stood up, leaning forward to peer over the half-wall. "Look, Ben Hayden's making my life miserable right now. Can we just leave it at that for now?"

"Sure, Jule. It's none of my business anyway."

"Bev?" She looked to the woman beside her for support.

"I'm with Tyler. I wouldn't be in your shoes right now if you paid me."

Julianne looked at Jack's empty office beyond the quad.

A familiar voice thundered through the office. "I know she's here and I want to see her now!"

Julianne put her elbows up on her desk and leaned into her hands. "Oh God, not now."

"Did you hear about that guy that started shooting up an office down the street because his girlfriend broke up with him?" Bev whispered.

"Julianne!" Steve shouted.

"Do you know that guy?" Bev asked. "He's not going to go postal or anything, is he?"

"No," Julianne reassured her. "At least I don't think so."

Julianne saw Steve's sandy head jerk to attention when he picked her out of the sea of creative staff and began pushing his way toward her.

"You got married?" He shouted.

Julianne rose from her seat, taking his arm and leading him back out of the office. "Let's go somewhere we can talk," she suggested.

"What's the matter, you don't want your new friends to know what you did to me?"

Julianne put her hands on her hips and stood to face him. "What I did to you? Would you like me to announce to all these people what you did to me? Let's not air our dirty laundry, shall we."

"Who is the guy?" Steve demanded. "I'll kill him."

Julianne pushed Steve through the glass doors and into the vestibule. She punched the elevator call button and began pacing.

"How long have you been cheating on me?"

"Shut up," she snapped. A light glowed over the elevator and a bell rang its arrival. "Get in."

She pushed the button for the cafeteria and turned on him like a cornered lion. "You better not make any more trouble for me or I'll really let you know how vindictive I can be. I work here now and I don't need you waltzing in jeopardizing my position when you have no idea what's going on."

The elevator doors opened and they stepped out. Julianne strode angrily into the cafeteria and sat down at one of the tables in the nearly empty room.

"Who is this guy you're living with?" he insisted.

"Well where was I supposed to go? You took over the apartment and I'm not about to move in with my sister. My mother's on her side and that leaves me in the cold." Julianne shook her head. "Why am I even trying to explain any of this to you? What do you care? Haven't you already screwed me over enough?"

"You did this to get even, didn't you?" Steve's head drooped like a wounded puppy's as he took a seat opposite her at the table. "I love you, Julianne. It hurts to see you just throw out the last two years like they never happened."

"It hurts for me to look at what a waste the last two years have been. The only reason you love me, Steve Montgomery, is because I left you. You didn't want me when you had me."

"Are you going to tell me you don't love me at all?"

"That's got nothing to do with it. Think about what you're saying Steve. I know you love me, but that wasn't enough for you, was it?"

"You can't just leave me like this."

"It isn't just like this." She let out an exasperated sigh and took hold of his hands across the top of the table. "It's been coming for a long time, Steve. I stayed because I kept expecting it to work out. I kept believing that maybe things would change. But I couldn't be happy that way. I'd always be wondering where you were, who you were with. That's no kind of life." She tilted her head searching out his eyes, trying to get him to look at her. "We haven't been together for a long time. Not really. It doesn't work anymore."

Jack's deep voice resonated from behind. "Julianne?"

Julianne's forehead hit the table with a thunk. Jack's appearance could only fan the flames that she was trying to stifle.

"Is this the guy?" Steve shouted, jumping to his feet. He pointed his finger accusingly, first at Jack, then at Julianne. "You did this. Stealing her away from me."

"Oh God," Julianne cried out. "If you say one more word, Steve Montgomery, I'm going to start advertising what you did and no woman will come within ten feet of you."

Steve's face suffused with blood as he visibly fought to control his temper, fists clenching and unclenching.

"This is a place of business," Jack told him calmly, "and you're disrupting the office. This is a private matter which we will be happy to discuss in private, after business hours. Can you leave quietly or do you need an escort?"

"Is that necessary?" Julianne asked, slowly rising to her feet in defense of Steve.

"Maybe we should just take out a full-page ad so everyone can read up on our private lives. Inquiring minds, you know," Jack said.

"I'm not finished yet," Steve shouted.

Jack stood in front of Julianne, shielding her. "Oh yes you are."

"I'll come to the apartment later and we can talk about it then," Julianne said, stepping out from behind Jack's broad back.

Jack put a protective arm around Julianne's shoulders. "You have class tonight."

"You and that damn class. Screw you," Steve spat out. "Screw you both." He pushed past them, hitting the backs of the chairs as he left the cafeteria.

Julianne buried her head against Jack's chest. His arms circled her before he rested his chin on top of her head. "We'd better get back to work."

Julianne closed her eyes, indulging in his embrace. She reluctantly pulled away from the wings of the gryphon, allowing him to lead her out of the cafeteria.

They rode back up to the 42nd floor on opposite sides of the elevator. Jack held the glass doors to the office open for Julianne and followed her in, walking back to his office while she detoured to the ladies room.

Julianne splashed cold water on her face and patted it off gently with a paper towel. She leaned forward against the marble countertop and closed her eyes, summoning whatever strength she had left.

"You all right?" Bev asked, walking in behind her.

Julianne straightened up and pulled down on her sweater. Steve had surely made her the focus of office gossip now. She wished she could blend into the background. "Yeah. Fine."

"The old boyfriend carrying a little baggage?"

"Yeah," she answered simply. Julianne brushed by Bev and back to her quad.

Tyler peered around the half wall. "You leave the poor guy standing at the altar or what?"

Julianne opened the package of information Dorian left on her desk, dizzy with the emotions swimming inside her head. Ben Hayden wanted her in Texas in three days. She got back to her feet and walked past Dorian into Jack's office. "Excuse me, Mr. Guilder?"

He sat behind his desk staring out the window. "What?"

"Is Ron Perkins going to fire me?"

Jack smiled. "Ron Perkins wants to clone you." He straightened in his chair and folded his hands on the desk in front of him. "Scared the hell out of Alec, demanding to know who the hell this Julianne DeAngelo person was. He was ready to give you a promotion. Had a hard time believing you hadn't finished your degree yet. Asked what firm Alec stole you from."

She shook her head. "No."

"Honest." Jack crossed his heart with one finger. "He saw the commercial screening. When he found out you were just starting your career, he said he'd never seen so much raw talent in his life."

Julianne felt the blush rising from her collar. "Yeah, but you did a lot of it, too."

Jack shook his head. "No. You did it."

CHAPTER 15

They walked into the radio station side by side. Jack kept looking sideways at her, making Julianne feel more self-conscious. She hadn't eaten anything since lunch the day before, a fact that Jack continued to bring to her attention. Her stomach wouldn't settle long enough for her to try.

Jack stopped her outside the control room and lay a hand on her shoulder. "Hold up a minute." He reached into his pocket and pulled out a ring box. Removing two bands, he slipped them onto Julianne's fingers, staring into her eyes. "So Hayden can stop asking," he explained. He held her hand a moment longer, curling her fingers into her palm. "Don't lose them."

Caught in his gaze, Julianne nodded silently. With all the activity around them, her mind was too numb to come up with a response.

Jack opened the door to the control room, and Julianne continued to the studio with the script, smiling and nodding to everyone who was trying to assist her. She turned the rings on her finger without looking at them.

From behind the glass, she saw Jack point to her, sending someone with a small black bag in her direction. While another person tried to help her with her headphones, a third person tried to point out her cues in the script. With so many people trying to demand her attention, it took all Julianne's concentration to figure out what she was supposed to do.

The woman Jack sent in from the control room pulled a stool up beside Julianne and opened her little black bag. Seeing the cosmetics inside, Julianne began to protest. "I did make-up today."

"It's for the camera, hon," the woman told her. "Besides, you're about as pale as the moon. And look at these dark circles under your eyes. You sick or something?"

Julianne reached for a mirror and held it to her face. Who was she trying to kid, pretending to be beautiful before the world? She forced a weak smile for the beautician. "Not sick, only ordinary."

The beautician graced her with a smile. "Far from ordinary, sweetie." She tilted Julianne's head back. "I love the color of your eyes, like sherry in wineglasses, and your hair, you can't pay for highlights like these. Look at this bone structure. And I can see the pallor, which means it isn't normal. I bet you usually have rosy cheeks. It's the circles under your eyes. They give you away." The woman reached back into her bag, digging around through her supplies. "I've seen these kinds of nerves before. We'll take care of you." With a wink, she began removing the make-up Julianne had applied earlier. "You listen to your run-through and pretend I'm not here. It'll all be over in a jif. No one's gonna see your face on the radio anyway."

"Julianne, we're going to play it through for you." Julianne looked up to see who addressed her from the control booth, his voice tinny through the microphone. She nodded while the beautician clucked her tongue at the sudden movement.

"Sorry," Julianne apologized.

Thirty minutes later Julianne was sitting alone in the studio, one hand on her headset listening for the cues. Doing the voiceover was more difficult than she'd expected, but it took her mind off the interview to follow. The reporter they'd lined up was already waiting in the control booth with the news team and she could see the red light on the camera at her side periodically going off and on.

Julianne visualized the palace in Mexico City and smiled. She closed her eyes and lifted her arms, waving them in the air the way she would if she was doing the "queen's walk." She heard the cue and recited the lines for the radio ad, pausing to wink at the news camera beside her.

The red light went off and the music in her head stopped. She looked to the control booth where Jack stood smiling. He leaned forward to press the speaker button.

"Ham," he teased.

She stuck her tongue out. They were on stage again. "Am I done?" she asked.

She watched the orchestration going on in the control booth and removed her head gear, crossing her legs until the parade made its way into the studio.

With a deep breath, she prepared for the next act in their drama. Her only wish was that she didn't have to be the star of the show.

Jack sat beside her, the loving husband, holding her hand. Julianne fielded questions from the reporter sent to promote the husband and wife team that was about to wow the advertising world with their Clio-bound commercial waiting in the wings.

The interrogation came at them rapid fire, but Julianne and Jack had been up half the night preparing. The answers flowed easily, playing up the gimmick of Hayden's quirks in choosing Julianne instead of a commercial model and their impulsive jaunt to Mexico to shoot.

Jack fielded the matter of her experience neatly, giving her the credit for his Preston slogan as another noteworthy contribution and pulling the rest of her resume under a generic blanket of "less public efforts."

With the formalities completed, lunch was laid out for them in a conference room. Away from the cameras and microphones, Julianne realized she was ravenous.

By three o'clock, she was back at her desk, struggling to stay awake. The nervous energy left her drained, and she still had class to get through.

Jack walked past her to his office. "Go home," he suggested.

"I have to finish . . ."

"It will still be here tomorrow."

She gratefully accepted defeat and rose to her feet while she closed down her workstation.

* * *

The cleaning people were gone. Only the emergency lights were still on in the office space. The hairs stood up on the back of Julianne's neck in spite of her irritation at having forgotten her computer at her desk. She was relieved to see the security guards in the lobby.

She re-locked the glass doors of Perkins & Stone behind her and rode the elevator down. With the announcing "ding" she bowed her head as if prepared to plow through the normal onrush of people, but the lobby was silent except for the guard watching television at his post.

"'Night, Mr. Guilder," he called out.

Julianne opened her mouth to reply, wondering why the man called her Mr. Guilder until she heard Jack respond "See you tomorrow." A flood of relief swept over her. She never expected he would still be at the office after her class finished. Now she could catch a ride home with him.

Then she stopped cold in her tracks when she heard another woman's voice.

"Jack? Jack Guilder?"

Julianne ducked behind the corner.

Jack lifted his head slowly, his attention directed toward the glass doors that opened to the street. "Gloria?"

"It is you, isn't it?"

The woman wore a short fur jacket, her long legs stretching interminably from beneath, almost as if she wasn't wearing anything at all beneath the jacket.

The woman flew at him in a cloud of long blond hair and dramatically overused perfume, throwing her arms around him.

"You look wonderful!" she said, standing back to take inventory.

"So do you. In fact I feel guilty. It's been so long."

"Well I was in the city and I figured you'd be working late - you always did. Thought I'd take a chance. It's been five years, Jack."

"You'd never know it by looking at you. What brings you to town?" He steered her out of the building and onto the streets of Chicago.

Julianne hesitated, her heart in her throat. She felt like an intruder and as curious as she was, her common sense slapped her with the fact that she held no ties to Jack.

The couple walked slowly down Michigan Avenue. Julianne came around the corner of the elevator bank, feeling somewhat exposed and yet anxious to get home after her exhausting day.

"'Night Ms. DeAngelo," the guard greeted her.

"Night."

And then as a second thought, he got up from his post. "Oh. Did you want me to call you a cab. You just missed Mr. Guilder. Maybe I can . . . "

"I'm fine," she assured him, waving him off and wishing he would speak more quietly even though there was no one else in the building to hear.

"Well see you tomorrow then," he said, sitting back down at his station.

"Tomorrow," Julianne replied, eyes still on the couple outside the glass doors. Gloria slid an arm insinuatingly around Jack's waist and dipped a hand just inside his belt. Jack continued to walk, not missing a stride.

Julianne's heart sank. She wanted to stay hiding inside the building or to run in another direction. She didn't want Jack to see how much he meant to her. "Don't be silly," she whispered to herself, walking onto Michigan Avenue.

The echo of Gloria's high heels stopped and Jack turned to take one more look at her long, long legs. Her voice carried in the crisp night air. "Well where are my manners?" She walked up to hug him, pressing tightly against him and lifting one leg almost unnoticeably between his. "Congratulations. Actually I did see something on the news, but I couldn't believe it."

Jack just smiled.

Gloria's smile broadened while her fingers played up his chest. "Surely you have a few minutes to have a drink with an old friend. We are old friends, aren't we?"

Jack looked up toward the dark sky hidden behind the towering skyscrapers and Julianne resisted the urge to duck. Instead, Julianne turned away to hail a cab. She hid, slouched into the back seat, and let her hair cover her face. With one last look to the couple on the sidewalk, Julianne saw Jack lean over and kiss Gloria, then whistle for a taxi. Julianne pretended she dropped something and ducked, hoping she wouldn't be noticed.

As Julianne's cab passed the couple, another stopped. Julianne looked through the back window, unable to resist, and saw Jack open the cab, help Gloria in and lean in one last time before waving her off.

Julianne twisted the rings on her finger. Her life was spinning out of control. Like a bad dream, it was as if she were an onlooker instead of a participant.

Gone were the nights she was able to type all her feelings down and have JGGuilder answer back, making sense of all the things she couldn't. Their expectations had been so simple then. They'd lost that, and she didn't know how to compensate. She felt as inanimate as the statue that guarded her desk.

CHAPTER 16

Jack walked past Julianne to the kitchen. It was odd having someone else around while she was getting ready for work.

They moved past each other in silence, reaching for coffee cups, toasting bagels, pouring cereal, reaching into the refrigerator. Julianne's feelings were still bruised after witnessing his encounter the night before and she didn't trust herself to make small talk.

They arrived home within minutes of each other the night before and Julianne wondered if he was resenting having a faux wife disrupting his personal plans.

"Maybe I should move out," she suggested, offering him the release.

"What?" He stopped to look at her.

"This has to be a great imposition to you," she continued. "I'm sure you're used to your routine, a different type of lifestyle. I feel like I'm in the way."

"Don't be silly. You're not in the way."

She licked her lips, debating if she should tell him she saw him leave the office. He couldn't very well bring the woman home. But couldn't he have gone with her?

They had the image to keep up. He would probably be more discrete. Before she could think of a good way to open the subject, he cleared his throat and took a seat at the kitchen table.

"Do you have a picture of Steve?"

It seemed an odd question. She furrowed her brow before answering. "Yeah, why?"

"I need to borrow it. Just for today."

"What for?" She raised her head to look at him, tried to see past those brown eyes into his motives.

He made a conscious effort to look away and poured a cup of coffee. He grimaced as he took a drink of the steaming liquid. "Do you trust me?"

She rested the side of her head in her hand as she considered the point, her hair falling to one side in a cascade of soft copper.

"I'll give it back to you later," he pressed. Jack leveled his eyes on Julianne's. "Do you trust me, Julianne?"

It was her turn to grimace. Julianne rubbed her forehead and rose from the table. She walked through the great room to her desk and took out her wallet.

Jack bowed his head and set his coffee mug on the counter. With his hands on the smooth surface, she was aware of the tension in his arms.

Julianne removed an old photo from her wallet, taken in a photo booth at the mall. A momentary prickling of nostalgia drew her back to happier days before she turned to offer it to Jack.

Jack walked up behind her, then slowed when he saw the photo in her hand. He took it from her gingerly. "I'll have this back to you by tonight."

She shrugged her shoulders. "I don't expect it really matters. You won't hurt him, will you?"

Jack shook his head and stared at the photo of the happy couple, the moment forever captured on film.

* * *

She was distracted again. It was becoming a habit.

Did she trust him?

The picture didn't really matter, but what did he intend to do with it?

After Steve's appearance she was sure the gossip was running rampant through the office. In spite of the fact that she had never liked Megan at Kimball Brothers, Julianne was certainly feeling sympathetic toward her now.

Bev tried to make small talk, hoping to glean more information that she could process through the office. The truth of the matter was no one really knew Julianne's status. Was she dating? Engaged? Married to Jack Guilder?

Julianne's eyes wandered back to Jack's office where he sat poring over documents on his desk. She watched him answer his phone and considered how many things she didn't know about him. He looked up and Julianne self-consciously turned back to her work. From the other side of her quad, she heard Tyler push back his chair and saw him charge into Jack's office and close the door.

Through the glass sidelight, Julianne saw Tyler raise his arms making a heated point. She could see Jack's eyebrows pulled together and that now familiar clenching of his jaw. Jack looked out the window directly at her and Julianne quickly averted her attention.

She wasn't only distracted, she was a distraction. The speculation about her position had probably taken on a life of its own. Rifling through her papers, she came across the packet Dorian had given her the day before and pulled out the travel itinerary.

Jack was leaving tonight for Los Angeles. She was leaving tomorrow for Houston. Maybe their absence would quiet the rumor mills. Or add fuel to the fire.

Julianne was startled to see Jack striding toward her moments later. He cocked his head indicating she should follow and she rose discretely from her desk to meet him in the vestibule.

"Your sister," he began, his eyes still flashing from his discussion with Tyler. "Her name is Suzanne DePalma?"

Dread made her shiver. "Yes."

"Why would she want to see me?"

Rising anger made her dizzy. "She thinks she needs to protect me from the world. She'll proposition you to prove that you're not good enough for me."

Jack nodded. "Ok, I get it." He turned to press the elevator call button.

Apprehensively, she called after him. "Jack?" But her courage evaporated just as quickly. She shook her head and turned away. She couldn't lose what she didn't have. "Never mind."

* * *

"I hear you got married," his message read.

It was so much easier to talk to him online and yet the condo felt colder, emptier with him gone. The moonlight crept across the hardwood floors while Julianne typed out her response. "It's like déjà vu."

The cliché answer would be, "all over again," and Julianne half expected to read that as his next line. Instead, she read: "I hear he's a great guy."

The smile crept to her face. "My mother thinks he's a serial killer."

"So don't keep any Wheaties in your kitchen."

Julianne furrowed her brow, confused for a moment. With a groan, she started to laugh and put her fingers back to the keyboard. "Nearly missed that one – but maybe better to be a cereal killer than a celery stalker."

"Still got your wit, I see."

"Speaking of my family – what did you think of my sister?" She hit send before she could second guess her decision to ask.

"She must own stock in make-up," came his reply. "Is she always so overdone?"

The smile broadened across her face. "Afraid so."

"It was like Halloween in the reception area. I think I made her mad."

Julianne laughed out loud. "What did you do?" She bounced in her chair, anxious for his next line of type.

"She tried to worm her way into my office, until I told her she had a smudge on her cheek. She panicked, then got real cool toward me when she couldn't find it."

Julianne laughed again. There weren't many men who could see through Suzanne's ploys the way Jack seemed to. He had braved not only her mother, but now her sister. "Well now you can get some sleep," she typed, choosing a safer conversation. "California can turn back the clock for you."

"You should be sleeping," came his reply. "Did you finish your paper?"

Julianne toggled over to the word processing program and saved her paper, then toggled back to his message. "Nearly. You must have bribed the teacher. He's been very nice about my schedule."

"He owed me a favor."

Julianne frowned. She didn't want to get her degree on favors and she was preparing to tell that to Jack when his next message forestalled her.

"Don't get mad. The favor was letting you complete the assignment early, not giving you an "A". You'll get whatever grade you deserve (as if there's any doubt about that)."

With a sigh, Julianne relaxed into her chair. "Well I suppose it isn't as if I'm slacking off the whole class. There's only a couple of weeks left and this is the end game."

The cursor blinked mutely for several minutes. Julianne closed her eyes and felt the fatigue settling in. She would be on a flight tomorrow and it wouldn't do much good to meet Hayden half asleep. The chiming of Jack's next message brought her back to the computer screen.

"I miss you."

Julianne stared at the words in the box for several minutes. There was so much she wanted to say. She wanted to tell him she missed him too, but images of a leggy blonde on Michigan Avenue halted her fingers from exposing her feelings.

"It seems strange," the words continued, "chatting online with you now. I've gotten used to talking to you in person."

Julianne smiled and felt her heart glowing. "You could always call," she invited. "I think you know the number."

As she hit the send button, the phone rang behind her. "Hello?"

On the other end of the line she heard the ding of her message on his computer screen. Jack chuckled. "I guess I do know the number."

Before she could stop herself, she said, "I miss you, too."

"I wanted to say goodnight." The tenor of his voice vibrated along her spine.

"Good night." She looked at the gryphon perched above her computer and reached up to touch it.

"Call me when you get to Houston," he told her.

"Ok."

"I'll see you in a couple of days."

All coherent thoughts seemed to escape her. All she could say was "Ok."

"Get some sleep, Julie."

"You too."

* * *

The cell phone created dissonance through the headphones. Julianne pulled one off her ear to be certain she had heard it and then turned off her portable CD player with the insistent confirming ring.

"Hello?"

"I'm very proud of you, Julianne," her mother said.

She hadn't expected to feel the flush of gratification at her mother's words. "What did I do?"

"I just saw your commercial, and you know what? I'd buy Hayden Casualwear."

Julianne laughed and reached for the remote control. "You do buy Hayden Casualwear. What are you watching?"

"Channel Two, but it's already over."

"He sponsored the first half hour. There's another one."

"Then let me go so I can watch it. I love you."

Julianne felt a tear sting the corner of her eyes. "I love you too, Mom."

As soon as she disconnected, the phone rang again.

"Did you see it?" Jack asked.

"No. I was listening to a CD but my mother just called. The other one will be on, won't it?"

"Should be before 9:30. It looks great, Julianne."

"My ten minutes of fame."

"You got that before you showed up on commercial television."

She felt shy suddenly, exposed. "Maybe I'll just go back to the CD."

"Watch the commercial, Julie. Give yourself something to feel good about."

She wrapped one arm around herself. "How's the weather back home?"

"Cold. Did you get the message about the awards banquet on Saturday night?"

"What am I supposed to wear?"

"It's formal. Do you have something?"

Frustration swelled inside her. "The only formal gown I own right now is my wedding dress."

"Probably a little too formal, huh?"

"Actually, it's more of a cocktail dress. I could probably get by with it. But do I really have to go?"

"It'll be like making the commercial, Julie. Just relax and step into character."

"Feels more like a bad B movie."

"Then I'll be King Kong and you can be Fay Wray."

"Why do I get the feeling you're enjoying all this?"

"I'll see you Saturday, Fay."

* * *

Without her makeup, Suzanne looked more like the sister Julianne remembered. Suzanne sat on one of the twin beds in the room they shared growing up painting her toenails the way they had when they were in high school.

Suzanne didn't look up while Julianne took her wedding dress out of the closet, concentrating on her toes instead. "Taking it back?"

"No, I need it for a formal dinner tomorrow night."

Suzanne raised her eyebrows, but continued to stare at her feet, wiggling each toe to test the color. "Aren't we special?"

Julianne shook her head. "It isn't as if I even want to go."

"Poor you." Suzanne lifted her head and gave Julianne a plastic smile.

"Well hopefully you'll think I'm doing better for myself." Julianne closed the closet door.

"Did I tell you he invited me to his office?" Suzanne said casually.

"Don't you just love the ducks on his wall?"

"I don't go for that hunting theme. Maybe you could talk him into some art nouveau."

"Maybe you'll pay attention the next time he invites you to his office," Julianne muttered, catching her sister in the lie.

"He did invite me."

"Yeah, right. The same way Steve invited you to lunch. How stupid do you think I am, Suzanne?"

Suzanne shrugged her shoulders. "It was just coincidence that Steve and I met for lunch that day."

"Steve would never go to lunch at Berghoffs. He never goes to lunch, period. Unless he has a date."

Suzanne shrugged again. "I don't know why he was there. He just was."

Julianne huffed out her indignation. "You're a terrible liar."

"So what if I had lunch with him?" Suzanne countered, sitting up on the edge of the bed. "There's no crime in that."

Julianne rolled her eyes. "The same way showing up at John's office was innocent? He doesn't even know you. Why would he invite you?" She put her hands on her hips knowing full well what her sister's response would be and yet unable to stop herself from asking the question.

"I wanted to see what kind of man would make you break off your engagement to the man you truly love."

"Who says John made me break off the engagement? And what business is it of yours how I conduct my life?"

"I'm your sister. I care about you."

Julianne laughed. "That's rich."

"Well why else would I go to his office?"

"Why else indeed. And why would you be having lunch with my fiancé in a cozy little restaurant in the city when he's supposed to be working? And why would you call a guard on the high school basketball team that you didn't even know? Shall I go on?"

Suzanne heaved an exaggerated sigh. "Are we going to go over Tommy Bennett again? Honestly, Julianne. That was high school. Get over it. Can I help it if he liked me better than you?"

"No, but you can help the fact that he had no idea who you were until that day. You didn't even know what he looked like."

"How was I supposed to know you had a crush on him? I called him on a dare."

"You called him because you knew he was going to ask me out and you couldn't stand the thought of me having a boyfriend when you didn't. What I don't get, Suzanne, is why you haven't grown out of that. For heaven's sake, you have a husband. Why are you still chasing after my boyfriends?"

"Really, Julianne. You're just being paranoid. I have no interest in the men you date."

"And what about Bill? Do you remember how you snagged your husband?"

Suzanne scowled. "You never dated Bill."

"One thing you never knew, sister dear, was that I never developed enough of an interest to date Bill. You should have waited until he actually asked me out. When you swooped in for the kill, I figured it wasn't worth the effort."

"That's a nice thing to say about your brother-in-law."

"Any man who could buy your act that easily isn't worth my time. I just feel sorry for him because he actually is a nice guy."

Suzanne rose to her feet, hands on her hips to stand nose-to-nose with Julianne. "What act are you talking about?"

"Stop it you two," their mother scolded from the living room beyond. "Why don't you stop bickering and try getting along for a change."

Suzanne sat back down on the bed with a pout. "You know Steve's really broken up that you left him."

"What's the matter, spoiling your love life?"

"I'm sorry, Julianne, okay? For every little perceived injustice you think I've done you. Can I help it I'm prettier than you are?"

Julianne rolled her eyes again. "You just don't get it, do you? I don't care how pretty you are or aren't. How is it that you know all of Steve's moves?"

"He thinks I can change your mind. He picked up his tux, you know. He's still ready to marry you."

Julianne turned her head with a jerk. "You're joking, aren't you?"

"That Jack seems kind of like a dud to me. Hardly gave me the time of day."

"I thought he invited you into his office."

Suzanne shrugged her shoulders. "He was kind of rude, you know."

"He's a busy man. Doesn't like being interrupted at work."

Suzanne hugged her knees up tight. "Why are you doing it, Jule? You're not the impulsive type."

Julianne looked beyond the door of their childhood bedroom. "We're kind of past the point of sisterly confidences."

"But you couldn't love the guy. Besides, he looks like an owl."

"He's been a good friend."

"So you marry the guy? Wait a minute," Suzanne scooted to the edge of her bed. "You're the one who's always saying life is a trade off. What are you trading for, Julie?"

Julianne hesitated, afraid to confess to her sister how much she wanted Jack. "Maybe I'm done trading. Maybe I found my happily ever after."

"And maybe the tooth fairy will put a quarter under your pillow tonight."

"You should be concentrating on working things out with Bill."

Suzanne backed up against the wall behind her bed again, stretching her legs out in front of her. "We're going to counseling, but you probably know that. You talk to him more than I do. A person could get the wrong impression, you know."

"I could do a lot worse."

"You did. I still don't know what you see in the Owl."

Julianne smiled in secret amusement. There would only be one reason Suzanne would give up on a prospect. "That's because he turned you down."

Suzanne leaned forward, wiggling her freshly painted toes one more time. "Good in bed, is he?"

"Couldn't say."

"You haven't slept with him? Now I know there's something wrong. 'Fess up, Julianne."

Julianne reached across and switched off the light. "Good night, Suzanne." She walked out of the bedroom with a smile on her face.

"Hey! Turn the light back on. Is he gay?"

"Probably."

"I hope the payoff is worth it."

CHAPTER 17

Jack wasn't there when Julianne got home. She remembered the leggy blonde and her stomach knotted up again.

"It's all an act," she reminded herself.

Julianne checked her wristwatch, then made her way to the desk in the great room. Tired from her return flight from Houston, she still had homework to make up.

* * *

City lights shone through the tall windows casting eerie shadows around the room. The hardwood floor cold on her bare feet, Julianne raised her head from her folded arms and sleepily acknowledged the chime that woke her up. She hugged herself to ward off the chill. Force of habit left her anticipating a message from JGGuilder to help her through the night.

For a moment she thought she was back in the apartment in Schaumburg, Steve snoring obnoxiously in the next room. Then she shuddered.

The screen chimed at her again, announcing a message. Julianne opened her eyes and saw the instant message. "Trouble sleeping?"

"A lot on my mind," she typed automatically.

The computer showed his response. "Want to talk?"

She sat upright in the chair behind the desk, suddenly remembering where she was. She turned to look up to the loft overhead. "John?" she called out.

"Can you see me?" His disembodied voice carried eerily in the darkness.

"No."

"Can you hear me well enough?"

"Yes."

"Welcome to the chat room."

On the floor beside her the moonlight outlined the panels of the window, casting an elongated shadow of her body along the edge. It was strange to hear his voice in the dark rather than to read his words one line at a time.

She stood up, looking for him in the darkness overhead, but all she could see was the glow of his monitor. "I didn't hear you come in." She took a deep breath and sat back down.

"I didn't want to wake you." His voice floated down to her with that same hypnotic cadence the all-night disc jockeys used.

She squinted to see him, but he remained concealed in the shadows. The squeak of chair wheels let her know that he had shifted position.

Should she tell him she'd seen him with his girlfriend on the street? But what right did she have to say anything about his personal life? "I know this whole arrangement is an imposition on you," she said, fumbling for the words. "I'm sorry if I've disrupted your home."

"You said that once before. How have you disrupted my life?"

Julianne shrugged her shoulders in the dark. "Invaded your privacy, put a crimp in your personal life."

His laugh echoed in the great room. "What personal life? I work too much to have a personal life."

"Well it must be an imposition to pretend you have a wife say, when you run into an old friend, or want to make plans with someone you want to know better. I can still find my own place."

The chair squeaked again overhead. "I asked you to stay here. When you're imposing on me, I'll let you know."

"Maybe if I was more provocative, more like Suzanne. . ." she said quietly, almost to herself.

"No." She heard the chair slide across the floor overhead and heard the ringing of the cast iron railing that lined the loft when his hands took hold of it. "You can't be something you're not."

"What does that mean?" She demanded.

"Do you really want to be like your sister?" His voice sounded strained, fading slightly as if he had turned away from her.

In the silence that followed, she saw the shadow disappear and heard the sound of a lockset overhead. It was an odd sensation, as if he had exited the chat room.

Julianne powered down her computer, frustrated by his departure.

Overhead came the sounds of metal clinking against metal as weights fell against locking pins. Julianne closed her eyes, unable to block out the pictures of bulging biceps, skin glistening from exertion. She imagined the essence of male musk.

She walked back to her bedroom and flipped onto her stomach on the bed. Steve had never aroused in her the feelings she experienced just thinking about the man upstairs from her - the shadow that projected animal magnetism - who always seemed to know just when she needed a friend.

The difficulty in bringing their online relationship into the real world disturbed her. She missed his friendship; she missed the closeness they had shared online. They never left an online chat as abruptly as he left their conversation just now, but then it had never been this personal before.

Julianne turned over onto her back, and stared at the ceiling overhead.

* * *

Although she heard him bustling around, Julianne hadn't seen Jack all day. When Alec arrived, he disappeared upstairs into Jack's inner sanctum, but Julianne was too nervous about her own appearance to wonder what the two of them were up to.

Her dress was three-quarter length, the princess waist accented with a blue-turquoise inset. The top of her fitted bodice lay off her shoulders in a flounce that matched the color of the vee at her waist, cinched by three red ribbon rosettes. The full skirt was white satin beneath blue taffeta.

It was her wedding dress, but she wasn't getting married anymore. At least she had been practical and now there actually was another use for her gown. Ironic that she would be wearing it with the man the world thought she was married to.

Julianne checked her hair, twisting the tendrils of auburn that she hadn't caught up on top of her head into soft curls. Her heart was racing, caught up in the excitement of playing dress-up although she continued to remind herself that it wasn't her party. "I'm not Cinderella, he's not Prince Charming. This is not the ball. We're not really married." She repeated the mantra while she smoothed her make-up and then cast a glance to the reflection of her bedroom door when she heard them descending the steps.

"I still think you look funny with makeup," she heard Alec tease.

Julianne furrowed her brow. Make-up?

"My face hasn't seen the light of day in over nine years. I look like Fred Flintstone, for God's sake."

Fred Flintstone?

"Julianne?"

"I'm almost ready," she called out. Julianne took several measured breaths to calm her nerves and smoothed her skirt one more time. "Show time," she told her reflection.

In the center of the great room, Alec checked his watch, frowning. "The limo's going to be here any minute."

Both men were gawking as she made her entrance, but it was Alec who broke into his smile first. "You're lovely, Julianne. Stunning. Breathtaking." He reached his hands out to hers and pulled her close, planting a kiss on her cheek. She felt the warmth rising to her face and looked at Jack. For a moment she wasn't sure it was Jack – his face was clean-shaven.

"What happened to your beard?" she asked.

Jack reached up a hand to feel his naked jaw and then stopped the impulse to rub it. "Close encounter with a razor."

She couldn't resist the urge to walk up and lay a hand on his smooth face. And then she realized what Alec was referring to. "Are you . . ."

The phone on the pillar rang out with a call from the lobby. "That will be our limo," Alec predicted. "And yes, he's wearing makeup. He's worried that he looks like Fred Flintstone."

Jack scowled while he answered the phone, and then nodded to confirm that their ride had indeed arrived.

* * *

The banquet hall was filled with people Julianne didn't know. She felt horribly out of place and wondered if her gown was suitable. Had things gone according to plan, she would have been wearing it at her reception tonight. This would have been her wedding day. That thought left her light-headed and suddenly short of breath.

The chandeliers seemed much too bright, the temperature in the room too hot, the music too loud.

Her full skirt swung gracefully below her knees with each carefully measured step. Julianne's fingers played Jack's arm where she gripped it like a concert pianist.

She rocked onto her toes and whispered into his ear: "I need to freshen up."

Jack nodded toward the bathrooms, patted her hand and dismissed her with a smile.

She wanted to run but she was afraid she'd fall. Spots blotted her vision and Julianne felt sure she would faint. Once inside the restroom, she took a seat in the plush powder room area and leaned over, pretending to examine her shoes while sending the blood flow back to the brain that was determined to abandon her.

"I brought you a glass of water. You know the gossips are going to have you pregnant if they see you like this."

Julianne looked up to see a blonde woman seated next to her. With a forced smile, Julianne sat upright and accepted the glass. Meeting the woman's eyes, the last vestiges of her self-control crumbled. She was looking into the face of the woman she saw on the street with Jack. The water slipped through her hands, spilling across the carpet while the glass rolled silently away.

Julianne began to gasp for air, reaching for the counter to keep from sliding off the chair.

The blonde woman raised one eyebrow and lent a supporting arm around Julianne's back, massaging between her shoulder blades until Julianne's breathing began to return to normal.

"I," Julianne gasped, "I don't quite know what's wrong with me."

"Dress too tight?"

A brief flash of anger sent the adrenalin boost Julianne needed and she moved away from her new friend. "Must have been something I ate."

"Maybe I should get Jack."

Julianne bristled. "No, I'll be fine, thanks. You know Jack, then?"

The blonde woman slid back in her seat, crossing her long legs in front of Julianne. "We're old friends. From college days. By the way, I'm Gloria Bennett. You know I saw your interview on television the other night. Very impressive. What did you do to have Hayden eating out of your hands like that?"

Julianne turned to face the mirror, opening her handbag to retrieve her makeup. She brushed at the corners of her eyes with her fingers and decided not to fuss with the work she'd already done. Already she felt horribly painted. Like Suzanne.

"He's a bit eccentric is all. And a bit of a gambler," Julianne answered, smiling sweetly. "No accounting for taste, is there?"

"How sweet," Gloria replied. "Such self-deprecation. It must be one of the things that endears you to Jack."

Julianne fought to maintain the casual smile on her face. "Speaking of Jack, he'll be wondering what happened to me."

"Are you sure you're feeling better?"

Julianne smoothed the skirt of her dress and checked the alignment of her bodice. "I'll be fine, thank you. I'll be sure to let Jack know how kind you've been to me."

The smile slid from Gloria's face and Julianne knew she'd scored her hit. With a renewed sense of self, Julianne walked out of the bathroom. She hadn't come to be the most beautiful woman at the banquet, although for a brief moment the Cinderella complex had almost taken hold. She was here to make contacts that would advance her budding career and Jack was her introduction.

Julianne snapped her purse shut and looked around the banquet room, searching out her pseudo husband when Alec appeared beside her.

"You look stunning, Julianne."

Julianne grimaced. "Thank you, but the compliments really aren't necessary."

Alec placed an arm around her shoulders and led her toward the table arranged with hors d'oeuvres. "Why is it so difficult for you to accept a compliment?"

With a shrug of the shoulders, Julianne took a deep breath. "I suppose because it always seems a game of superlatives. You look pretty. She looks prettier. How clever you are! But wasn't that a clever thing that person just said." She offered Alec a conciliatory smile.

"You don't even know your own worth," Alec scolded, turning Julianne to face him. "You need to enjoy the moment."

Julianne's eyes followed Gloria, who had just emerged from the restroom. "Too many snakes biting at my heels."

Alec raised Julianne's hand, admiring her rings. "I see he gave them to you." He studied Julianne's face intently. "Remind me to tell you a story about these rings one day."

"Another fairy tale?" She shook her head. "I'm not ready for any more stories right now. I need a good healthy dose of reality, and it probably ain't gonna be tonight. Show's still on 'til the party's over."

With a light touch to her forehead, Alec brushed back a stray lock of hair. "No girl should ever give up her fairy tales entirely. Besides, I think you'd like the story about the rings."

"Are you flirting with my wife?" Jack accused, taking his place beside Julianne.

"Prettiest woman here." Alec winked and leaned over to kiss Julianne's cheek.

"The night's still young," she countered.

Jack took hold of Julianne's hand, wrapped it under his arm and led her into the sea of plastic smiles.

The crowd seemed welcoming to their newest member, but like her own carefully positioned façade, Julianne found most of the people only superficially pleasant. Like a masquerade ball, she wondered what secrets the others kept concealed behind warm smiles and firm handshakes. At the same time, she wondered how many of them knew or even cared about the secrets she and Jack harbored for the sake of the business.

When they took their seats for dinner, Julianne was dismayed to discover Gloria Bennett seated across the table from her. It took an extra measure of control to maintain her smile while Jack greeted and introduced.

"Josh Baxter, Gloria Bennett, this is my wife, Julianne." Jack laid a proprietary hand across Julianne's shoulder,. "Josh is an account executive with Blackman Schroeder, and Gloria . . ." he paused, tilting his head, "I'm not sure I've kept up with where you are now, Gloria." Jack turned to look at Julianne. "Gloria and I go back a long ways. We went to college together."

Gloria smiled, batting her eyelashes at Jack. "Yes, we've been close friends forever." Her attention returned to Julianne, appraising her one more time. "Julianne and I met in the ladies' room earlier. Are you feeling better dear?"

Josh Baxter adjusted his tuxedo jacket and glanced at Jack somewhat nervously. "Gloria is a sales rep in our Cleveland office these days."

Julianne extended her hand to Josh. "It's nice to meet you." She turned her attention to Gloria. "What brings you to Chicago? Certainly you didn't come in just for this function?"

Gloria smiled sweetly. "No, I came in for a visit." She grabbed hold of Josh's arm and attached herself firmly. "Josh asked me to join him tonight."

Jack lay his napkin across his lap. "You didn't mention you'd met Gloria in the ladies room," he whispered discretely to Julianne.

"I didn't know I was supposed to."

Jack smiled at Julianne, his eyes searching for a hint of what lay hidden. Julianne returned his smile, but gave nothing away.

* * *

Outside the banquet hall, Alec lit a cigar, pulling in the smoke and then blowing it back out slowly. "You two look well together," he told Julianne.

The cold night air felt good after the stuffiness of the banquet hall. "Then we're accomplishing our goal," she answered.

He pulled at the ascot around his neck and squinted into the night. "You can push a horse to water . . . ," he said.

"Some things just aren't meant to be." She exhaled a loud sigh. "You're not going to fire me if he doesn't take the bait, are you? And remember, this wasn't my idea."

Alec chuckled, chewing on the end of his cigar. "No, Julianne. I'm not going to fire you unless there's a reason for it. I didn't hire you just to tease him."

"That's not what you said in the limo at the airport."

Alec put an arm around her and squeezed her shoulders tight. "I think I said something about being tough competition," he reminded her, "or an ally. You and Jack? That was just an experiment on my part. Nothing to do with your employment, Dear."

"I'm sorry your experiment failed."

Alec took a step to face Julianne, his cigar hooked between two fingers. "Who says it failed?"

Julianne nodded a head at Gloria, standing in the entrance to the banquet room on the other side of the glass doors, insinuating herself into Jack's personal space while her date watched uncomfortably. "I can't compete with that."

Alec chuckled again and shook his head. "You don't have to. That was over long ago."

"This isn't the first time I've seen her with him," Julianne confessed. "And let's face it, Alec. He hasn't expressed any interest in me apart from the job."

Alec laughed out loud. "I'm not getting in the middle of this, Julianne. You're just going to have to find out on your own. Now get back in there and claim your husband before the press starts thinking about Gloria the way you do."

With a frown, Julianne let Alec push her back through the glass doors, looking over her shoulder in dismay. It was nearly midnight and many of the guests had already gone. She was ready to go home, too.

Exhausted from her week, Julianne couldn't find the energy to paste on one more forced smile. She rested a hand on the back of Jack's shoulder. "The limo's here," she told him.

"There you are," he greeted, turning slowly. The smile he wore to greet her was replaced in an instant with a look of horror while he looked over her shoulder.

There was an explosion of glass following Alec back into the building and squealing tires in the parking lot.

"Alec!" Jack shouted.

Julianne pushed her way through the crowd rushing to the lobby. "Alec," she whispered, falling down beside him. She took his head in her lap.

His voice was strained, but he struggled to be heard. "Black Trans Am. Blond man." He closed his eyes with the effort and licked his lips.

Julianne froze. She cast a furtive glance at Jack who was yelling into his cell phone for an ambulance. "Are you sure?" she whispered.

Alec nodded, wincing with the effort.

"What happened?" Jack yelled, replacing his cell phone in his tuxedo.

Alec looked up at Jack and nodded for Julianne to pass along his words. Her mouth was dry and her hands were cold. "Black Trans Am," she repeated, "blond man."

Alec nodded and grimaced.

Flashing lights colored the banquet hall red and yellow. The approaching sirens increased in volume as the emergency vehicles lined up outside.

Nothing seemed quite real. Julianne was only vaguely aware of the paramedic that pushed her aside. She panicked when she saw the blood on her hands and the stains on her dress.

"Everything's going to be alright," a paramedic assured her and handed Julianne a towel to clean her hands. "Are you hurt?"

Julianne stared blindly at her ruined dress and shook her head. "No!" she answered finally, tears streaming down her cheeks.

The fireman put a hand on her shoulder. "He's going to be ok," he promised, while another man strapped Alec to the gurney to transport him to the hospital.

Jack stood between Julianne and the ambulance, looking from one to the other. "I'm going to ride to the hospital with him. Can you get home okay?"

Julianne looked over her shoulder at the Perkins & Stone limousine and nodded uncertainly.

"Alec," she sobbed.

Jack put his arms around her, holding her close. "I have to go with him," he said to the top of her head.

Julianne stepped out of his embrace, her head bowed. Jack stepped away slowly and climbed into the ambulance. The paramedics held bags and tubes over Alec while the firemen closed the doors.

The same way they had when they took her father away.

CHAPTER 18

The wedding dress hung on a hook behind the bedroom door. Julianne lay in semi-darkness staring at it, seeing only the dark spots that stained it. The coppery smell of blood hung in the air, the sound of breaking glass still ringing in her memory.

She rolled over again, staring at the wall for only a minute more before she threw off the covers and approached the phantom dress guarding her exit. Pushing it aside with a swish of satin, she opened the door and walked out into the great room. With a glance at her computer, Julianne went instead to the tall window and looked out at the city beyond.

Sniffling, the tears began streaming down Julianne's cheeks. When had she become so involved? Not just with Jack, but with Alec, too. And now Alec lay in the hospital because Steve was looking for her. She knew the temper all too well. It wouldn't have taken much to bring Steve to the point of throwing the bottle that smashed into Alec's back.

"I have to move," she told the moonlight. "I can't stay here." How long could they play out the charade before someone found out the truth? Certainly if Jack wanted more of a relationship he would have given her some indication by now. By staying she would only subject him to the same danger she brought to Alec. And she would subject herself to more heartache.

* * *

She'd been out early to get the apartment hunting brochure and a cup of Starbucks. Sitting cross-legged on the futon sofa, she flipped through the pages, circling possibilities.

Upstairs Jack's door opened followed by tenuous footsteps as he made his way down the staircase. Without raising her head, she could see his reflection in the television set. He was concentrating on buttoning his shirt, giving only a brief look in her direction. Julianne flipped another page, pretending not to notice him.

In the television, the reflection stopped moving except for the hand passing over his face. She heard the rasp of his beard already thick with new growth. "You're up early."

"Going to the hospital," he answered with the deep morning voice of disuse.

"Aren't you going to shave?"

Again she heard the bristles on his chin. "Keeps me warm in the winter."

"Or leaves you exposed without it?" She turned slowly to face him, her legs falling out from underneath her, one foot dropping to the hardwood floor.

"I promised Alec I'd be there first thing."

"I'll get dressed." She rose from the sofa with her apartment guide in hand and started toward her bedroom at the rear of the great room.

"You don't have to," he said quickly, raising a hand to halt her. "I think I'd rather you stayed here."

She stopped and turned to face him once more. "This is my fault."

"No," he said unconvincingly.

"I'm going with you."

"I don't want you to."

She needed to know Alec was okay. And she was afraid of being alone after what happened. "What if he's out there?" Her voice shook. "Waiting."

They stood across the room from each other, eyes locked. "He's probably long gone," Jack said. "The police think he probably scared himself more than anyone else and ran."

"Aren't you afraid?" she whispered.

"You know him better than I do. Should I be?"

She knew just how impulsive Steve could be. "I'm going with you."

"I'd rather you stayed here."

She tucked her book under her arm and put her hands on her hips. "If you leave without me I'll go by myself."

He turned around, letting out a sigh. "And if Steve is out there?"

"He'll listen to me."

"I doubt that."

"I won't have you on my conscience, too." The guilt of Alec's injury produced a corresponding pain in her chest.

"Is that it?" When he turned back to her, his eyes were blazing. "You don't want to bear the guilt if he hurts me?"

She backed up toward her room, pointing at Jack. "You do blame me."

He cast his eyes to the ceiling and raised his arms. "I don't blame you, Julie."

"Alec wouldn't be lying in the hospital now if it wasn't for me."

"You didn't throw that bottle."

"Maybe not, but certainly I triggered the man behind it."

They stared defiantly at each other for several minutes before he spoke again. "You'd better get dressed if you want to go."

* * *

Alec lay on his side in the hospital bed, looking from one to the other of them. "Can't stand the smell of a hospital," he grumbled. "Can't imagine being here another day."

"Good thing you didn't get hit in the head then," Jack pointed out.

Alec put a hand to his bandaged side gingerly. "Lucky for me he's a lousy shot."

Jack sat solicitously in the chair beside his godfather while Julianne turned to look out the window. It was difficult to look at either of them.

"Jack, would you go down to the gift shop and buy me that new Ken Follett novel?" Alec suggested. "I'm going to need something to read while I'm laying around the next couple of days trying not to scratch these stitches."

Jack nodded obediently and left his godfather alone with Julianne.

"It's like that, is it?" Alec said quietly to Julianne.

"Like what?" She turned from the window and stood beside his bed, resting her hands on the metal rail.

"Married life not agreeing with you?"

"I don't know how much longer I can go through with this whole farce. And he's not interested, Alec."

A low rumble of laughter rose from Alec's chest. "Forgive me for saying so, but I think you're missing some key indicators."

"He as much as told me his interests run in other directions."

"Now you're listening to gossip?"

"He suggested it. Dorian tried to warn me."

"So you've decided it's safer to keep your distance just in case it's true?"

"Look, we aren't really married. Remember?" She looked around cautiously, realizing her outburst could quickly bring her new account to a close. "It's all show to protect your precious firm," she whispered. Her knuckles were white around the bars on the side of his bed. "We've both been slinging so many lies it's hard to tell where they stop any more."

The guilt bubbled out of her. "After last night I can't even believe you're still talking to me. I'm so sorry, Alec."

Alec coughed with the sudden intake of air that choked him. "You mean that wacko that threw the bottle? He's not your responsibility."

"I don't want anyone else getting hurt because of me. I'm going to get my own place."

Alec shifted in the bed, grimacing with the effort. "If you're looking at it from the security standpoint, you're probably safer where you are. You're free to do what you want, but considering the amount of traveling the two of you are doing, does it really matter? Obviously it looks better when Hayden comes nosing around if you're living together, and if you two are hardly crossing paths as it is, is it really necessary?"

Julianne wrung her hands as she struggled with her emotions. How could she explain to Alec how increasingly difficult it was to walk away from the game?

Julianne looked up as Jack reappeared and turned back to the window.

"Is this the one you wanted?" Jack asked, handing Alec the book.

"It serves the purpose."

"Good morning, Mr. Stone." Julianne moved away from the window when the new voice entered the room. The doctor was dressed casually in brown trousers matched to a striped shirt and pullover sweater. Without a lab coat, he was only identifiable by the badge he wore around his neck.

He had coal black hair and hazel eyes and spoke with the slightest hint of a Southern dialect. "You can probably go home this afternoon, I want to wait for those last test results to come back in." There was a casual friendliness about him that brought a smile to Julianne's face.

"I'm fine," Alec argued. He struggled to sit up, falling back against the pillows and closing his eyes.

"Still a little dizzy?"

"That's because I've been lying down so long."

"You lost a fair amount of blood," the doctor replied. "If you would have let us give you some . . . "

"I've lost more blood donating," Alec growled.

The doctor smiled a wide, warm smile and reached down to check the dressing on Alec's side. "I'll be back later and we'll talk about releasing you, Mr. Stone." He raised his eyes to look at Julianne. "Will your daughter be taking you home? Or your son?"

Alec managed a chuckle. "Not my daughter. Or my son for that matter."

"I'll be taking Alec home," Jack answered tersely.

Julianne was startled by the tone in Jack's voice. He often referred to Alec as a surrogate father, so it didn't make sense for him to be annoyed when the doctor referred to Jack as Alec's son. Was he upset about being the one to take him home?

The doctor turned to face Jack. "Then I'll see you later." He gave Julianne a bright smile and left the room.

Alec straightened the blanket on his bed. "Have you been to the police station yet, Julianne?"

"Jack filed a report last night, didn't he?"

"They have laws against stalkers," he told her.

"He's not stalking me."

"If this is what he did to me, I can't imagine what he would have done to you." Alec winced, reaching for his bandages with his hand but stopping short.

Jack's Adam's apple bobbed beneath the stubbly growth of beard and the muscles along his jaw tightened. "I'll take her on the way back home."

"But he hasn't done anything to me. And we don't actually know that it was him yet," Julianne protested.

Both men stared at her, waiting for her to make the inevitable decision. "All right," she conceded.

"Go on, then," Alec urged, settling back into his bed. "Let me flirt with the nurses by myself."

"I'll be back later," Jack promised his godfather.

Alec shooed them away. "You have other things to do. I'll see you tomorrow."

Jack smiled. "Any nurse in particular you might be waiting for?"

"Ever had a sponge bath, Jack my boy?" Alec closed his eyes and smiled.

"Let's go," Jack laughed, standing back so Julianne could pass.

CHAPTER 19

Julianne sat quietly beside Jack in his black BMW, growing increasingly uncomfortable. He had shaved again and now retained the fresh scent of his after-shave. His silky brown hair lay softly against the collar of his charcoal gray suit coat, muted maroon stripes sparking similar highlights in the thick growth on his head.

"I wish you'd let me go to the hospital with you," she said once more.

"There isn't anything you can do," he answered. Jack glanced sideways. "If you want to see the doctor again, make an appointment."

"See the doctor?"

She saw his hands tighten around the steering wheel as he shrugged. "You know."

"Know what?"

He shot her another sideways look. "I can't blame you for noticing."

"Noticing what?" She shifted sideways in her seat, half facing him.

"Well it wasn't as if he didn't notice you, too."

She noticed him all right. A woman would have to be dead not to notice Dr. McCullom. Julianne couldn't suppress the smile when the realization flooded over her: Jack was jealous. "So you think I ought to pursue him?" she asked.

The color flooded the tender skin of his cheeks. "Well . . . "

"I won't embarrass you or make a fool of you. So far as the rest of the world is concerned, I am your wife. And until this gig is over, I don't want you fixing me up with every attractive man that walks by."

He looked up at the buildings towering over the Chicago Loop and then back at the road, avoiding the sudden emergence of a taxi into the intersection. "I appreciate your consideration." He looked out his window and back at the stream of traffic, anywhere but at the woman beside him until he maneuvered into a space in front of Perkins & Stone.

Julianne stared at him while he continued to avoid looking at her. "You're so damn perfect, aren't you?"

He turned to face her, his eyes wide with surprise. "Excuse me?"

"Always know what to say, how to act."

"I'd say by the tone of your voice that's a problem."

She folded her arms and sat back. "Here we are, acting in this ridiculous play. When does it end? When do you stop being perfect? When Hayden fires Perkins & Stone? We just keep walking around like little wind-up toys until the client says stop?"

He cast a glance at the traffic on the busy Chicago street around them, flexing his fingers around the steering wheel. "You wanted to be in advertising."

She lifted her hands, pantomiming her words into separate boxes. "There's work," she shifted her arms to the other side, "and there's home. You act a certain way around people, and then there's the way you are when you're alone, relaxed."

"Okay," he nodded, his eyebrows close together.

"With you. . . ." she motioned as if she was pushing the two boxes together, "I can't see the difference. Are you always on?"

"On?"

"Yeah. Mr. Perfect. Take your house. Nothing out of place."

"Is there a point to all this?" he asked with a pained look on his face.

"I liked you better when you were on the other end of a modem. At least I didn't feel it was part of the act. Maybe you treat all your online friends that way - like you really care."

His eyebrows shot up. "You don't think I care?"

"All part of the show, isn't it?"

He turned to the front and slammed a hand against the steering wheel. On the street, cars honked angrily. "What do you want from me?"

She leaned back against her door, feeling the blow of his words like a slap in the face. The memory of Gloria draped around Jack wasn't just going to go away. "Maybe I'd like the same consideration for my feelings."

"What are you talking about?"

"Making out with your girlfriends in the middle of Michigan Avenue isn't exactly discrete."

The color flooded to Jack's face, starting from his neck and working its way up. "Get out."

Julianne stared at him, stunned.

He nodded his head toward the door. "We're here. Get out of the car."

She turned to look at the building, wrapping her fingers around the straps of her purse.

"I wasn't going to mention that," she whispered. "I'm sorry."

A traffic cop knocked on the window of the car, motioning for Jack to move.

"Go on," he told her more gently. "We'll talk about that later."

Julianne opened the car door and turned back once more. "What if he's out there?"

"If you even think you see him, call the police," he told her firmly.

Julianne flashed her office pass for the security guard on her way to the elevators. As she waited for her ride up, she saw the picture posted at the security station and felt a shudder go through her. In the photo, enlarged and separated from hers, in a place where he could be easily recognized, Steve's face smiled rakishly.

Minutes later she walked through the glass doors on the 42nd floor. She was painfully aware of the cessation of conversation. With her eyes downcast, she made her way to her quad and sat down behind the half-wall of her desk, grateful that Bev wasn't there yet.

She could smell cappuccino coming from one of the executive offices and reached for her own coffee cup.

In the kitchenette, her presence scattered a small group of the creative staff back to their desks, but not without several backward glances. She poured herself a cup of coffee and raised it to let the steam warm her face.

"So how was awards night?"

Julianne turned to face Bev, the first line of fire. "Interesting," she answered.

"Oh, come on. I want to know all about it. Are you really married to Jack?"

Julianne held out her left hand, looking at the ring Jack had put there as if seeing it for the first time.

"So how long before they put you in one of the offices?" Tyler asked.

"Why would they do that?"

"Most people just sleep their way to the top. Perfectly acceptable in this day and age. Why marry him?"

"Oh shut up," Bev scolded. "There are plenty of women who would die for a chance to marry a man like Jack Guilder."

Tyler laughed scornfully. "And a few men."

Julianne pushed past the two of them, returning to her desk. She felt exposed, on display.

"C'mon, Julie," Tyler prodded, following her around the partition. "Tell the truth. It's all just a front, right?"

"For what?" she answered testily.

"To keep him in the closet."

Julianne shot him a dark look, pulling her sketchbook from her portfolio. "Speaking from experience?"

Tyler stood directly behind her. Putting his hands on her shoulders, he bent over to speak confidentially into her ear. "I told him I had hoped to date you. He told me I might still get that chance. Doesn't sound too much like a loving husband to me."

Julianne turned and brushed his hands off her shoulders. "You never had a chance."

"What happened to Mr. Stone?" Bev asked.

"What?" Tyler echoed, suddenly interested.

"Betty says he's out today. Had some kind of accident over the weekend."

All eyes turned to Julianne, waiting for her to supply the answer. She sat down at her desk and looked around the group. "Ask him yourself. I'm sure he'll be back tomorrow."

"Oh come on," Bev pleaded. "You know."

Office gossip was the same no matter where she worked. "Yes," she stated simply. "I do."

A new buzz started around the office with Jack's appearance.

Jack pushed resolutely through the staff area, his smile twisting with the catcalls and comments about his new, clean-shaven appearance. Heads popped up over the quads while news of his arrival passed from station to station.

"Julie," Bev whispered when she caught sight of him.

Jack shook hands as he passed, his eyes wide as the creative staff began a round of applause.

He continued through the staff and stopped beside Julianne. "Would you step into my office?" he asked, his naked cheeks bright red.

Julianne couldn't resist smiling. "Can you give me a minute."

He pulled his lapels straight and with a quick nod, disappeared into his office.

Bev sighed. "Who'd have thought that underneath that beard . . ."

"Wow," Tyler muttered.

"You want a crack at him?" Julianne teased.

CHAPTER 20

The tapping of her fingers on the keyboard echoed through the great room. Julianne stopped and leaned over an open reference book for the highlighted text that she wanted to incorporate into her final paper and then nearly jumped out of her chair when the telephone rang.

Two short rings signaled a call from the lobby of the building. Julianne stared at the phone in the center of the room nervously. *Was it Steve? Was he really capable of hurting her?*

The phone rang again and she walked across the room to the girder where it was mounted. Maybe it was just a package - *a bomb?* - or Alec - *so soon after the incident?* "Hello?"

"Yeah, Miz Guilder, it's Tommy downstairs. There's a lady here wants to come up. Says her name's DePalma. Says she's your sister but she don't look that much like you."

Julianne squeezed the phone. "Is she alone?"

"Yes, ma'am."

The image of Steve and Suzanne at the restaurant crept into her mind and Julianne squeezed her eyes to shut it out.

"Miz Guilder?"

"Is she very pretty?"

"Ma'am?"

Julianne pounded her fist against the post. *Why did she ask? Conditioned response.* "Send her up."

Julianne took a deep breath. It was always that way - since they were old enough to date. A game. I'm prettier than you are. Anything you have I can take away from you. If Suzanne had any brains, she might be dangerous.

"Not this time," Julianne promised herself. She opened the door in time to see Suzanne step off the elevator.

"What brings you downtown on a Tuesday night?" Julianne greeted with as much enthusiasm as she could manage.

"Julianne!" Suzanne hurried down the hall, arms outstretched.

Julianne flinched, her guard raised another notch. "I wasn't expecting you." For an awkward moment, the two women remained in the corridor until Julianne took a tentative step backward to admit her sister into the condo.

Suzanne swept all the visible areas with a slow, critical eye before looking at Julianne again. "Oooh. And a loft. Very nice. I'd say you've done all right for yourself, little sister. Where's the man of the house?"

"Away on business. How do you happen to be in the city?"

"Well, I came to see you."

"Overcome with sisterly love, no doubt."

"I said I'm sorry already. If Bill can forgive me, why can't you?"

"Did he?"

Suzanne dropped her purse on the end table. "He will. We're going to counseling, you know."

"Yes, I know."

"Oh I forgot. He tells you everything."

"Why are you here?" Julianne folded her arms across her chest. "I have a paper to write."

"I wanted to see your new place." She turned to face Julianne, swinging back her dark hair. "And I wanted to talk to you."

Julianne sat with one leg underneath her on the futon sofa, motioning for her sister to take a seat. "So you've seen it. And I don't imagine you want to talk about what to get Mom for her birthday."

Suzanne studied the backs of her hands. "I wasn't sure if I should come, and I told him you probably wouldn't listen to me anyway."

Julianne stiffened. "Him?"

"He just wants to talk to you, Julianne." Suzanne leaned forward on the sofa, her painted eyes imploring Julianne's understanding.

Julianne rose to her feet, fighting off the dizziness and the urge to vomit. She still didn't want to believe it was Steve that hurt Alec. "After he goes to the police. Tell him to clear his name first."

"After what you did to him . . . How is he supposed to trust you?"

Julianne's hands went to her hips. "After what I did to him?"

"How would you like it, if someone threw you over and then just turned around and married someone else you'd never heard of?"

"Threw him over?"

". . .without any warning."

Julianne began to pace behind the futon sofa, struggling for composure. "What would you think if you came home one day and found me and Bill in flagrante?"

Suzanne's eyes opened wide, her mouth set in a thin line. "I knew it."

"What?"

"You and Bill. And all this time you've been denying it." She rose to her feet, her eyes flashing.

"I said 'what if,'" Julianne emphasized. "I have the good sense to know when to say no, unlike certain other people."

"You were always jealous of me."

"Think again."

"I can't help it if your old boyfriends liked me better."

"Oh can't you? What happens when you wave a carrot in front of a rabbit, Suzanne? You think he's going to say, 'no, I'll wait until dinnertime'?"

Suzanne flushed and turned away. "Well maybe you'll remember that they didn't stay around very long once they got a bite of the carrot."

"Sometimes it's better to make them wait for dinner." Julianne watched her sister closely. While Suzanne certainly attracted men, it was true that none of them stayed very long.

"You didn't make Steve wait," Suzanne sniffled.

"Oh yes I did, and he still didn't stay home." Julianne's voice caught in her throat. She took a deep breath.

"But he loves you," Suzanne cried, turning back to her sister.

"There's more to love than sex."

"Like what?"

"Commitment, trust, respect."

"Yeah right. Like you and Mr. Wonderful?"

Julianne sat down beside her sister, crossing her arms.

Suzanne cleared her throat and continued. "Anyway, that's why I'm here. You two got married so fast. You couldn't possibly have thought it through, much less meant it."

"Why not?"

"Look. Steve wants to talk to you. He wants to make everything right."

"It's a little late for that now."

"No it's not. This guy's out of town. How well do you really know him, anyway?"

"No."

"Steve just wants to talk to you. I wish someone cared enough about me to beg for another chance."

"If he cares so much, why did he send you?"

"He can't get close to you. He's seen his picture plastered everywhere. He knows they're watching for him." Suzanne leaned in to whisper. "He thinks the police are looking for him."

Julianne rested her head in her hands, exhausted by Suzanne's rapid-fire argument. "Then he should clear his name. And while we're at it, you have someone that cares for you, Suzanne. Think about it. Why does Bill keep giving you another chance?" She turned to look full into the heavily made-up face of her sister. "Tantamount to begging if you ask me." She got up from the sofa and returned to her computer, releasing a long withheld sigh.

"What could it hurt to talk to him?" Suzanne asked.

Julianne's laughed. "Now that's a dumb question."

"Steve just wants to talk to you."

"There isn't anything left to say."

"Oh come on. You were engaged to the guy. You ought to at least hear him out."

Julianne turned on her sister. "I'm married." She shouted. "It's done."

"Two years ought to count for something."

"That's what I told him every time he came home from another woman's bed." Her breath caught in a half-sob and she turned quickly away from her sister.

"If Bill's willing to give me another chance, why can't you do the same for Steve?"

"And did I intervene with Bill on your behalf?"

"Steve can't get to you."

"I just don't know."

"You can't possibly love this guy enough to give up the emotional investment you've already made with Steve."

Julianne wiped at her eyes, stubbornly silent.

"Well at least show me around the place," Suzanne suggested, looking around the great room with undisguised envy.

Julianne made a sweeping arc with her arm. "Go ahead." She turned to her computer, saved her work, and closed out of the program.

Suzanne scurried through the condo, opening and closing doors upstairs. She ran back down, wandered into the kitchen and out into the great room. It wasn't until Julianne saw Suzanne's hand on her bedroom door that she recognized her mistake.

"Suzanne," she called out, hoping to distract her, but the door was open.

The amusement in Suzanne's face was obvious. "Separate bedrooms?" She closed Julianne's bedroom and sauntered to where Julianne sat helplessly watching. "You really haven't slept with him, have you?"

"That's where I left all my stuff when I moved in."

"He is gay, isn't he? Does he have AIDS? Why does he need a wife?"

"It isn't any of your business!"

Suzanne wore a smug smile. "It can't be you - unless . . . Are you one of those women who hate sex, Julianne? Are you gay? No wonder Steve's sleeping all over town."

"And now I think you should go."

"I have to know!"

"No you don't." Julianne's patience had reached its limit. "What should I tell Steve? Will you talk to him?"

Julianne opened the door for her sister. "Goodbye, Suzanne."

"Julianne," her sister whined.

"Leave me alone, Suzanne."

"Why won't you talk to him?"

"I'm afraid of him, okay? For God's sake, Suzanne, he put a man in the hospital!"

Suzanne skulked through the door, turning one last time to address her sister. "I think I'd be more afraid of living with a man I hardly knew."

* * *

The snapshots flashed so quickly Julianne could hardly see everything that was happening around her. Suzanne's face loomed in front of her, menacing, her make-up running until she took on the appearance of a witch.

Two beady eyes peered out of the darkness, coming into focus in the face of the "rat sniper." A friend of Steve's, the man sat in the alley by his house and shot at rats with his BB gun for entertainment. He looked more than a little like a rat himself. In the whirlwind of images, Julianne saw Steve sitting beside the rat sniper, laughing and taking shots at the rodents alongside the sniper until he directed the gun at her.

She was out of breath and although her feet were moving, Julianne didn't feel as if she was going anywhere. Too terrified even to scream, she continued to run from her pursuers, from Suzanne's maniacal laughter, from the gun Steve had trained on her, from the rat sniper watching her with unrestrained glee.

"Do you trust me?" she heard Jack's deep voice reaching out to her in the void that surrounded her in the dream, and in the next instant she heard Suzanne's parting words: "I think I'd be more afraid of living with a man I hardly knew."

A rush of wind blew her hair from her face and a steady cadence, like the flapping of wings, beat through the air above her. Shielding her eyes, Julianne raised her face just as the gryphon's talons grabbed hold of her.

"Julianne?"

The voice cut through the bedlam that shrouded her dream and Julianne sat upright in bed, startled to awareness and eager to escape the danger that pursued her. She let out a residual cry of fear and put her hands to her mouth when she saw the shadow standing at her bedroom door.

With the flick of a switch, light flooded the condominium behind him. "Julie, it's me," Jack reassured her. "What happened?" He sat at the edge of the bed.

"Don't touch me!" she screamed, reaching for the lamp beside the bed.

Jack jumped to his feet, holding up his hands in front of him. "I won't . . . I just. . . "

The lamp chased away the remaining dark corners in her room. Jack shielded his eyes, not prepared for the brightness.

"John?" she gasped. Remnants of the dream evaporated with the illumination.

"It's me, Julie."

Instinctively, she grabbed hold of him. "I dreamed he was here," she gasped.

Jack wrapped his arms around her and rested his cheek against her hair. "It's only a dream."

Julianne continued to tremble. "He told me everything was going to be just the way it used to be, but I wouldn't go." She choked out the words. "And then he turned into this monster, and he was laughing. Oh God."

Tears spilled down her cheeks and her skin radiated heat.

"It was a dream." Jack's voice was hoarse. His arms slid easily around the smooth satin of her nightshirt.

"Hold me, John. Don't leave me." Her grip tightened around his arms and she felt him flex against her stranglehold.

She could feel her heartbeat slowing back into a more regular rhythm. He eased down beside her, comforting her and smoothing her hair. "It's ok," he said again and again. He kissed her forehead, petting the back of her head like he would a frightened kitten. She curled up against him, her head snuggling into his neck. Her viselike grip relaxed and she took a deep breath.

As the dream slipped away, rational thought returned. "I thought you weren't due back from Atlanta until tomorrow."

"I caught an earlier flight. I just walked in the door." He held her at arms' length, his eyes filled with concern. "You were crying out."

Julianne shivered once more and Jack reflexively pulled her close.

The tears slid down her cheeks. In that moment she didn't care how he felt about her, she only knew she felt safe in his arms. "Stay with me," she whispered. "Just hold me."

It seemed he held his breath, but then he eased down beside her, letting her head rest in the crook of his neck.

* * *

She woke from the dream of a gryphon, guarding her, close beside her. He had a decidedly gamey smell about him, not yet offensive and yet definitely in need of bathing. Julianne opened her eyes and wrinkled her nose. His arms were still wrapped around her, clutching her tight against him.

She moved slightly and his grip loosened. He rolled onto his back, sleep tousled and peacefully unaware.

In the morning light, Julianne propped herself up on one arm to look at the man beside her. Steve's body type didn't allow for the same muscle definition. Even with the heavy manual labor he did, his arms were relatively straight and thin. John's were curved and sinewy.

His torso was well-defined, making her wonder if he had also developed the "six pack" abdominal muscles.

Jack's great owl eyes fluttered open. His brow creased for a moment and then relaxed.

"Good morning," she greeted.

He stretched his arms over his head and rubbed his face with one hand. "What time is it?"

"6:00."

Jack rolled over her, kicking his legs over the side of the bed. "Are you okay?" He turned to look for her response.

Julianne nodded and turned away. Jack reached for her hand and he slid one knee back across the bed. Julianne shied back, staring at the floor.

He hesitated for a moment and then said, "I promised to tell you about Gloria."

A chill ran the length of Julianne's arms and down her spine. "You don't have to explain anything." She smiled. "I'm sorry about last night. I guess I had a bad dream."

"Don't be sorry." His voice was husky and he reached for her hands again. "Julianne," he ducked to meet her lowered eyes, but Julianne avoided him. She heard him exhale a loud sigh and he released her, turning back to the edge of the bed. "I have a nine o'clock this morning. I have to get cleaned up."

Julianne nodded, sitting quietly while he left her room.

CHAPTER 21

Alec walked by Julianne's desk with a glancing touch to her shoulder. She looked up from her work and Alec crooked a finger for her to follow. Julianne rose obediently, grabbed a pencil and pad of paper, and stood behind him a moment later in Jack's office.

His face set in a scowl, Jack's mood didn't improve with the two visitors. "What now?" he asked Alec.

"Hayden wants to shoot on a cruise ship."

"He'll have to wait."

"I told him that. In the meantime, he wants some sketches in that setting."

Jack looked to Julianne, clearly ready to delegate his interest in Ben Hayden. "Will that be a problem?"

Julianne shrugged her shoulders. "Depends on how quickly he wants them. I'm working on that Foster layout right now."

"Foster can wait a week," Alec suggested. "Hayden wants you in Houston again."

Julianne rolled her eyes. "I've already missed a lot of school. How long does he want me this time?"

"Can you put in three days? That's two nights and we can try to work around your school schedule if that will help," Alec offered.

The pace was beginning to overwhelm her. Night school wasn't so bad when she was working 9 to 5, but since starting at Perkins & Stone, 8 hour workdays were a thing of the past. "This week?"

"That would be preferred."

Julianne looked to Jack for help, but she knew his schedule was just as full as hers. She was beginning to understand why he'd never married.

Their online relationship began to make more sense. When he told her nobody probably knew him any better, he wasn't kidding. Would her life become just as caught up in her work as his to the point where the only relationship she could have would be with a virtual stranger in a city somewhere across the country at all hours of the night?

"Julianne?" Alec brought her back to the conversation, waiting for an answer.

With a sigh of resignation, she nodded. "I'll go."

All because of one innocent lunch. Somewhere in the back of her mind she remembered the proverb, "be careful what you wish for."

"Thank you," Jack said. The set of his jaw relaxed and she saw his shoulders slump slightly. He offered her a half smile and turned his attention back to Alec. "I thought Ben was going to leave us alone until the end of the year if we promised him a Super Bowl commercial."

Alec shrugged. "In his eyes, he is leaving us alone. I'll remind him when I send him Julianne's itinerary." Alec turned to Julianne. "We'll try to keep you home until you can finish up. Are you having any problems at school?"

"My instructor has been very cooperative." She gave way to a shy smile. "He's pretty impressed that I've already landed a job and he said he'd help me get through the end." She reached over and gave Alec's arm an appreciative squeeze.

"I'm not surprised. If you weren't a good student, it would probably be somewhat different."

Julianne looked over her shoulder back to her cube. "I'd better go finish up with my Foster layout. Do you want me to hand that over to Bev?"

"When can you fly out?" Alec asked.

"I have class tonight. I could go tomorrow. I just want to get this done."

"Foster will still be here at the end of the week. Bev's got something else right now. Let Tyler know your time frame and if he has any questions, he can take it up with Jack."

Jack rolled his eyes.

"What's that for?" Alec asked, not missing the gesture.

Jack pursed his lips and shook his head. "Tyler's a little unhappy with me at the moment. I'm sure he'll have something to say. It'll be fine."

"Do you think he's at risk?"

Jack shrugged his shoulders again. "Probably not." Then he looked directly at Alec. "If he is, it would be your fault for bringing in new staff that he feels has an unfair edge." Jack raised his eyebrows.

"I think I should just get back to work now," Julianne excused herself, stepping backward out of the office.

* * *

Julianne's conscience continued to trouble her. She'd spent all day in Hayden's offices and then he'd insisted on taking her to dinner. Every time he started to talk about Jack, she found herself trying to change the subject, afraid of saying the wrong thing or telling him the truth outright. The longer she thought of herself as Jack's wife, the harder it was to step out of that role. Especially on those nights when the dreams haunted her sleep.

Julianne had hoped to do more homework after she returned to the hotel room, but after her dinner with Hayden, it was already 10:00 and she was exhausted from spending all day "on." She wanted to hit her off switch and fall into bed.

The computer sat closed on the desk in the corner of the room and Julianne thought once more about her connection with Jack. She'd never thought about it from his perspective before. Was that his only personal time? Unable to resist the pull, Julianne went to her computer and turned it on. It wasn't just for herself this time, she wanted to be there for him. As the connection went through, she remembered Gloria once more. There seemed significance in the fact that he didn't get into the cab with her, and yet all Julianne could picture was the way the woman draped herself across Jack.

"Where are you?" she whispered, searching the computer for traces of JGGuilder, but the gryphon wasn't on duty. Instead, she opened up an e-mail to report her day for both Jack and Alec.

* * *

Exhaustion closed in around her and she wondered if Hayden would let her go back to the hotel room to work, but she knew if she did she'd probably fall asleep. Julianne shrugged her shoulders and decided the only way she could keep on task was to stay put in the office she had been provided at Hayden Casualwear's corporate offices.

"And don't forget about your homework," her brain reminded her. Julianne turned to stare out the window, her focus hopelessly scattered. At least in Houston she didn't have to worry about Steve shadowing her.

Julianne yawned and from somewhere in the back of her mind she recalled the fairy tale of a princess locked in a tower to spin straw into gold. Sure she'd done it once, but could she do it again?

In her computer, a CD of the Boston Pops played Gershwin. Julianne hummed along with Rhapsody in Blue. The sketch of a princess sitting at the spinning wheel began to take shape on her pad of paper. Julianne continued to draw the princess dressed in sweats instead of a long gown. The idea expanded from there until the door to her prison opened.

Julianne shook her head for a moment, not sure if she'd actually fallen asleep and was dreaming again. "Jack?"

"I hear you're struggling a little.

"I'm hallucinating," she said half to herself.

Ben Hayden laughed, moving out from behind Jack. "I thought you might like a friendly face."

Julianne smiled in spite of herself. Jack walked in and looked over her shoulder. "Just waiting for Prince Charming?" he teased. "What are you listening to?"

The temperature in the room seemed much warmer than it was before. Julianne turned off her music and rose from her chair. "Boston Pops. And I didn't think I was allowed to see Prince Charming until I'd spun gold."

Jack wrapped his arms around Julianne.

"I'm glad to see you," she whispered.

Hayden cleared his throat. "Well I promised Jack here I'd let you two put something together without bothering you for a few hours." He tipped a hand from his forehead and closed the door as he left.

"I am so tired," Julianne said. "I can't even think anymore."

"I can see that." He picked up her sketchpad. "We might be able to take an angle on this idea. I'm just surprised to see you resort to fairy tales."

"Oh shut up and tell me what your angle is."

Jack took his seat beside her and opened his laptop. "We do make a great team, you know."

"You didn't seem to think so in Mexico."

"Not true," Jack said as he shook a finger at her. "There were other issues to consider."

"And now?"

"And now we have to get Hayden off our backs so we can have a month's peace."

* * *

When Hayden's limousine left them at the hotel, the only sign of life in the lobby was a television set in the office behind the desk.

"I didn't even think about a room," Jack sighed. "I'll have to see if they have another one available."

"Hayden won't pick up the tab for two rooms, Dear," Julianne reminded him sleepily. "And it isn't as if we haven't bunked together before." She motioned to the elevator with her head.

"Are you sure you don't mind? I wouldn't have to run the room through my expense report."

"I'm too tired to argue with you. If you want your own room, get one. I just don't see the point."

"I think you're beginning to trust me just a little," he teased, toting his overnight bag in one hand and his computer case over his shoulder.

Moments later she unlocked the door to her room and invited him in. "Two beds. I slept on the inside one last night in case it makes a difference to you."

"Doesn't matter. I'll sleep by the window."

Julianne set her computer beside the bed and fell across the comforter. "Another useless night," she sighed.

"What do you mean useless? At least Hayden didn't throw the idea out completely."

"No, I mean as far as homework goes. I keep expecting to find time to work on my final assignment and by the time I'm done for the day, I'm too tired to do anything but hit the bed."

Jack sat beside Julianne and pulled off her shoes. Then he pulled back the comforter and patted the sheets for her to roll over. "It'll all be over in a couple of weeks."

"And then Ben Hayden will own me for the next year."

"Sorry you got the job now, aren't you?"

Julianne opened her eyes and saw the grin on Jack's face. "Some days," she conceded.

Jack stood up and pulled his overnight case onto his bed. "Do you need to use the bathroom?" he asked as he pulled out his shaving kit.

Julianne shook her head and pulled herself up to a sitting position. "Go ahead."

While she listened to him brush his teeth, she changed her clothes and considered the familiarity they now shared. In the short time Steve lived with her she was always self-conscious and nervous about him being in her apartment, but from the first night she shared the hotel with Jack in Mexico, they slipped into a comfortable routine.

Her turn in the bathroom. His turn to shut off the light. And then, comfortable silence.

Julianne stared into the inky darkness toward the ceiling, exhausted and yet unable to sleep. "How do you do it?" she asked quietly.

"Do what?" Jack's deep voice seemed disconnected in the darkness.

"Hayden's going to find out. Then what?"

She heard the rustle of sheets in the other bed. "Attack of conscience?"

"Don't you ever have those?"

Jack exhaled a short laugh. "All the time."

"I'm lying to everyone I know."

"Except me and Alec."

"Put this in perspective. Do you lie to Alec?"

She heard an intake of air as if he was about to speak, and then he was quiet again. It was several minutes before he answered, and Julianne had almost given up, assuming he'd fallen asleep. "I didn't want to do this, you know. Remember me? The one who wouldn't give you a job?"

"So I should blame Alec?"

Again she heard a quiet laugh. "Well I have been. But on the other hand, I have also been considering a solution to this whole mess."

"So it does bother you?"

"Yes, but probably not quite the same way it bothers you."

"What's your solution?"

There was another rustling of sheets in the darkness and Julianne heard the rasp of his hand against his beard. "As things stand now, I'm not sure you'd trust me if I told you."

His answer pricked her temper. "So it gives you peace of mind and I have to wrangle with this some more?"

"To me it's peace of mind. To you it could be one more stick of dynamite."

In spite of her annoyance, the disembodied voice in the dark held a calming effect that kept her from building into a rage. Julianne closed her eyes and hoped her brain would slow down enough to let her rest.

Half an hour later, she rolled over and stared at the digital clock between the beds.

"Are you still awake?" Jack asked.

She stretched her arms over her head. "Yeah."

"Worried about nightmares?"

Julianne smiled to the darkness. "No. The bogeys are a thousand miles away."

"Homework?"

She wriggled uncomfortably with the reminder. "Just restless, I guess."

"I'm going to fix things, Julianne."

"We just keep getting in deeper," she sighed. "The longer we go, the better our chances of getting fired. And not just by Hayden."

"Well on the one side of the coin, once we do the Super Bowl ad, we can lay him to rest for a bit. As long as we come up with a blockbuster ad he should be set. That will cut down on our exposure."

"And on the other side of the coin?"

"We're already exposed. There will be damage control - more for you."

Julianne heaved a great sigh. "Thanks for that."

"What do you want to do with your career, Julianne? What are your long-term goals?"

"Oh great. We're going to do a goal setting session now? Can we just go to sleep?"

"Now that's the question of the hour. Can you go to sleep?"

Julianne looked at the red numbers on the clock between them. They'd been laying awake for three hours. "We're going to be useless tomorrow."

"Today," he corrected her.

"Today," she repeated.

"I'm serious. What do you want to do with the rest of your life? I'm not talking to you as a boss, pretend I'm asking you online. This is me. As in 'you and me.' Think of this as the chat room."

"I want to do advertising. Marketing."

"But you're regretting getting into the business, I know you are."

"No, I'm regretting getting caught up in a web of deceit."

"To a certain degree, it goes with the territory."

Julianne sat up in the bed and gathered her knees to her chest. "We're not talking casual omissions or little untruths."

"I want to leave Perkins & Stone."

Her head turned blindly in his direction, stunned by his last statement. "Can you do that?"

Jack laughed and she heard him move. "Why not?"

"What about Alec? I mean isn't it a family kinda thing?"

"I love Alec, he's all I have. I suppose in a lot of ways that's what keeps me there."

"So why leave? Ron Perkins doesn't seem like such a bad guy."

"The company's gotten too big. We go after the big fish now, like Hayden, and forget about the regular guys."

"And you have more resources at your fingertips. You don't have to worry quite so much about budgets and understaffing on short time frames."

Jack chuckled. "Alec's got you right where he wants you, doesn't he?"

Again, Julianne bristled. She refrained from addressing his comment. "So what do you want to do if it isn't Perkins & Stone?"

"Maybe go into teaching."

"Why don't you?"

"You and I make a great team."

"Perpetuate the illusion," she muttered.

"We can end this illusion anytime." His voice was suddenly cold. "If you like, I'll just tell Hayden tomorrow."

"Is that the solution you came up with?"

"I could tell you, Julianne, but somehow I think you'd believe it was another gimmick."

"And is it?"

Jack sighed in the darkness. "No. And that's why I'm not ready to tell you yet."

She hesitated a moment, almost willing to hear any crazy scheme he'd come up with to clean up the mess they made, and then thought better of asking again. She was already operating beyond what she thought to be maximum capacity, and here she lay, spending the night talking rather than getting much-needed sleep.

"Kinda funny, isn't it?" she pondered, giving way to a yawn.

"What's that?"

"Actually talking in the middle of the night."

"You mean instead of sending computer messages?"

Julianne smiled. "Yeah. That too."

"Have you ever done anything like this before?"

Julianne eased back down into her bed, pulling her covers up around her neck. "Yep. I spent a week in Mexico with a guy once."

"No, I mean stayed up all night just talking."

With a smile, Julianne closed her eyes. "No."

"Hey, Julianne?"

"Hmmm?" she felt herself drifting off the sandbar in the middle of an ocean of sleep.

"Where'd you get the statue that you keep by your computer?"

"You mean the gryphon?"

It was a moment before he confirmed her question. "Yeah."

She yawned and rolled toward the wall. "My dad gave it to me. Kind of a good luck charm. It's supposed," she interrupted herself with another yawn, "to keep me safe. It's just a trinket, really, but it reminds me of him."

Julianne opened her eyes for one more brief moment. "You lost both your parents. That must have been difficult, even if you were an adult."

Her ears pricked up to hear over the whir of the ventilation system for his next words, but he remained silent. After several minutes, Julianne closed her eyes once more and floated off to sleep.

CHAPTER 22

She was almost finished with the task that occupied her morning. Julianne checked the clock one more time. Her mind was already switching gears to her school assignment. Over lunch she planned to complete her homework, one more step toward her final grade.

Tyler Stern tapped an open palm against the top of her cube in passing. "Alec's looking for you."

Julianne's heart sank and she rolled her eyes. She was anxious to put the last touches to her projects. As fond as she had grown of Alec, if he was looking for her in the office, it generally meant more work. The phone on her desk rang and she gave it a sidelong look, pondering if she should just ignore it.

"He'll only show up at your desk if you don't answer it," Bev pointed out.

Julianne smiled reluctantly and answered the call. "Julianne DeAngelo."

"Can you step into my office a sec?" It was Jack. Julianne looked over her left shoulder and saw him watching her. She raised her hand in a small wave. "What are you two up to now?"

"As if I'm responsible for my godfather's whims?"

"Give me a minute. I'm almost done with this layout."

"Would you rather go to lunch?"

"No. I have to finish my homework at lunch."

"You can do that later."

"I have to hand it in tonight."

"Can you miss class tonight?"

Julianne sighed, closed her eyes and massaged her temples. "Now what?" When there was no response, she looked back into his office where he crooked a finger, summoning her. She scowled, then hung up her phone and walked into Jack's office.

"You know that award I won at the banquet?" He began.

"Yes?"

"Well it put me in contention for another one in New York this weekend. I think it was already on your itinerary anyway. Will you go with me?"

"What's the catch?"

"It will be a good opportunity for you. Play ball with the big boys."

"Alec's suggestion?"

Jack fidgeted behind his desk. He picked up a pen and twirled it between his fingers. "Actually it was my idea."

In the jealous corner of her mind she struggled not to ask him why he didn't invite Gloria to go instead. "So why would I miss my class tonight? It's only Thursday."

He avoided looking directly at her, a trait Julianne was coming to recognize when he was uncomfortable. "Well there's also a presentation Friday afternoon that Alec wanted you to sit in on. In New York."

"Well now that you mention it, my Cinderella dress is ruined. I don't have anything to wear."

He cringed, both of them sensitive to the reason it was ruined. "Well, we could go shopping after the presentation tomorrow – in New York."

"I get it. We're going to New York." She chewed on the inside of her cheeks to try to keep her expression neutral. She didn't want him to see how he affected her. Gloria continued to haunt her. Julianne recognized that she was in love with Jack, but she wouldn't let another man make a fool of her.

Her feelings for Jack eclipsed anything she'd felt for anyone before, but her track record wasn't very good. There was always someone prettier waiting in the wings. She stood silently, afraid to say anything.

Jack misread her hesitation. "Julianne, we can get a suite. Two rooms with a locking door between them. I'm not trying to seduce you or harass you." He bowed his head. "I apologize if it sounded that way."

She eased into a chair, staring at the floor. When had things become so awkward between them? "When would we have to leave?"

"Dorian's looking at a 7:00 flight tonight."

"I have to turn in my homework," she repeated. "I can take a flight in the morning."

Jack cleared his throat and looked out the window. "The awards banquet is Saturday night." He turned to meet her eyes. "Maybe we could see a show Friday night, since we're already there."

"There you are, Juju Dee." Alec swept through Jack's door and took a seat beside Julianne. He gave her a quick pat on the knee.

Julianne grinned at his new nickname for her. As meddlesome as he had been, she'd grown very fond of Alec Stone. "Shipping me off again, are you?"

"You won't have any trouble at school, will you?"

"My professor has been very cooperative, as long as I get my assignments in. And I have one that's due tonight."

"Can you turn it in earlier in the day?"

"I don't know if that's really necessary, and I have to finish it first. May I be excused?"

Jack nodded, and held a hand out toward the door.

She rose to her feet and accepted a hug from Alec. In spite of her misgivings, she was giddy with excitement. She and Jack were going on a date!

CHAPTER 23

As the Town Car crawled through traffic, Jack rubbed his jaw, pulled his hands through his hair, then rubbed his forehead. It made Julianne wonder what kind of nightmares this New York client had in store for her.

Would she be a liability in his meeting? "I didn't get much information about the presentation today."

"You won't need much," he reassured her.

"So why are you so nervous?"

He sat upright, too stiff. "I'm not nervous."

"Preoccupied then. You're definitely not yourself."

Jack licked his lips, and ran a hand through his hair once more, smoothing ruffled wings back into place. "I suppose there is something else on my mind." He looked out his window, then at the driver in the front seat before he turned back to her. "You said something the other day. . ." The car came to a stop and so did Jack's conversation. He grimaced, exhaled noisily, and shook his head. "We're here."

"What did I say?" Julianne asked.

Jack gave her a reassuring smile and patted her hand. "We'll have time to talk later. When we go shopping." He opened his door quickly and jumped out, then stopped by the driver's window to take care of the charges.

Julianne watched him. What had she said that would require so much thought? Since she moved in, he seemed increasingly distracted. How much of that was her fault? A pang of guilt pricked her conscience. She felt like an untied shoe he had to keep tying.

Fifteen minutes later she shook hands with Andrew Bellock, a small man with close cropped blond-white hair moussed to stand straight up. His chartreuse suit underscored his flamboyant sense of style.

"So this is the wife," Andrew held her hand a moment longer and raised it to his lips. "I saw your interview. Jack, I never knew you were married!" His voice carried an effeminate cadence and was slightly higher pitched than

Julianne was accustomed to hearing from a man. Andrew motioned for them to sit with an exaggerated sweep of his arm.

Parched from the morning's flight, Julianne reached for a bottle of water and poured it into a waiting glass.

"I figured it was time to bring her out of the closet," Jack quipped.

Julianne almost choked on the drink she'd taken and turned away from the table to cover her mouth.

"Oh really, dear, you don't need to get choked up about it," Andrew teased. "Jack and I are old friends." With a flip of the wrist he laughed and continued. "If you can't joke with your friends, what have you got left?"

Julianne smiled and winked. "Some of us are still a little shy about the exposure."

Andrew laughed in quick breathy bursts. "Oh Jack, she's adorable! What a treasure."

Julianne felt another stab of alarm. How many other clients had seen their interview? Their innocent make-believe lunch was taking on a life of its own. Hayden wasn't the only patsy any more. "You saw the interview?"

"National account," Jack pointed out. "The interview had a national feed."

Julianne took a deep gulp of water. Their little white lie was growing very quickly into a wall of snow and ice. The avalanche from the fallout would bury them both.

"Don't be so shy," Andrew assured her. "The commercial was wonderful! I saw it, you know. You're going to have all Jack's clients begging for you to be in their commercials."

Julianne shook her head. "No. It was just a one-time deal."

"She's so modest!" Andrew cooed. "Jack she's just charming! I can't imagine why you haven't put her on the front line before this."

"She's been working toward finishing a degree," Jack answered. "With that behind her, she'll be able to concentrate on blasting out all the competition. And she will too."

Julianne put her hands up to stop the accolades. "Ok, ok. We didn't come here to flaunt Julianne. Andrew, tell me about your company. Are Jack's ads flooding you with business?"

"Of course! Jack has been brilliant for us."

"And that's why I'm here," Jack stepped into his opening, "so I can continue to be brilliant for you going forward. Let's talk about what you want to see for the new ads."

Julianne marveled at his smooth transition and sat back to watch Jack work.

Intimate Distance

* * *

The meeting had been brief enough as to almost have been unnecessary. By lunch time, they were walking the streets of Manhattan.

"I've never met anyone like quite Andrew Bellock before," Julianne laughed.

"He can be overwhelming," Jack agreed, a smile on his face.

"He's got so much energy! His ideas are very good."

"Makes my job that much easier."

Snow flurries floated around 5th Avenue. Julianne clung to Jack's arm to ward off the bitter chill, toting her growing number of purchases.

In spite of the numerous shops to choose from, Julianne decided on a dress for the awards dinner fairly early in their trek, pleased with her quick success. After that, the shopping became more leisurely with stops to pick up accessories, a side trip into the chocolate shops or pausing to admire the window displays.

Her legs and feet began to protest the extended amount of walking, but the thrill of Gotham City propelled her forward.

The November wind playfully nudged at the bags they carried. Jack slid rope handles to his elbow, took hold of Julianne's gloved hand and smiled. The aroma of roasting chestnuts carried through the streets replacing less pleasant smells as they neared the corner vendors.

They looked in at Tiffanys where Julianne admired sparkling jewelry that winked through the window. "What a beautiful necklace."

"Do you want it?"

She shook her head immediately. "No. I'm not that frivolous. It's lovely to look at, but how practical would it be to own?"

"It would go well with the dress you got at Saks."

"That's too showy for me. I have much simpler tastes."

Jack pulled at her arm, inviting her into the store. With a smile, she followed.

"Why don't you see if anything catches your eye," he suggested.

"Everything's so expensive," she whispered. "I don't want to spend my entire bonus and I've already gotten so much." She held up the bags on her arm to illustrate.

"Well there's no harm in looking."

She let go of his arm and surveyed the jewelry cases.

A clerk appeared quietly beside her. "Is there something Madam wishes to see?"

"Oh," Julianne sighed. "Well I just don't know yet."

"A lovely diamond, or maybe an emerald to complement your coloring?"

Julianne reached for her neckline with her free hand. The old budget would never have allowed for Tiffany and suddenly it all seemed excessive.

"What do you think?" Jack asked.

"I don't think so."

"We could stop at Cartier if you prefer."

She raised one eyebrow. "Cartier?"

"There's a Tiffany's on Michigan Avenue back in Chicago. It might be easier if we need something shipped, in case you wanted something personalized, but that doesn't mean we can't buy at Cartier."

Overwhelmed at the ease with which he minimized the price tags, Julianne pulled him out of the store. "Maybe we should just look in Chicago. Then we wouldn't have to worry about any shipping. I'm still a little shell-shocked. You know we can find better prices."

"But then it wouldn't be Tiffany's."

"Do I strike you as a name-brand type of person?"

Jack laughed and gave her a squeeze across the shoulders. He turned his wrist over to look at his watch, the bags on his arm swinging precariously. "We need to get back to the hotel and get ready for dinner," he said.

They walked back to the Plaza by way of Carnegie Hall. "The Pops!" Julianne exclaimed when she saw the "one night only" poster, but she pouted at the black "Sold Out" sticker pasted over it. "They were in Chicago," she told Jack, "but I couldn't get tickets there either."

"I did."

"See them in Chicago?"

"No, I got tickets."

Julianne came to an abrupt stop. "You got tickets?"

Jack nodded.

"To the Pops?"

His grin spread.

Her eyes grew larger. "Tonight?"

When he continued to nod, Julianne threw her arms around him, hitting him with her bags in the process. She pulled back, gathering in her purchases. "I can't believe it! We're going to see the Pops?"

"Not if we don't get moving."

* * *

Jack held her hand throughout the concert. The orchestra was exactly as she expected, and she nodded her head and tapped a foot in time with the music through most of the performance. In her peripheral vision, Julianne noticed Jack glance at her often and wondered if he was embarrassed by her open admiration for the music. She made a mental note to ask him when they left. Meanwhile, she continued to enjoy the buoyant conductor swaying in tempo with the instruments.

When they left Carnegie Hall, it took them several minutes of brisk walking to negotiate the crowd. Julianne continued to hum, bouncing with each step to keep warm.

"That was wonderful," she gushed. "I'm going to be humming those songs in my head all night. I love Scheherazade. I can't believe you got tickets to the Boston Pops! And at Carnegie Hall! Those seats must have cost a fortune. Oh," she took one step sideways to look at Jack and then fell back in stride, "and dinner was wonderful, too. Have you eaten there before? I've never been to New York before, you know. I bet you've been here dozens of times. I can't believe all the beautiful flowers they had in that restaurant and at this time of year. It was so much fun to speak French to that waiter. I haven't used my French since high school Did you know La Grenuoille means frog?"

She stopped her prattle long enough to wait for an answer and realized he hadn't spoken since leaving the Hall. With the excitement of the evening, Julianne walked in a bubble, oblivious to the discomfort of the chill. Jack's collar stood up around his neck against the icy wind that blew them down the street. He showed no indication that he had even heard the question. Julianne stepped in front of him, to command his full attention. "Where were you just now?"

He looked startled and almost walked into her. "What?"

"You haven't heard a word I said. Not that you missed anything." He hadn't been that preoccupied since she arrived. And then she remembered with a shiver. "What was it I said to you that's got you thinking so hard? Did I embarrass you at the concert?"

Jack smiled and squeezed her gloved hand. He stood silently, just gazing into her eyes for several moments before he spoke. "There's so much I want to tell you." He looked around and caught sight of a hansom cab. He nodded toward the horse. "Let's take a ride."

Julianne hesitated. If he was upset with her, the last thing she wanted to do was climb into a horse-drawn carriage. It was one of the last vestiges of romance left in her wounded psyche. If Jack meant to quash her mood, she didn't want to forever associate the moment with the carriage.

"Jack," she began, deliberately keeping a step behind.

He stopped and reached for her hand to coax her along. "I want to ride around Central Park. I've never done it before."

Unable to resist his reassuring smile, she nodded and kept in step with him. Julianne climbed in first and Jack took the seat beside her. The driver placed a blanket across their legs and closed them in. Jack grasped both Julianne's hands in his.

His breath steamed white in the frigid night air. "This may all seem a little corny to you. Call it the ad man in me. Some clichés are just meant to be used, regardless of how old they are."

"Why do I feel like I should be raising my guard right about now?" she laughed.

Jack turned toward her and pressed her gloved hands to his chest. "I have had the most wonderful day with you."

She smiled and looked shyly past him to the park outside. It wasn't like him to be so attentive and it made her wonder what bombshell he had yet to detonate.

"Julianne, I want to tell you about Gloria."

She inched away and tried to retract her hands, but he held them tight. "You don't have to..." she said, afraid to hear more.

"The truth. I was engaged to her when we were in college. Everything seemed to be going along fine and then my parents had that accident. Suddenly everything wasn't quite so fine anymore, including Gloria. That's about the time I realized that I wanted to marry her for all the wrong reasons. Once I faced that, it became even more apparent what a poor match we were. We broke it off, but left it kind of open-ended. Over the years, we've gone out whenever she's in town, but I've never felt the same about her."

Julianne squirmed in her seat. The icy chill sent out tentacles to tear open her cocoon. "Really, you don't have to tell me about her."

"Let me finish. When you saw us on Michigan Avenue, she asked if I wanted to go out. It was after the interview so naturally I told her I was married." He paused a moment, leaning across the seat toward Julianne. "That didn't seem to matter to her, but it was important to me." He ducked to get her attention, drawing her eyes to his. "More important was the part where it didn't matter to her."

Julianne frowned, not fully comprehending his point. "Well now you have some closure for yourself."

There was an intensity in his gaze that she hadn't seen before. "Julianne, I'm crazy about you. I have been since before I asked you to that stupid lunch. I couldn't say anything then; you were engaged." Jack's voice grew hoarse and he hastily swiped at his cheek.

Julianne took the opportunity to pull back her hand and adjusted the blanket across her legs. Was she dreaming? JGGuilder wasn't really sitting across from her, in a hansom cab, professing his love for her. She remained still, afraid to move, afraid to speak, afraid she would wake up and find it was all a dream.

Jack's eyes glittered in the lamplight of Central Park. Through the gloved hand he still held, he fingered the circles of her rings and then a thought illuminated his face. "The rings," he announced triumphantly.

Julianne looked to her left hand briefly and then narrowed her eyes. "You want them back?"

"No, I want you to have them. Not just for the length of the contract. Julianne, I want to marry you."

The cab bumped over a pot hole, taking all of Julianne's breath with it. More propoganda?

Jack blew out a slow, white breath, not taking his eyes from her face. Transfixed, she studied him for any sign of insincerity.

"I'm not doing this for the sake of Hayden or the firm." He tightened his grip on her hand. "I can't imagine my life without you."

"Is this your solution?" she asked, scarcely able to find her own voice.

Jack sat back and released her hands. "Julianne, I've never felt this way about anyone before. That lunch, I thought if I could just see you one more time, I might be able to get you out of my system, once and for all." He shook his head and laughed. "Instead, you lodged yourself in tighter and I began to panic."

Julianne fought back the smile threatening to creep across her face. "So you uninvited me to the meeting."

"Yes."

She began to understand a lot of things. "And you kept me at arms-length all through the Mexico trip."

He leaned forward again and raised one eyebrow. "You were never at arms-length."

"You slept in the chair."

Jack rolled his eyes. "Did you want me to seduce you?"

She felt the warmth of embarrassment flushing over her. "No." Was he just trying to ingratiate himself? Maybe he was counting on tonight being his payoff.

The horse clip-clopped around a corner, swaying its occupants to one side. When the next street lamp lit up the inside of the cab, Julianne saw Jack wearing a silly grin. "I lose more women that way. All they want from me is sex."

Julianne laughed and sniffed indelicately. "You're too good of a liar."

He reached for her chin to get her to look at him.

Julianne swallowed hard, wanting him to mean it and still afraid it was a hoax.

The horse came to a stop. Outside, the driver set up the stool for them to step down.

Jack frowned, squeezing her hands one more time. When she didn't respond, he let her go and stepped out of the cab to pay the driver. Jack offered his hand and she stepped out of her fantasy.

They walked the rest of the way back to the Plaza in silence. Julianne hated being so skeptical, but she'd seen him lie too easily to so many people. As much as she knew her own feelings for him, she didn't want to be exploited. What if he had been preoccupied all day trying to figure out the easiest way to seduce her? Maybe he'd finally gotten a read on her personality and this was his sell.

They lived together. They shared hotel rooms. They'd even shared a bed. Tonight, their accommodations seemed inappropriate.

When Jack unlocked the hotel room, Julianne felt exposed. With Steve it was a running battle to keep him away until after the wedding, even after he'd promised to honor her wishes.

"Why did you go to Houston with me?" she asked him.

A sideways grin crept across Jack's features. "Hayden called me. He said you missed me." Jack put an arm around her shoulders. "But I went because I missed you." He crossed his heart with two fingers and held them up in the air. "That's the truth."

"I'm not going to . . ." she began, still unable to say the words. She sighed and closed her eyes to gather her strength. "I don't want you to think. . ."

She couldn't look into his face. He stood directly in front of her, his hands squeezing her shoulders gently. "I'm not going to. Not until we make this real. I'm not that kind of guy."

The eyebrow she raised underlined her misgivings.

Jack lifted his arms. "I'm going to get another room."

Was he gay? Was he looking for a marriage of convenience? "What kind of guy are you?" she asked.

She saw his jaw tighten and realized after the words were out how they sounded. "I'm not the type of guy that shacks up with his girlfriend before their wedding and then steps out with her sister."

His words stung her already open wounds. Julianne clenched her teeth while she fought back the tears. "His moving in was a matter of convenience before the wedding, not a premature honeymoon."

"I'm not judging you,"

"Then why make the comment?"

Jack closed his eyes and turned away from her. "Maybe I mistook your meaning."

She stood her ground firmly, her hands on her hips.

"You did share a bed with him, didn't you" Jack pointed out.

"Actually we had separate bedrooms, but he was always pressuring me to give in. Why does that suddenly seem more normal?"

"That's what society expects from a man. I set my standards a little higher than that."

Julianne bit her lip. She wanted to believe him and yet she was frightened of yet another mistake. "Why should I believe you? I saw the way Gloria was draped all over you on Michigan Avenue."

Jack scratched his forehead and looked away. "I never slept with Gloria."

Julianne sank into the chair by the window and stared at him.

Jack shook his head. "Alec was right."

"What's Alec got to do with this?"

"When I asked him to bring me my mother's rings, I told him they would be the one piece of truth in this whole mess of a lie. He told me the foundation would be too soft to build on. And therein lies the problem. I can't expect you to believe anything I say." Jack shook his head and walked away.

"Your mother's rings?"

He nodded.

"You gave me your *mother's* rings? But you hardly knew me."

"Julianne, this may all have started out as fabrication, but there isn't anything bogus about the way I feel about you."

Was that what Alec meant when he told Julianne there was a story behind the rings? Surely Jack wouldn't give her his mother's rings as part of the scam just as she would never part with her statuette of the gryphon. It was the last thing she had of her father.

"I love you, Julianne."

And in that moment she believed him.

He held his arms out in supplication. "I don't know what else I can say."

This time she reached for him. She pulled him back into the room, gave him a smile and tilted her head, determined to alter the mood. "Do you think I'm a cold fish?"

Jack furrowed his brow, confused by the question. "I think you're warm and vibrant."

"But you haven't made any passes at me."

"Sex doesn't define love, it's the perk that comes after real love has already been confirmed. For me, that means after marriage."

She nodded. "A couple of weeks ago my sister called me a cold fish and suggested the reason Steve was looking for outside entertainment must be a shortcoming on my part. She assumed we'd already done the deed and that I didn't like sex." Julianne started to laugh.

"I'm still waiting for the funny part."

"My mother said something, too. Remember in Mexico when you asked me what 30-year-old man didn't date much? Well that isn't exactly what you said, but my mother made a similar comment to me, about me. Not that I was still a virgin, but that maybe because I hadn't landed a husband by the ripe old age of 25 that I maybe preferred women. Particularly since I was willing to pass on such a prime piece of real estate as Steve."

Jack's shoulders relaxed and the frown on his face receded.

Julianne held a hand open in front of her. "Okay, you ask me and then I'll ask you."

"It's different for women. Double standard."

"Maybe but for some women, having sex is more an affirmation of beauty rather than any level of emotional attachment."

Jack let out a short laugh.

"You know I'm right," she pressed.

"I'll bite," he conceded. "Are you gay?"

"No. Are you?"

"No," he stated firmly.

Julianne broke into a wide grin. "Would you lie to me?"

Jack pulled her close and wrapped his arms around her. "I will never lie to you. Please don't confuse the way I sometimes misdirect my clients with who I am." His lips touched her hair and then he smoothed the spot down with his hand.

"You just want to get laid," she teased.

"We already covered that. You're just stalling now."

Jack held her at arms' length and stroked her cheek.

Julianne turned away, afraid to let him see her feelings. "I understand you met my sister."

Jack smirked. "Yeah, I met her. She seems a bit more like your mother than you."

Julianne laughed. "Well you're right about that. But she is pretty, don't you think?"

"She seemed a little superficial to me. My first reaction, and please forgive me for judging her on a first impression, wasn't very positive." He pulled Julianne's head against his shoulder. "I can't say I'm going to like your sister, Julianne. I'm sorry. Did she want to do some modeling or something?"

Julianne shook her head. "You may have noticed my family is somewhat dysfunctional, particularly since my father died." The tears fell before she had a chance to check them.

Jack gave her a gentle squeeze. "Let me get you a tissue." When he returned, they sat down on Julianne's bed while she blew her nose.

"Sorry for the waterworks," she apologized. "But I do miss my dad."

"That must be why you seem to have adopted Alec."

She turned to face him. "Adopted Alec?"

"JuJu Dee? When did he start calling you that?"

Julianne laughed.

"You know he loves you. I'm sure he'd gladly step in for your father. And I speak from experience."

Julianne threw her arms around Jack, clinging to him tightly. She didn't want to let go. Ever. But could she believe him? "You'll have to give me a little more time."

"Just think about it?" Jack prodded.

Julianne mustered a smile. "Of course I'll think about it." It was all she'd think about. It would be so easy to say yes. Steve had been ready to marry her, wanted to marry her still, and yet Steve's values were a long way from hers. Maybe Jack would be faithful, but there was so much she didn't know about him. And still so much she didn't trust.

She needed to talk to someone to get her bearings, but was there anyone she could trust? Julianne was just as guilty as Jack in fostering their scheme. To share her feelings with anyone would be to admit her part. That could ruin their public image and their respective reputations permanently.

And then a thought occurred to her. Julianne rifled through her purse until she found her address book, aware of Jack's eyes fixed on her. "Please stop staring at me like I'm going to explode."

He took a deep breath. "I'm going to get another room."

"You don't have to."

Jack raised one eyebrow. "Yeah, I do." He pulled a hand through his rumpled hair.

"You're mad at me."

With a sigh, Jack picked up his suitcase. "Julianne, that night I came home from Atlanta . . ." he stopped with another sigh, "even if you would have said yes to me tonight . . ." he held his hands out. "I still need to get another room."

"We've done this before."

Jack turned to the door. "And each time the intensity increases."

"Is this some sort of emotional blackmail?"

Jack set his suitcase down by the door. "No. This is who I am." He turned slowly. "I want to hold you, but I'm afraid I won't be able to let you go. I want to sleep beside you, but the temptation is just too great. The more time we spend together the more time I want to spend together." He shook his head. "That was eloquent," he said sarcastically. "Look, until we get this figured out, I think we could benefit by some time apart."

It was a strange twist of fate that didn't escape Julianne's attention. This was just the sort of thing she would talk to JGGuilder about online at 2:00 a.m. The thought made her glance at the clock and she couldn't suppress the smile. It was 1:37 a.m. and JGGuilder was in the room with her. And he was just as confused as she was.

Maybe he was right.

"Alec has me at professional education classes in St. Louis starting next Tuesday. I plan to hand in my final paper on Monday night." She took a deep breath. "I'll be gone most of next week."

Jack nodded.

"Listen, there's someone I want to look up while I'm in New York. Do you mind if I spend some alone time tomorrow?"

"You are planning to go to the dinner tomorrow night, aren't you?"

Julianne smiled. "That's the reason I came to New York, isn't it?"

CHAPTER 24

If Barbara DeAngelo knew Julianne planned to visit her uncle, there would be hell to pay. The levels of dysfunction expanded as Julianne crossed generations. Although she'd only met her Uncle Vinnie a handful of times, she remembered him as being very much like her father. Whatever the dispute between her mother and her uncle, the man she remembered fondly seemed her best choice for a sounding board. Or at least one last tie to family.

He had sounded happy enough to hear from her when she phoned. As she checked the house numbers against the piece of paper in her mittened hand, Julianne slid precariously on the thin layer of snow that remained on the Brooklyn sidewalk. She caught her balance and marched resolutely up to the brick home.

He was waiting on the screened-in porch, the same man she remembered from their last visit, her father's funeral.

Uncle Vinnie opened the door and held his arms out to her. "Once you get retired you look forward to company." Unlike her father, his gravelly voice made her want to give him a throat lozenge.

Julianne pulled him close and kissed his cheek. "Uncle Vinnie. It's good to see you again."

"I would have liked to see more of you girls," he said, drawing her inside the porch and through the front door, "but your ma and me, we didn't get along too good. You, you were always something special, Julianne."

Julianne smirked. "I'm just your average, everyday Midwestern girl."

Uncle Vinnie closed the door behind them and motioned her to a chair in the sitting room. "You're the spitting image of your dad. Just prettier. I was so glad he used to bring you and your sister to Akron."

"I remember when Grandpa took us to watch them move that house. I was fascinated to see an entire house roll down the street." Uncle Vinnie had been the one to hold her hand. The man who sat across from her had her father's eyes, the same washed out brown that was passed along to her. The hawkish nose looked as if it had been broken once, and he had deep dimples that Julianne remembered poking her fingers into as a child.

They took measure of each other silently for a moment. His thick, unruly hair had gone completely white. "I'm glad you looked me up, Julianne," Uncle Vinnie finally said with a sigh. "With your dad gone, I don't hardly know how to get in touch with you anymore, and That Woman certainly wouldn't give me the time of day, let alone give me your phone number."

"What is it with you and Mom, anyway?" Julianne asked, letting her attention wander around the old-fashioned sitting room. She saw photos on shelves of her grandparents in Akron, her father, her uncle and his family. So many of them gone now.

"Oh we were never good enough for the likes of her." As if he could read her mind, Uncle Vinnie got up to hand her the photos. "She was always so high and mighty, like the Queen of England. Don't know why she thought Tom was any better than the rest of us, but she certainly didn't care for the family. Bless his soul, I don't know how he put up with her all those years. Sometimes I think she drove him to an early grave."

Julianne sorted through the picture frames one by one, feeling that familiar tug at her heart while she looked into the faces of her grandparents. There was one photo of all of them: her father, her aunt and uncle, Julianne and Suzanne, but her mother was noticeably absent. "It's a shame you never had kids. You would have been a great father, Uncle Vinnie."

The older man's dimples deepened with his smile. "I guess God had other plans for me and Bonnie."

Julianne handed the pictures back to him and watched him replace them lovingly onto the shelves.

"So what brings you to New York?"

"Business," she answered with a sigh.

"Didn't I hear something about you getting married?"

"Well that didn't quite pan out."

Uncle Vinnie cocked his head to one side, then sat forward in his chair and folded his hands, his elbows on his knees. "Why do I get the idea you didn't just stop by to keep an old man company?"

Julianne turned her rings while a smile spread across her face. It seemed she was easier to read than she thought. "Well I was kind of looking for a sounding board – someone who might give me some advice."

"You miss your dad, don't you?"

The question made her throat swell and brought tears to her eyes. She nodded, not trusting herself to speak.

"I miss him too. I don't mean to be disrespectful, Julianne, but your dad used to tell me a lot about how things were for you girls growing up." He stopped, opening his mouth a couple of times only to close it again. "Don't imagine you can talk much to That Woman, can you?" he finally asked.

Julianne shook her head.

"I'm just a Dumb Old Dago, but I've got two ears." He sat back in his chair and crossed his legs.

Julianne laughed. "You're not a dumb old Dago. You're my Uncle Vinnie."

"So what's on your mind?"

Shyness closed in on Julianne and she wondered if she should burden her uncle with her problems.

"You'll tell me when you're ready, Cara." He pushed himself to his feet. "Do you want something to drink? Maybe a cuppa joe? And I have some cookies from one of the neighbor ladies who keeps trying to get me to take her on a date."

Julianne laughed again. How could her mother have disliked him so much for so many years? "I'd love a cup of coffee. And I have a particular fondness for cookies. Let me help?"

He waved her down. "Not on your life. I don't get company very often. Let me take care of you."

Julianne watched him disappear behind a swinging door into the kitchen. No one had called her "Cara" since her father died. It was one of the few Italian words his family carried into the "new world" through the two generations that had been Americans before him. She wrapped her arms around herself and looked at the faded chintz curtains that hung at the window shading the nearly antique furniture scattered around the room.

He returned moments later with a tray, chewing his lower lip and wearing a fierce look of concentration fixed on the coffee cups on his tray. His bushy eyebrows lifted and lowered with each slosh of coffee until he set the tray on a round table beside her. With a sigh of relief, he gave her a smile that brought out his dimples while he handed her a cup.

"We got cream and sugar, too." He pointed to the tray. "Help yourself to the cookies. I don't need so many just for myself."

Julianne added some cream to her coffee while Uncle Vinnie took his cup back to his chair and reached back for a couple of chocolate chip cookies.

"So tell me about your job, then," he prompted.

"Well I just started a couple of weeks ago."

"Do you like it?" He blew across the top of his cup, his eyes fixed on Julianne.

"Hard to say." She turned her attention to the swirls of white in her coffee cup. "It's a little complicated."

"Sounds like you got a lot going on. A wedding that didn't happen, a job that's complicated . . ."

And then the dam broke. Julianne told him about night school and Jack Guilder, the engagement to Steve, the online conferences, losing her job at Kimball Brothers and being hired at Perkins & Stone. Three cookies and two cups of coffee later, she told him about her proposal from Jack.

Uncle Vinnie sat back in his chair. He made a tent with his fingers and studied the structure attentively.

"So what are you most worried about right now?" he asked. "Finishing your degree?"

She took a deep breath, purged of her burdens. "No, I think that's about finished. I'm hoping to hand in my final paper on Monday night when I get back and that's all but done."

"What about the job? They working you pretty hard?"

"The job is fun," she told him, sitting upright. "Without all the garbage, I've been enjoying what I do."

He nodded slowly, then rubbed at his eyes. "All the garbage," he repeated. "You mean this thing with John?"

Julianne nodded.

"But that's really all separate, isn't it? I mean you like the job, you just don't like the pretending part."

It felt good to tell someone the truth. "Yeah, but the pretending complicates the job."

"Well you're in advertising, Julianne. Seems to me it's all pretending, isn't it? I mean you got actors pretending they like somebody's product. Seems to me the industry will forgive you for your little gimmick, your angle on the whole deal."

"You don't understand," she told him as she leaned forward. "This client wants integrity. All we've given him so far is lies."

"You're selling his product," Uncle Vinnie pointed with a finger. "His bottom line is all he's gonna care about."

"He came into the office breathing fire when we got back from Mexico. If he finds out we've been duping him with this whole marriage thing, I can't imagine what kind of blood vessels he's going to pop."

Uncle Vinnie continued to wag his finger at her. "Did you ever stop to consider maybe he already knows and he's just playing with you two? Wants to see how far you'll carry it?"

Julianne sat back to consider his point. "I hadn't thought of it before. But I can't imagine he'd let it go quietly."

"So now John wants to make it legitimate and you doubt his intentions?"

"We've told so many lies. I just don't know where the truth is anymore."

Uncle Vinnie nodded and folded his hands behind his head. "Let's step back a minute. You met this guy in the classroom, right?"

"Right."

"Then you started talking to him on the computer?"

"Yes."

"And all the while you were engaged to this bozo?"

A layer of guilt darkened Julianne's perspective. "Yes."

Uncle Vinnie leaned forward to shake a finger at her again. "Now stop that. I can see your feelings all over your face. You didn't do anything to feel bad about."

"It's kind of like cheating on him."

"Now I'm not saying what's good for the goose, you understand, but what you did isn't anything compared to what he did to you." The older man sat back again, his hands on his knees. "So tell me what you thought about this other guy while you were talking to him on the computer."

"I thought he was very intelligent. I found him sympathetic. We formed a close friendship."

"You might even say you were falling in love with him?" Uncle Vinnie prompted.

Julianne lowered her eyes and nodded.

"And you felt guilty about that."

"I was still engaged."

"To a bozo."

Julianne couldn't suppress the giggle. Her uncle had a unique way of presenting the facts. "I suppose so."

"So you're falling in love with this guy, he's falling in love with you. Then you have this lunch? That seems to be the turning point to all of that, yes?"

"Yes."

"And what happened at lunch? Forget about bozo for a minute, I mean with you and John."

"It was strange. I felt a little exposed. On the computer I kind of endowed him with the attributes of a gryphon, you know, kind of my protector from the world, and he developed into this ideal."

"Like you fell in love with the man you wanted him to be."

"Exactly. And then to see him in real life. It was as if he stepped out of my imagination, off the page in a manner of speaking."

"And he didn't measure up to what you built him up to be?"

Julianne shook her head. "On the contrary. He was everything I imagined he was." Her breath caught in her throat.

"So this is the perfect man we're talking about here. And then you look across the room and see bozo sitting over there with your sister." Uncle Vinnie leaned forward again. "And instead of thinking, 'what a loser he is, sneaking around behind my back once again,' you think, 'look at me enjoying the company of the perfect man when I'm supposed to be stuck with that loser over there.'" Uncle Vinnie closed his eyes and waved his hand to erase that thought. "No, you wouldn't have thought of it that way, but you would have felt guilty that you were enjoying yourself when you were supposed to be loyal to that bozo, am I right?"

Julianne reached for her coffee cup, surprised by how closely he'd hit on her feelings. "Something like that."

"So now you feel guilty about liking Mr. Perfect."

"I don't know if it's just the guilt . . ."

"And you don't think you can trust him. It's all just a game to him?"

"Yeah." She lifted the cup and drained the remains of her coffee.

"But you love this guy?"

Again the tears stung the corners of her eyes. "Yeah."

Uncle Vinnie sat back, tenting his fingers and collapsing them several times. When he finally looked at Julianne again, his face was stern. "You know I can't tell you what to do."

"I feel better just being able to talk about it."

He nodded and studied his hands again. "Well this is where I tell you a little something more."

Julianne laughed. "Oh yeah, I know. I'm a Mafia Princess and you're gonna whack this guy, right?"

The dimples dented in. "And you say you got no imagination." He leaned over, his arms resting on his legs. "I saw you on the TV. The interview on that entertainment show that's on at dinner time."

Julianne felt a flush of pride.

"I even called That Woman," he continued.

Her eyes opened wide. "You called my mother?"

He nodded. "Must have been a bitter pill for her and that sister of yours to swallow. All these years of making you believe you're the ugly duckling and then you go and make a commercial on TV. Bet it sent them into a spiral."

His point felt like a blow to the head. "I hadn't thought of that."

"Don't you feel bad about it," he threatened, shaking his finger at her again. "What you've got they'll never have. That's what sets you apart from them." He thumped his chest. "It comes from in here. When your mom and dad told me they were getting married, he started in about how beautiful she was. I reminded him beauty is only skin deep and that it fades with the years. Your mother heard me and I don't think she ever forgave me that. Now she's old and probably not quite so beautiful anymore and what does she have left?" He shook his head. "But I'm getting away from my point here."

Julianne smiled, moved by his intensity.

"I saw that interview," he repeated. "I saw that man sitting beside you, holding your hand, looking at you as if he was watching a star shooting across the sky. It was the look of a man who knows he's seeing something spectacular and can't believe his good fortune in being there to witness it." Uncle Vinnie reached across and closed his hands around hers.

"Cara, I'm a pretty good judge of character. I don't know Mr. Perfect from Adam, but I know that look. He's definitely in love with you. Maybe he's just caught up in the act, but he's not pretending. That probably doesn't help you any, but when you think about it, think about what you know about him. Is he the kind of man who would get carried away with the moment and forget his footing? Or does he consider his steps carefully? Maybe he's told a lot of lies – that goes with the territory, I'm afraid. But has he lied to you? You said bozo hasn't lied to you, but he was running around on you. You knew about it but chose not to see it. Learn from that lesson. Open your eyes and look at everything. Then make your decision." He rubbed her hands, watching to make sure she understood.

"Don't look at this as all one big lump. There are other jobs. There will be other clients. If it takes changing that to find out if John really is Mr. Perfect, do that."

From her purse, Julianne's cell phone rang out. She leaned back reluctantly and reached for it, seeing Jack's name on her caller ID display. "That's him now," she told her uncle, connecting the call.

"Where are you?" Jack asked.

"Brooklyn."

"Then you better think about heading back unless you're going to the dinner in your jeans."

Julianne looked at the clothes she was wearing and then to a mantel clock. "Oh my! I didn't realize what time it was! I'm on my way." She disconnected the call, dropped the phone back in her purse and jumped to her feet. "I have to go."

"But you only just got here," her uncle protested.

Julianne threw herself into her uncle's arms. "I know. I'm sorry. Thank you, Uncle Vinnie."

"Now you know where I live, don't be a stranger, eh?" he wagged his finger at her one last time.

"I won't. I promise. And I want you to come visit me in Chicago." She shrugged back into her coat and pulled on her mittens.

Uncle Vinnie shrugged his shoulders. "I don't get out that way much anymore, Cara. But if there should be a wedding in your future . . ."

Julianne laughed. "There's a good chance of that."

"Of course your mother might just have a stroke if she were to see me walk in."

"She's kept you from me long enough. But for now I really have to go." Julianne planted a kiss on her uncle's cheek. "You made my day, Uncle Vinnie." She saw his eyes glisten as she hurried out the door. Julianne offered up one last wave when she turned onto the sidewalk with a lighter load on her shoulders.

CHAPTER 25

When Julianne walked back into the hotel suite, she found Jack in front of the mirror, pulling out the bow in his tie. He cast an irritated look at her reflection and started over. "Where have you been all day?"

Buoyed by her visit with her uncle, Julianne smiled inwardly. "I'm sorry, I guess I lost track of time." She hurried to the closet and pulled out her new dress, carefully removed it from the store bag and cut off the tags.

She looked up to see Jack tighten the knot around his neck, take a cursory look and pull it out one more time. "Is there someone else?" he asked. Jack stood frozen in front of the mirror, the ends of his tie in either hand.

"Someone else?"

"It was probably presumptuous of me to assume I was the only one you were talking to online."

Julianne lay the dress on the bed and put her hands to her hips. "You think I went to see someone I met online?"

"I was just asking the question. You seem a little cloak and dagger about it. And now you come bouncing back into the room like you've just had the time of your life."

Julianne's mouth gaped open. A rendezvous with her Uncle Vinnie? She broke into a fit of giggles. "You're not serious."

His face turned red and she recognized the familiar clenching and unclenching in his jaw. Her mirth seemed to add to his irritation.

"You don't really believe that," she said. And at that moment she decided she wasn't going to tell him where she'd been.

"You haven't answered the question."

"And I don't intend to with that attitude." In a moment of déjà vu, it occurred to Julianne that she'd heard a similar argument with her in the accuser's seat. From the other perspective, she wondered if she'd falsely accused Steve. With a quick shake to clear her head, she stopped herself from second-guessing that decision. "There isn't anyone else," she reassured him. "Do I strike you as the black widow type?"

Jack heaved a sigh and headed for the door. "I'll leave you alone to get ready. Maybe I'll be able to tie this cursed thing around my neck in the lobby."

* * *

Julianne surveyed the opulent ballroom inside the Waldorf-Astoria and felt a renewed sense of confidence. It helped that they were in a different city. No panic attacks. No Steve waiting outside to bash someone's brains in. No Gloria Bennett lurking in the shadows waiting for the opportunity to throw herself at Jack.

There was something electric about New York. For a fanciful moment Julianne envisioned herself in an office on Madison Avenue and then realized that the room was filled with people who could help her get there. With a shake of her head, Julianne dismissed the idea. She wasn't ready for Madison Avenue.

Julianne wrapped one hand around Jack's arm. His arm stiffened in response, and she could see his jaw clench. Secretly, Julianne was flattered he cared enough to be jealous. She'd tell him about her visit with Uncle Vinnie when they returned to the hotel.

"George, Marguerite." Jack gave a nod to another couple. "Do you want a drink?" he asked Julianne.

"Yes, I think I would," she replied.

"Jack!" A booming voice rushed at them from the right. "And this must be the infamous Julianne."

Jack stopped and released Julianne's hand from his arm. He clasped the man's outstretched hand in both of his. "Good to see you. Julianne, may I present David Kent?"

"Mr. Kent," she repeated, and took the hand of a tall blond man. Visions of Vikings came to mind and she pictured David Kent in a hat with horns on his head. She camouflaged a giggle behind her hand with a short cough.

"None of this Mr. Kent business. Jack and I are old friends." He slapped Jack on the shoulder. "Even prettier in person."

"You'll make me blush," Julianne said.

"David is a partner at Brakrog, Block and Kent," Jack introduced.

"I'm the Kent part," David said with a wink.

Julianne laughed. "So I gathered."

David turned to look over his shoulder and crooked a finger at a woman standing nearby. "You'll need to meet my wife, Melissa. She'll have my head if she doesn't get to meet you."

"Will you do the intros?" Jack asked. "I'm headed over to get us a couple of drinks."

"Have at it," David replied. "We'll watch out for your bride while you're away." The woman who appeared at David's side had straight brown hair that hung limply on either side of her head, but her eyes were a sparkling shade of blue that matched the sequins on her columnar gown. "Julianne, Melissa. Melissa, Julianne."

"THE Julianne?" Melissa asked, taking Julianne's hand. "Jack Guilder's Julianne?"

"Guilty," Julianne replied with a laugh.

Melissa turned Julianne's hand over and held it higher to examine the rings. "He gave you his mother's rings."

Julianne's raised her eyebrows. "You knew his mother?"

"Our parents were friends," Melissa went on. "When we were kids we sometimes took vacations together. Fishing trips. I remember those rings though. I always thought they were so unique. The etching and the filigree. Unusual for a bridal set, you know."

"Yes, I thought so, too."

"You'd think Jack could have sprung for the Hope Diamond," David teased.

Melissa smiled at Julianne. "I think I'd rather have these. They have so much more sentimental value." She let go of Julianne's hands and gave her a quick hug. "Congratulations. He looks so happy with you, or at least he did in the interview. He seems a little out of sorts tonight. You two have a fight?"

Julianne's face grew hot. "You might say that."

"You know there are a lot of doubters in the room, and with him in that mood he's going to give them more to talk about, but these rings say it all for me."

Julianne nodded her affirmation. "I wish I'd had the opportunity to meet his parents."

"They were good people," Melissa told her. "I know they would have liked you. They never liked Gloria much. You have met Gloria, haven't you?"

A prick of jealousy unsettled Julianne's good mood. "Kind of hard to miss her."

Melissa patted Julianne's shoulder. "Ancient history, Julianne. If he'd have wanted her, he would have had her. She stills throws herself at him every opportunity. He walked away from it and never looked back."

"You're not giving away any of my secrets, are you?" Jack asked with two drinks in his hands.

"You mean like the time you put a frog in that woman's swimsuit in Carmel?" Melissa teased.

"You didn't!" Julianne exclaimed.

Jack grinned boyishly, the color rising in his cheeks. "What do you expect from an adolescent boy?"

"I like you much better without the beard," Melissa told him matter-of-factly.

"What do you think of New York?" David asked Julianne in an obvious attempt to redirect the topic of conversation.

"You know I've never been before, but I'm finding it very embracing."

"Maybe we can lure you away from Perkins & Stone, then," David suggested. "Bet we could make you a better offer."

"You can't ask Jack to leave Alec," Melissa objected.

"Who's asking Jack?" David teased.

"An office on Madison Avenue?" Julianne suggested.

Jack put a proprietary arm around Julianne. "Knock it off."

Julianne couldn't resist the urge to push him a little further. "Well it would solve your problems. You didn't want to hire me in the first place."

Jack gave his friends a wink. "Conflict of interest, you know." He directed Julianne away and called back over his shoulder, "we'll catch up with you later."

"I was just getting to know them," Julianne protested. "I like Melissa."

Jack led her to a quiet corner of the ballroom. "You'll have plenty of time to disparage my character later."

"Are you still mad at me?"

"Is there a reason you won't share where you were today, or are you deliberately trying to make me jealous?"

Julianne set her drink on a nearby table and put her hands to her hips. "Life has been a challenge lately. I haven't had a whole lot of bright shining moments in the past couple of months. Every time something good happens, something else happens to cloud it over. Case in point: I got hired at Perkins & Stone, a job I wanted, a job I asked you for. Alec hired me. That was a bright moment: one you clouded over." Her temper took over and she forged ahead.

"I had a bright shining moment today. Something really special that helped me clear a lot of the dark corners that have been hovering around me and I wanted to keep it to myself for a little while. I didn't want anyone to muck it up. Not even you. You asked me once if I trusted you. Well how do you plan to marry me if you don't trust me?"

Jack cast a panicked look around him. "Keep your voice down."

Julianne grabbed her drink back off the table and leaned closer to Jack. "I'll tell you where I went when I'm good and ready," she told him in a low voice. "Until then, you're going to have to trust me. Because if you can't trust me, I guess we have our answer to the million dollar question, don't we?"

They stood toe to toe, their eyes fixed in a deadlock. Julianne tightened her hand around the glass and fought the urge to throw it.

"You do understand why I didn't want to hire you, don't you?"

There had been moments where she thought she did, but this wasn't one of them. "Why don't you explain it to me?"

Jack took the drink from her hand, set it on the table beside them and placed his hands on her arms. "I didn't want to screw up what we had and I didn't want to mess up your life either." He fixed her with a glare. "Well I did screw things up, didn't I? I'm a mess, you're a mess." He took a deep breath and looked at the crowd in the ballroom finding their dinner seats. He shook his head and rubbed his chin. "I'm sorry if I ruined your excitement about the job."

"You didn't exactly ruin it," she admitted, letting some of the tension slip off. "I guess you just helped me keep it in perspective a little. I can't exactly run the company as a new hire, now can I?"

Jack gave her a crooked smile. "That's about all you haven't done."

Julianne pursed her lips and looked away. She blew out a long, slow breath and extended a hand. "Truce?"

"Truce." But he didn't shake her hand. Instead he put one finger under her chin and broke into a slow smile. For a few interminable seconds, his round eyes danced with the light from the chandeliers overhead just before he pressed his lips gently to hers.

CHAPTER 26

The first one up always made the pot of coffee, and this morning Jack not only made it, he handed Julianne a cup just the way she liked it, with the cream swirling gently around the cup. He gave her a kiss goodbye and it was like she'd never had a life without him. Every day with Jack was better than the day before.

It was going to be a long week apart, but classes Perkins & Stone required would make the time pass quickly. Her final paper was complete and she was tired of studying. Julianne needed to make a conscious effort to keep her momentum.

One hotel room looked like every other one to her now. This one seemed empty without Jack. A second suitcase indicated that her roommate had arrived sometime during the day. With the dinner hour approaching, all the sessions would be ending soon.

The lock clicked and Julianne looked up, prepared to meet the person sharing her room for the next two days.

Bev juggled a laptop and briefcase while she tried to push the door open. Julianne rushed to help and blocked the door open for her. "At least you're someone I know."

Bev gave her a short smile. "No one told you?"

"Haven't been in the office much."

Bev lumbered into the room and heaved her bundles onto the unclaimed bed. "Off on more secret missions, I suppose."

Julianne bowed her head. "I'm sorry if I've been rude at the office. I'm a little embarrassed about certain aspects of my private life, as you've no doubt seen."

Bev looked up, one eyebrow raised.

Julianne grabbed a handful of hair and held it over one shoulder. "Remind me to tell you about the job I came from. I'm not used to people being genuinely friendly. Everyone always had some agenda."

"It ain't any different at good ol' P&S." Bev plunked down in a chair. "And you don't need to apologize. Maybe I was being a little too nosy. But you have to admit you did cause quite a stir."

Julianne rolled her eyes and took a seat behind the desk. "I prefer to be a little more inconspicuous."

"Will you at least tell me what the deal is with the old boyfriend?"

Julianne closed her eyes and heaved a sigh. "Unpleasant breakup. He's having a hard time adjusting."

"Duh!"

"What do you say we go get something to eat?" Julianne suggested.

"I had a boyfriend like that once."

"What did you do?"

"I moved to a different city." Bev rolled her eyes and laughed.

* * *

She wondered if Jack would be online or if they'd left all that behind them. With a sideways glance at the telephone, she opted for the computer. It was time to share Uncle Vinnie with him and she thought it might be easier to convey in type. No tone of voice to analyze, no wondering what he thought of the news. Some things were easier from a distance. If he wasn't online, she'd send him an e-mail.

But he was there. In the forum. Already she forgot he led the Tuesday night discussion. She missed the forum, but she needed the break. With a surreptitious glance to the bathroom where Bev showered, Julianne sought out JGGuilder.

"I thought you might call instead," he replied to her greeting.

Her fingers moved rapidly over the keyboard. "More privacy this way."

"I heard you're rooming with Bev?"

She nodded her head and typed out the affirmation. With another look at the closed bathroom door, she began her confession.

"I have an Uncle in New York," she started, sending her statements in short bursts. "On my father's side. I don't see him very often and my mother doesn't like him."

A reply popped up in the middle of her essay. "Why doesn't that surprise me?"

Julianne paused to grin and continued. "I spent the day with him. In Brooklyn." For a moment she wondered if Jack might think she made up the story. Did he really think she wanted to be with someone else?

The cursor blinked silently for several minutes. "I told him the truth," she typed deliberately.

"No wonder you came back feeling so much better."

Julianne stared at his response and then wondered about his tone. Would it have been better to tell him on the phone? Once it had seemed so personal chatting with him like this. "Are you angry?"

"No."

And then her cell phone rang. Julianne looked over her shoulder to where her purse lay on the bed.

"That's me," came his next line of type.

Julianne abandoned her keyboard and answered the phone. "Hi."

"Turn off your computer," he said gently, in that deep, disc jockey voice that was so soothing to her nerves.

"I was just looking for a friend," she answered softly. "Someone I used to chat with online quite a bit."

"Anyone I know?"

"He hangs out in the advertising forums. Used to hide behind a face full of hair."

"Oh THAT guy. I hear he got married."

Julianne fell back on the bed. "You're not upset that I told my Uncle?"

She heard Jack take a deep breath on the other side of the connection. "I didn't realize what a strain I was putting on you until you told me just now."

"What?"

"You came back that day like the weight of the world had been lifted off your shoulders. I couldn't imagine what would make you feel so much better about everything."

"I told you, I don't like to lie." She looked up nervously when she heard Bev turn off the water. "And there was no one I could tell."

"Then I'm glad you told him."

A movement on her computer caught Julianne's eye, and she saw words pop into her instant message from Jack. "I love you." With a grin, she went back to the desk and typed the same sentence. She heard the ding on Jack's end as the message went through.

"Then marry me."

"Okay," she whispered.

"You have to know I'm serious about this . . . did you say yes?"

"Yes."

Bev came out of the bathroom toweling her hair.

"When?" Jack asked.

"We can talk about it when I get back."

She heard him struggle for words and she grinned.

"What kind of wedding should we have? I don't want to cheat you."

Intimate Distance

Julianne cradled the cell phone in both hands. "We can talk about it when I get back," she repeated. "Considering my family, I'm not too concerned about anything fancy."

"If we went to City Hall we could get married right away," he suggested. "After we get the license, that is."

"No." she paused and looked over her shoulder, then put her next words into an instant message. "I want a church wedding."

Jack was silent for a moment. "Is Bev there with you?"

"Yep."

"Do you want to IM about this?"

"No. I'm going to turn off my computer now. We can't do anything until Friday anyway."

"I'll pick you up at the airport."

"But my flight comes in at 2:30."

"I know."

Julianne smiled and twirled the rings on her fingers.

"I love you," Jack told her once more.

"I love you, too."

Bev started making gagging noises and Julianne disconnected the call. "Let me guess," Bev said, "Jack?"

"Yeah," Julianne sighed.

"Planning Thanksgiving?"

She'd almost forgotten how close the holiday was. It seemed a plausible explanation. Julianne nodded.

"Do you have a big family?"

With a shrug of her shoulders, Julianne thought about Thanksgivings past. "My mom, my sister." She looked vacantly at the curtained window. This year was definitely going to be different. "Maybe I can invite my Uncle Vinnie."

CHAPTER 27

Julianne got off the train in Arlington Heights and pulled her hat over her ears against the chilly November wind. Her hair blew over one shoulder while she made her way to the café on the street parallel to the tracks.

She stopped momentarily and glanced back over her shoulder, feeling the small hairs on the back of her neck rising as if she was being hunted. She shuddered from the cold and pushed into the storefront.

Bill sat inside nursing a cup of coffee. With a broad smile, he hesitated a moment. She closed her eyes to bask in the warmth from the ovens and the smell of freshly baked cinnamon rolls.

Bill rose and wrapped Julianne in a quick hug. "You look fantastic! Life with the agency must be agreeing with you."

Julianne shrugged her shoulders, suddenly shy. "They're working me hard. I've been doing a lot of traveling."

"Ahhh." Bill nodded. "That explains it."

"Explains what? I told you about New York in my last e-mail."

"We'll get to that. Do you want a cup of coffee?"

Julianne nodded. "I need something to thaw out my insides." She inhaled the mouth-watering aromas. "And something to go with it."

"I thought you might." Bill held up a hand to attract the clerk's attention. She nodded and brought over a tray with Julianne's coffee and a cinnamon roll.

Julianne took her seat across from her brother-in-law, wrapped her hands around her cup and blew gently across the top. "The best part about being cold is the way something warm makes you feel."

"I don't know if I've ever seen you so happy. Married life must be agreeing with you."

Julianne cringed. A gust of arctic wind followed another customer into the café and chilled her mood. Another sip of coffee chased some of the uneasiness. She and Jack had been to City Hall the day before to get the license. The pretense would be reality soon.

Bill turned his head to look out the window. "Does this feel odd to you?"

"Does what feel odd? Me and Jack?"

"No. You and me. Sitting here like this."

Julianne furrowed her eyebrows. "What do you mean? We've had coffee before."

"Well people might get the wrong idea, seeing us here like this. Maybe like Steve and Suzanne, you know? Maybe they were just having lunch that day you saw them in Chicago."

Julianne drew in a deep breath. "Maybe." There was little room for doubt, but if Bill wanted to take the road to denial, it wasn't up to her to steer him back in the right direction. She'd seen Bill and Suzanne go through the ups and downs too many times.

"Seriously," he pressed, looking straight at her. "What if it was all just a misunderstanding? What if you called off your wedding for all the wrong reasons?"

Julianne shook her head. "Suzanne isn't the reason I called off the wedding. Add to it that little incident at the banquet and I think the case is closed."

"But didn't you move into this new thing a little fast?"

Julianne cocked one eyebrow and stared at him. "Didn't you push me into this? And don't you already know where I stand?"

Bill wove his fingers tightly into his hair. "I'm starting to sound like her, aren't I?"

Julianne's hands tightened around her mug. "Is there something going on I don't know about?"

Bill took a gulp of his coffee and grimaced again. "It's scary, Julianne. She's actually got me believing her, even though I know better."

"Maybe I shouldn't have come..."

"I'm sorry, Julianne. I should have talked to you about all this sooner."

Julianne sat back and tried to quiet the nerves prickling her skin. "You're scaring me, Bill."

Bill cast a glance around and leaned forward to speak in hushed tones. "It seems Steve is having great fun playing cops and robbers. The police are still trying to get him to come in for questioning about that banquet deal but he's doing a fine job of avoiding them. Evidently the police aren't too concerned about the whole deal, either. They seem to be almost writing it off as a kid's prank."

Julianne's pulse raced. "It's been two weeks. They can't just write off what he did to Alec."

"According to Suzanne, Steve took a leave of absence. Some sick relative or something."

Julianne scoffed. "He'd never take time off work."

"Like I said – he's playing cops and robbers. And he's still trying to get to you. He thinks he can clear up this whole mess if he can just talk to you, but he hasn't been able to reach you."

Julianne took a deep breath. "Because I've been out of town." She shook her head. "I don't want to talk to him, Bill."

"I don't blame you, Jewel."

"And Suzanne is your source for all of this?"

Bill nodded and concentrated on his fingernails.

Was Suzanne playing Bill to get to her? Suzanne was very good at manipulating men, particularly her husband. "Does she know you're meeting me?"

Bill shook his head. "No." He rubbed his forehead. "I swear sometimes she just steals all of my common sense." He looked Julianne directly in the eye. "I've told her and I'll tell you, what's between you and Steve is between you and Steve and it's none of our business, but I won't let him hurt you, Julianne."

Julianne shuddered. "Do you think he wants to hurt me?"

"I have no idea what he's capable of these days, but it does make me nervous that he's been so hard to pin down. Maybe you are better off with this other guy."

With a short laugh, Julianne nodded. "I'm fairly positive of that."

"You sure it isn't all just a gimmick? A front? Maybe this elopement or whatever you guys did is just meant to add credence to the whole spiel." He cocked one eyebrow. "That is if you're really married."

Julianne squirmed. "It's not a front. Although I think about that every day." Bill's eyes were the clear blue of a cloudless sky. They had a way of conveying both his kindness and his vulnerability. She wondered if she was as transparent. "There is one thing I'm sure of and that's the way I feel about him. Maybe love is blind, but I believe in him."

"I can't help but feel he's setting you up for something. Something just doesn't ring true."

"I've never felt this way about anyone. We complement each other so perfectly; it's like each of us fills in what the other is missing."

Bill smiled into his coffee. "I can tell you you're pretty too if you just want compliments."

Julianne laughed. "You know what I mean."

"Yeah, I guess I do." Bill nodded toward the untouched roll on the plate in front of Julianne. "Are you planning to eat that?"

She handed him a knife and fork. "I'll give you half."

Bill cut the roll, his mouth screwed in concentration. "You know I love you, Jewel."

"Bill . . ."

"I'm trying to work things out with Suzanne," he continued. "When I see some of the things she does I can't stand to be in the same room with her, but I can't seem to get her out of my system. I won't let them hurt you."

Julianne pushed the rest of the roll across the table to him, her appetite gone. "What aren't you telling me? You asked me here for a reason, didn't you?"

"She has me feeling so guilty."

"I understand." Julianne wanted to remind Bill how often Suzanne had lied to him, how often she kept secrets. "You haven't done anything wrong. What is it you want me to know?"

Bill leaned over his elbows on the table. "I don't know why I'm even still trying to work things out."

"Because you love her. Now tell me what's going on."

Bill rubbed his hand across his mouth, his eyes darting around the restaurant. "She came home with a black eye the other day. She said she hit it closing the car door."

"You don't sound like you believe her."

"I don't. She was drunk when she got home and she looked scared."

Another chill shuddered through Julianne.

"Watch your back, Jewel."

CHAPTER 28

The dark restaurant reflected her mood. Julianne pushed the potatoes around on her plate, against the piece of prime rib that still remained and then away again. It was her only distraction from the uncomfortable conversation and her own personal dilemma.

If she invited Uncle Vinnie, her mother would be upset. If she invited Bill, her sister and her mother both would be upset. The lies poured like gravy over the potatoes, taking away all their substance.

"I thought it might be nicer to have a member of each side of the family," Jack told Alec, "but there are complications."

"Well that's a shame, but we can work around it. That is, as long as the project is still on track?"

"We got our ticket to the dance last Friday," Jack answered, "so after today we can move ahead any time."

Julianne smiled at Jack's veiled reference to their marriage license.

Alec leaned toward Julianne. "I know this isn't the way you'd hoped it would be."

Julianne set her fork down. "I have modest tastes. It isn't as if I had a big guest list anyway."

"How big was the party you were planning before?" Jack asked.

"About 100 people, and most of them were his guests." She tensed her muscles against the sensation someone was standing behind her. Julianne looked over her shoulder, checking the sea of patrons for a threat.

"Is there someone else you want to try?" Alec watched her face a little too intently.

Julianne reached for the cloth napkin in her lap. "Unless we move the party to New York, I don't know who else to ask." Her eyes darted around the dining room. "There aren't that many people I can trust with this type of information."

Jack put a hand on her arm. "We could go to New York if you want. I'm sorry. I never meant to put you in this situation."

Alec wiped at his chin. "Ron Perkins is in town. If he's available I'm sure he'd step in for us."

Julianne reached for her glass of wine. Her head was already spinning around the circle her life had taken in the past few months. "And you wouldn't give me a job," she teased Jack.

He cocked his head to one side. "What do you mean?"

"Now I have Perkins AND Stone rounding out our little party. I'm overwhelmed."

"We don't have Perkins yet," Jack reminded her with a grin, "but we will."

"Are you sure you want to do this?" Julianne twisted the rings on her finger.

Jack leaned forward and took hold of her hands. "Absolutely. Are you having second thoughts?"

It was a question she asked herself over and over. Was she reaching for Jack to fill a void? Maybe she was being hasty. "Just a lot to think about in a short period of time," she said.

"How does your calendar look tomorrow?" Alec asked, addressing first one and then the other of them.

Julianne's eyes opened wide. "Tomorrow?"

"Unless you've had a change of heart?"

Julianne let out a short laugh. "When did I lose control of my life?"

"The same time I did," Jack answered. "A week after we picked up our relationship outside the classroom in the online forum."

That night was still just as clear to her. A melding of the minds culminated in a moment of recognition that said "I remember you." After accidental online encounters over the course of a week, they sought each other out, exchanging several e-mails every day and arranging times and places to chat.

Julianne retrieved her calendar from her purse. "I don't have any other appointments tomorrow."

Jack pulled out his PDA at the same time. "My afternoon is clear."

Alec smiled and rubbed his hands together. "Then why don't the two of you take tomorrow afternoon off. I'll talk to Ron and we'll see when we can get this party started."

* * *

Jack wasn't sleeping either. Julianne heard the clinking of weights against pins overhead. It helped to know he was nervous, too.

She considered going on-line, but she didn't want to run into him tonight. Instead, the ceiling loomed dark over her head, the shadows danced across the walls and sleep remained just out of reach.

The only other man she'd been halfway serious about was Steve. It had been a vulnerable time of her life and she let him comfort her. She shuddered. There was no doubt she made the right decision when she ended that relationship, but was Jack just another crutch to help her through a difficult phase?

She looked forward to Jack's name on the computer screen or as the sender of an e-mail. He had become a constant in her life. But did she really love him?

The days they missed contact, there was disappointment, but not despair. Steve created a dependence that left Julianne unsure of herself and afraid of being alone. Now, she was confident and independent. She didn't need to spend the rest of her life with any man.

She wanted to spend the rest of her life with Jack.

The certainty of that thought was more powerful than the only red flag: Jack was a very good liar. But hadn't he shared his most intimate thoughts with her? His dissatisfactions with his own life? His hopes and dreams? So many nights they had chatted online until dawn, and the night he'd come to Houston, they talked through the night.

Julianne remembered their fateful lunch with Hayden and how difficult it was to bridge to reality once the intimate distance between them had been breached. It was Jack who thundered his displeasure when Alec threw them into day-to-day proximity and Jack who invited her into his home.

There would always be that emptiness where her family should be. One man couldn't fill that void, but he did understand. He lost his own family in a much more real sense.

The clinking stopped overhead but Julianne resisted the urge to open the "chat room." It was a night to be with their own thoughts. She rolled over to look at the alarm clock and realized that the night had already passed. Her wedding day had arrived.

* * *

"You look great!" Bev exclaimed when Julianne sat behind her desk.

Julianne shrugged her shoulders self-consciously. "It's just a dress."

Bev shook her head and smiled. "More than 'just a dress.' Meeting a client today?"

"I have an appointment later."

"Nervous, huh?"

Julianne looked at the pale woman. "Why do you say that?"

Bev laughed and pointed at Julianne's hands. "You're shaking like a leaf and your voice is a bit breathy."

"I'll have to work on that."

Julianne was too nervous to make small talk. She tried to concentrate on the work demanding her attention, but her eyes kept straying to the glass doors in anticipation of Alec's arrival. When she felt a tap on her shoulder, Julianne jumped.

Jack stood beside her, smiling. "I don't think he'll come down." He nodded to where Julianne's attention was focused. "He'll probably call."

"Ron probably won't even be in today," Julianne said and reached into her desk drawer, "and this will all just be a fire drill."

"That's entirely possible. We could still go to New York . . ."

Julianne shrugged her shoulders. "You didn't sleep at all last night either, did you?"

"We can take a nap when we get home." Jack winked and returned to his office.

The phone rang on Julianne's desk and she jumped again. "Julianne DeAngelo."

Bev looked over and laughed. "I've never seen you so on edge."

Julianne frowned, listening to the voice of the printroom manager on the other end of the line.

"Were you that nervous when you met Ben Hayden?" Bev asked when Julianne hung up the phone.

"Actually, no. I just put on my presentation face and pretended I was in class."

"Another big fish on the line?"

Julianne scratched her forehead. "It's more of a personal issue."

"Well I'm glad to hear that. If you landed another of those big clients I was going to feel passed by yet again." Bev gave a dramatic sigh and then a light-hearted laugh.

"Julie," Jack called to her from his office. He leaned around his desk and waved for her to come in, the phone on his shoulder.

"I have a 10:00 with Grant," Jack said into the phone when she walked in. He motioned for Julianne to close the door.

She sat on the edge of the chair and folded trembling hands in her lap.

Jack nodded, twirling a pen with his fingers. "Yeah," he answered his caller, still nodding his head. "You know how Grant is. It won't be before lunch time." He looked up at Julianne and a smile spread across his face. "I could try that." He hesitated a moment, then nodded again. "I'll call you when I'm through then." He hung up and pointed one finger at Julianne. "We're on."

She took a deep breath and nodded once.

"Are you okay?" Jack asked.

"Just nervous. I've never gotten married before."

Jack laughed. "Just do that thing you do, that switch you flip that changes you from jelly to poised and confident, like with Hayden."

"I had nothing to lose then."

"And now?"

Adrenaline bounced inside her chest like Nerf balls, each shot producing a short breath. She felt dangerously close to hyperventilating. "This is our lives we're talking about, not an ad campaign."

"Julianne, I love you." He leaned further across his desk, appealing to her with his eyes. "No gimmicks. No hidden agenda. Just you and me for the rest of our lives."

Julianne studied her hands. "Maybe it's too soon."

Jack sat back. "Do you want to wait a while?"

She closed her eyes and took a deep breath. "There really isn't a rush, after all, is there?" Julianne raised her face to look at Jack when he didn't answer immediately. He was looking out the window across the City.

"I've waited this long to find you. I'll wait as long as you need me to, Julianne."

Like a blanket, his words stilled the bouncing indecision. Mentally she scolded herself. She spent all night weighing her choices. "I'll be ready."

* * *

After her second bottle of water, Julianne's mouth was still dry. It seemed impossible to concentrate on the layout in front of her. She alternately tightened her hands into fists and stretched her fingers out by her sides.

"Julianne?"

She nearly jumped out of her seat. Jack laughed and took hold of her shoulders. Julianne scowled. "Not funny."

Jack offered a patient smile and his voice took on a more sympathetic tone. "We don't have to do this today."

Julianne twisted out of his grasp. "I'm good."

"Then we should go."

Julianne's eyes grew large and her heart skipped a beat.

"You're not going to faint, are you?" Jack re-established his grip on her shoulders and turned Julianne to face him.

Hands curled tightly into fists, Julianne closed her eyes and let out a long, slow breath. "I'm ready."

"Are you sure?"

His eyes were fixed on hers. Warm, comforting, liquid brown. Julianne raised a hand to his tender cheek to recall the beard that he had so recently worn. Without it, he looked younger, more vulnerable. Pale. Beneath her hand, the muscles of his jaw were working. It was a less noticeable version of the clenching she'd seen when he was agitated. He was nervous too.

She slipped her hand into his. "Let's go."

Moments later, they stepped onto Michigan Avenue and into a waiting Cadillac.

"It's a nice day. We could have walked," Julianne said.

"Long walk in high heels."

"I have my gym shoes."

Jack smiled. "It's your wedding day. The least I can do is give you a ride."

Julianne's heart flip-flopped. She folded her hands tightly in her lap. Walking would have helped allay some of her jitters, given her something to do with her nervous energy.

The car pulled over in front of the large stone church. "Do you want me to sign?" Jack asked the driver.

"Mr. Stone already took care of it."

Jack nodded and reached around Julianne to open the car door.

Unable to move, Julianne just stared at the majestic building. "It's huge! Tell me they have a chapel or something that we won't get lost in."

"It may seem a bit imposing, but it's very intimate on the inside."

Julianne rose. Time seemed to slow down. A filter shrouded the world around them. Pigeons squawking in the towers over head didn't seem as loud as they should be. The sun refracted as if through a cloud. Car horns and sirens were muted. Each step Julianne took toward the cloisters played out in slow motion. Every movement imprinted her memory in meticulous detail.

Alec stood just inside the church holding an armload of flowers. As quickly as it had taken hold, the filter disappeared. Trucks thundered through the streets, the reverberations bringing to full speed the bustle of the big city.

"Am I allowed to compliment the bride?" Alec asked, reaching with one hand to draw Julianne into a hug.

She smiled. "If you must."

Alec extended his other arm to her. "You look beautiful. And these are for you. I thought you might like some flowers."

"Who told you I liked gardenias?"

He leaned in and whispered, "I called your mother. She told me they were what you picked out for your last wedding."

Julianne laughed and then put a hand to her mouth. "Oh, you didn't tell her why you wanted to know, did you?"

Alec put a finger to his lips and invited her inside.

"Where's Mr. Perkins?" Julianne asked. The men exchanged glances. "What?" she asked, not missing the gesture.

"We've got it covered," Jack assured her.

Alec cleared his throat and nodded to Julianne. "I believe Pastor Campbell wanted a few words with you ahead of time."

A voice echoed in the empty sanctuary. "Indeed I do. This must be the bride." Pastor Donald Campbell made his way down the aisle, running a hand through wavy brown hair peppered with gray. Bushy brown eyebrows arched over his glasses. He extended a hand away from his square frame, his lips curled into a smile.

Jack took his hand in a firm handshake. "Donald. Thank you."

The pastor held up a finger. "Don't thank me yet. I haven't spoken with your intended yet." Donald Campbell smiled at Julianne. "Although any judgments I might make before agreeing to this will probably already have been assessed by Jack, here."

The small hairs on the back of Julianne's neck stood up. "I beg your pardon?"

Pastor Campbell laughed and led Julianne toward the back of the church. "It's nothing to worry about. But in this church, you have to attend pre-marriage classes in order to have the ceremony performed here. Before I agree to waive that, as Jack has requested, I want to see for myself that the two of you know what you're getting into."

"Actually, I've been through pre-marriage classes. I was engaged a short time ago."

The pastor stopped abruptly. "To another man?"

Julianne nodded.

"May I ask what happened?"

"Well, I suppose you could say the marriage classes did what they were supposed to. Or that I came to my senses. Or a combination of both."

He started his progress again, inviting her to follow him into his office. "How long have you known Jack?"

"A little less than a year."

"In your opinion, are you rushing into things?"

"I've asked myself that question a hundred times."

"And?"

Julianne smiled, her attention distracted by the ornate carvings inside the clergyman's office. "The more I find out about him, the more sure I am that this is the right decision."

"The more you find out about him."

Julianne nodded. "How long have you known Jack?"

Donald tented his fingers in front of his chest. "Jack has been an active member here for a number of years. He's done a lot for this church and that's why I agreed to entertain his, in my opinion, extravagant idea here today."

"Now see, that's something I didn't know about him. I know his values, I know his shortcomings. I didn't realize the source of his values until just now. It's one more thing I appreciate about him, admire about him. It's something that's important to me and it reinforces my feelings. It chases away some of those scary jitters."

Pastor Campbell nodded. "And what about your own values? What is your source?"

Julianne inhaled the scent of the gardenias on her arm and smiled. "I've been a member of a church in the suburbs for several years. My father and I used to go regularly, but after he died, I grew a little lazy."

"And now?"

"It will be nice to have someone to go to church with again."

"You completed your prior pre-marriage classes?"

"Yes."

"When did you call off your wedding?"

"Five weeks before."

Donald's eyebrows rose over his glasses. "Cutting it a little close, weren't you?"

"Better than going through with a mistake."

"You had more time to consider it."

Julianne took a deep breath. "I've had lots of time to consider this, as well."

"And this isn't a mistake?"

She shook her head. "No. Every day I love Jack a little more."

"And what if one day you discover something about him that makes you love him a little less?"

"I can't imagine living the rest of my life with anyone else."

Donald rubbed his chin. "I've seen your commercial."

Julianne nodded.

"I know Jack pretty well."

"So I gather."

"I know he has a gift for telling a good story."

Julianne laughed. "That's a polite way to say it."

"My dilemma comes from the fact that you have also done some acting. It is my responsibility to marry people permanently."

"Then you'll need to talk to Jack, because it is not my intention to marry him temporarily."

Donald smiled. "I've already spoken to him. I'm confident of his motives." His warm, dry hands closed around Julianne's. "And I think the two of you make a wonderful couple. Now let's go get this party started."

Organ music echoed inside the church. Julianne paused.

"Oh," Donald said, rubbing his chin again. "The organist is here to practice. I hope you don't mind."

She cocked one eyebrow. "And the organist just happens to be playing the Canon?"

"Well it is a fairly common hymn, don't you think?"

Julianne shook her head and smiled. "Is there anything they didn't think of?"

"I think they wanted to make this as special for you as possible." Donald nodded his head in the direction of the pews.

Julianne saw her mother seated in the first row beside Uncle Vinnie. "How in the world . . . "

Alec rushed to Julianne's side and spoke in a low voice. "We told your mother you wanted to be married in the church and that you're sanctifying your vows."

"She's sitting next to my Uncle!"

Alec rubbed his forehead and gave a chuckle. "Well she was fairly put out when she saw him at first, but then he told her he'd been wrong, that the years had been kind to her and she looked just as beautiful as she did when she married your father."

Julianne couldn't contain her laughter.

Barbara DeAngelo rose to meet her daughter. "You look lovely, dear."

"Thank you, Mom."

"I don't know why all the secrecy, though. They wouldn't even tell me what this was all about until we got here. I would think you'd want your sister here."

"I didn't want a big fuss."

Barbara leaned in and whispered, "Did you know your Uncle was going to be here?"

Julianne smiled. "I didn't even know you were coming." She hugged Barbara. "But I'm glad you did."

"Now you're going to make me cry." Barbara raised a handkerchief to her eyes and sniffled.

"Uncle Vinnie." Julianne outstretched her free arm and pulled her uncle in.

Her uncle winked and put a finger to his lips.

"Do you mind?" Jack asked, taking hold of Julianne's elbow.

Julianne looked up to Jack, her eyes filled with tears. "Thank you."

Donald cleared his throat. "Are we ready to begin?"

Carved angels looked down from piers along the aisles, returning the echoing voices from the frescoes on the ceiling back to the wedding party. In that moment, there were no doubts. There were no fears.

"I'm ready," Jack and Julianne said at the same time.

CHAPTER 29

She sat at her desk daydreaming. Their first night together made Julianne believe that maybe she wasn't such a cold fish. Jack lit her up like a blazing furnace.

The open door to his office looked increasingly inviting.

She closed her eyes and remembered Jack's solid arms wrapped tightly around her in protective embrace.

"I want to take you for lunch," he said lying beside her, running a long finger down her arm.

"Where?"

"On my desk, in the elevator, in the bathroom. Anywhere I can get you."

The telephone on her desk jangled her out of her reverie. "Julianne DeAngelo."

"Haven't changed your name, then?"

She froze, all her attention riveted to the voice on the other end of the line. The phone nearly slipped from her hands. Julianne's eyes darted around the office. She wondered how close he was.

"Don't hang up, I have to talk to you," Steve insisted. "They're setting me up, Julianne."

"Who's setting you up?" she whispered.

"Those guys. That guy you married and the other one - the one who got hurt."

"Why would they do that?"

"I don't know, but it all makes sense, don't it? Think about it, Julie. Suzanne told me you're sleeping in separate bedrooms. What normal, red-blooded American man would shy away from a beautiful woman? Especially when he's married to her."

A familiar flush ran all through her body. They weren't sleeping in separate bedrooms anymore. "My sleeping arrangements are none of your business." Bev gave her a sideways glance, pretending not to listen. Julianne turned away.

"I'm worried about you. You know I love you. I was trying to protect you and instead that goon you married told the police I was stalking you. They wouldn't let me near the place. We've known each other forever, Julie. Do you really think I could hurt anyone, much less you?"

How do you know he isn't a serial killer? A wave of nausea swept over her. "Why would they set you up?"

"I don't know, and that's what's got me scared. I need to see you, Julianne. I need to know you're all right."

"John would never hurt me," she said more to reassure herself than Steve.

"What if he's a sociopath and you just haven't found out yet?"

"No," she told him, her voice husky and her hands shaking.

"Meet me for a cup of coffee. They know I'm innocent. Why do you think they're trying so hard to keep me away from you? Maybe they're afraid you'll find out."

Julianne rested her head in one hand, eyes squeezed tight against the doubts he raised. "But Alec saw you. He identified you at the banquet. Why would he lie?"

"They're setting me up. You know me, Julie. Do you really think I would do something like that? I just want to talk to you, to see you."

She shivered. Blood pounded in her ears like drums warning of an ambush. She was well aware of his short fuse and his impulsive reactions.

"Just a cup of coffee, Julie," he urged. "In a public place."

"I have a class tonight."

"Later then, after?"

"It's over, Steve." She hesitated a moment, remembering the times Steve had been there for her even when her family wasn't.

"Lunch. We could go to Oliver's, like we used to," he persisted.

She turned toward her desk, ready to hang up the phone when she heard his last words. "I miss you."

Julianne stared at the half-wall in front of her and tried to reconcile Steve's proclamation of innocence to Alec's edict of guilt.

"You look pale," Bev said. "Is anything wrong?"

Julianne pushed sharply away from her desk. "I think I'm going to be sick."

* * *

Half a dozen times the professor stared at her, trying to get her attention without embarrassing her. After class he'd asked her if she'd mentally checked out. Telling him she was preoccupied seemed an understatement.

Jack definitely did not prefer men. His response to her had been overwhelming. It made Julianne reconsider Steve's sexuality and his need to prove himself to every woman he encountered.

Julianne's eyes darted around the city street, danger lurking in every alleyway. In every shadow she imagined a blond head, waiting to jump out at her. Had Steve been responsible for Suzanne's black eye?

A block away, Julianne saw a black Trans Am parked illegally. "Taxi!" she shouted, running to the street and holding up her arm. Seeing one approach she repeated her cry more emphatically. "Taxi!"

The driver pulled closer and Julianne only saw a blond head behind the wheel. Fear pumped through her veins, sending her back onto the sidewalk and jogging around the corner, away from the Trans Am and away from the cab with the blond driver.

A police car pulled up beside her, bathing her in flashing blue lights. "Everything ok, Miss?" the cop called out across the seat.

Julianne stopped to catch her breath and looked back over her shoulder. No taxi. Nobody pursuing her. She nodded to the policeman and pointed up the street. "I'm almost home. Just in a hurry."

The man followed her pointing finger. "You want me to follow you?"

Julianne took a deep breath. "It's just another two blocks." He continued to study her, and then Julianne nodded. "Yeah. If you don't mind."

The policeman nodded, turned off his lights and did a U-turn in the street to follow behind her.

Minutes later, she stood in front of the door to Jack's condo, her home. Digging through her purse, she located her key and opened the door.

"Hey, I was beginning to worry about you," he called down from the loft. "How was school?"

She put her books on the desk in the corner of the room. "I don't know."

He came down the stairs slowly. "Anything wrong?"

"Working?" she asked to deflect his question.

"Picking up e-mail." He maintained his distance while he assessed her mood. She felt ready to jump out of her skin. "Feeling a little shy?" he suggested. "I don't want you to be afraid of me, Julie."

"I'm not afraid of you."

"You look a little shaken up."

Julianne forced a smile. "I'm fine."

He reached out to interweave his fingers in her hair. "Ever hear of Pandora's box?"

"Have you had a lot of girlfriends?" she asked, feeling the heat of embarrassment.

Jack lifted her chin with one finger. "You want to know all the sordid details of my love life?"

She looked up into warm brown eyes, wanting to know and yet afraid.

"I told you I was engaged." He stiffened, and she saw an emotion she wasn't sure of in his eyes for just a second. "After my parents died we decided to wait, and then we kind of let it go." He looked at her, his gaze shifting from one of her eyes to the other. "I never slept with her. I told you where I stand on that." He turned away, shaking his arms by his sides as he walked away.

When Jack looked back to her, his great, round eyes were shining. "Last night is the first time in a very long time that I can remember feeling . . ." and then he turned away again.

"Feeling what?"

"Just feeling. It scares me to death." He rested his forehead against the post in the center of the great room. "I haven't let many people get close to me."

Julianne sat on the back of the futon sofa. "Safer on-line."

He raised his head abruptly and narrowed his eyes. "Yes," he agreed. "Damn it, Julie. Sex is so personal. It leaves you so vulnerable."

She smiled in spite of herself. "Ours isn't the most conventional of marriages."

"Second guessing?" he asked.

"It's just that I never . . ." she began, wringing her hands. "There's just so much I don't know . . ." she fumbled for words to express her feelings. "I don't have that much experience."

He tilted his head as if to read her better. "You didn't like it?"

"That's not exactly what I meant."

He sat down on a step. "What exactly do you mean?"

"I don't know. I just thought it would be different."

He folded his hands together, leaning his nose on his fist before he looked up to address her again. "Different how?"

Her lip began to quiver. She wanted to speak, but she was afraid of making a bigger fool of herself by crying.

"Did I hurt you?" he pressed. He reached for the railing with one hand and propelled himself to his feet. "Are you sore? I didn't mean to hurt you, Julianne."

"You didn't hurt me," she whimpered, hating the sound of her own voice.

"But you didn't like it?"

"It was fine," she replied and turned away from him. "Forget I said anything."

He crossed to where she sat, staring at the floor with each carefully measured step. "I guess you didn't look very much like a warm puddle."

"A warm puddle?"

He reached out to pet her shoulder-length hair. "I remember an all night cram session in college - a group of us studying for our finals - and somewhere after midnight and before dawn the books lost their interest. We began talking the way guys will and I remember one of them distinctly saying you weren't done until your woman looked like a warm puddle."

Julianne kicked off her shoes and stared shyly at her feet.

"I didn't get it at first either, and so he proceeded to enlighten me, first by way of explanation and then describing in detail how he accomplished this feat." He lifted Julianne's face to look directly at her. "His next comparison was that of a woman to a fish on the line, flailing as if your every touch is charged with electricity and then when she's satisfied, your touch becomes a ripple of contented waves - a warm puddle."

"Please, let's not talk about this."

"I want to do it right."

She shook her head. "We've done everything wrong."

Jack cradled the side of her face. "Then let's make it right. After Christmas, after you get your degree and the Christmas ads are behind us, I want to take you somewhere. Just the two of us. Maybe we didn't count on things turning out the way they did, but we deserve a chance to try." He tilted his head to catch her eyes. "If you don't want me until then, I'll stay away, but I want the chance to make it right, Julie. I want the chance to change your mind."

"But I do want you," she admitted quietly.

Jack laughed. He pulled her into his arms, laying her head against his shoulder. "Do you want to go upstairs?"

"No."

He held her away, confused for a minute and then understanding as she pulled her sweater over her head.

He stepped forward and cupped each one of her breasts in his large hands. "Like a fax machine," he sighed.

Startled, Julianne pulled away. "A fax machine?"

He reached behind her back to release her bra. "One calls to the other. They call it a handshake." He bent over, his lips brushing her neck as he found his way up to her mouth. "The call is answered," he continued with his metaphor, "and they join, a sheet of paper pulled in and then expelled until they finish with the final sigh when the connection is broken."

Julianne laughed. "I never thought of two fax machines as having sex before."

"See what you've done to me? Everything looks different." He slid his hands onto her hips. "And you want to be in advertising?" He cupped her bottom, pulling her against him. "You'll need a better imagination."

"Maybe you'd better explain the concept a little more clearly," she whispered, reaching into his pockets. Then she laughed, pulling at his zipper. "Don't you ever wear underwear?"

"Too confining." He lifted her onto the couch, letting his pants fall before kneeling down to kiss the tender skin of her midsection. She arched her back in response inviting a seductive chuckle from her lover. "Like a fish on a line."

"Very funny." She tried to sit up as he moved further south. "What are you doing?"

"Turning you into a warm puddle. Relax, and don't forget to breath."

"But what . . . " she gasped as his mouth closed over her. Reflexing muscles pushed her back into the cushions and she grabbed an armrest for support. "Oh."

"Do you want me to stop?" he asked, stroking her with his fingers.

"What are you doing to me?" she moaned, writhing beneath his touch.

"Easy girl," he gentled, kissing the inside of her thighs.

"Don't stop," she encouraged, twisting to bring his mouth back to the source of her agony. She locked her fingers into the thick dark hair on his scalp.

"Slowly," he cautioned her.

"I can't . . .I don't . . .," she panted, holding handfuls of his long hair. "Oh God!" she moaned.

"Not yet," he teased, tracing wet fingers around her inner thigh and ever so gently across her lips.

"What are you waiting for?"

"Does it feel good?"

"What are you doing to me?"

"Catching fish," he reminded her. "Is this better?"

She struggled against her flaming desire, digging her fingers into his hard shoulders.

His mouth closed determinedly over her once more, playing her with his tongue.

She convulsed in response, gasping for air as her nails dug into his back, and then he was on top of her, driving into her, sustaining the sensation.

Arching, her body rose and fell against his with each thrust, every pulsation taking her farther into ecstasy.

He grunted, clenching his teeth. For a moment, he hesitated, but then she thrust hard against him, pulling him out of all the dark corners and full into the light.

He surrendered in a spasm followed by quivering waves until he fell on top of her, nearly suffocating her against the musky dampness of his skin.

"Did I hurt you?" he whispered, trying to catch his breath.

"Is it like that for you every time?"

He touched her tingling skin and she felt the lingering ripples. "You do look kind of like a warm puddle," he teased.

"You didn't shake like that last night."

"Shake?"

"Yeah, I don't know, vibrate, like a bell when it's been rung."

He smiled. "Last night was different."

"What do you mean?"

Jack ran his hand over her hair. "You said last night was fine. And so it was. How would you describe tonight?"

She let out a deep sigh of contentment. "I feel like I've been drugged."

"No drug on earth could make you feel that way." He pulled her gently down onto the floor, drawing her close beside him.

Julianne lay quietly and absorbed the warmth of his body, staring at the beamed ceiling overhead but doubts continued to haunt her. Even as their connection grew stronger, she wondered if it were possible their relationship was part of another grand charade he had manufactured. Was he making Steve out to be a scapegoat? She didn't want to believe it. In two years, Steve never lied to her. She had known Jack less than a year and knew without a doubt that he could lie with little or no effort. But would he go so far as to implicate Steve in a crime?

For several minutes she considered if she should say anything, and then finally she decided to ask.

"Do you think Alec could have been mistaken about who threw that bottle?" She turned her head and found his large eyes closed and his lips slightly parted. His broad chest rose and fell with each rhythmic, sleeping breath.

CHAPTER 30

Julianne sat in the kitchen gazing across the city. The rosy hues of the rising sun reflected brilliantly off building after building until she wasn't sure where the rays had found the temerity to peek through in the first place.

She had given him the ring at breakfast, the intricate gold filigree woven into a gryphon. It suited his large hands, standing out boldly against his long fingers.

In the great room, Julianne heard Alec arrive to take Jack to their breakfast meeting.

Alec's voice carried to where she remained out of sight. "She's given you a ring then?"

"What?" Jack sounded distracted. Julianne wanted to peek out to see if he was still staring at the ring as he had been moments ago. "I was just thinking about that new cola campaign."

"You were thinking about her."

She heard Jack laugh. "I guess I was at that."

"Can't be easy, what with living in the same house with her, working ten feet away from her."

Julianne giggled quietly, listening to Alec put his godson on the spot.

"Yes, well I suppose one could get used to it."

"I thought you two might get along if you gave yourselves a chance." Julianne peeked around the wall when she heard Alec groan. He grabbed his side and waved off Jack's overtures to help him. "I'm not supposed to move so quickly. I keep forgetting."

Jack closed his briefcase. "Did we do the right thing, Alec?"

"Second thoughts?"

Jack turned toward the kitchen and Julianne ducked back into hiding. "Not for my part, but I worry about how much I've unsettled her life."

"Didn't see anyone with a shotgun to her head."

Their voices faded and the front door closed behind them. Julianne carried her coffee to the great room, staring at the empty space where the two men stood moments before.

She set her mug down on the dining room table and grabbed her coat from the back of the chair. Fear was not going to rule her life.

* * *

She drove to McCormick Place as much to give her car the work as to avoid the paranoia that developed every time she had to wait for public transportation. At 9:00 on a Wednesday morning, there were enough commuters around the City to insulate her in a crowd, but that did little to ease the nerves left over from the night before.

At the convention center parking garage, Julianne scoffed at herself for imagining every Trans Am on the street was Steve's. In the light of day, it seemed foolish to believe he might actually have been behind the wheel of the cab she hailed. Would his specter hang over her for the rest of her life?

Julianne's high heels clicked against the cement floor, fluorescent lights leading her through the underground toward the passage to the expansive building overhead. Footsteps echoed all around, but Julianne kept her eyes straight ahead, her chin tilted up to read the signs that directed her into the exhibition where she would be representing Perkins & Stone for the morning. The safety of other voices echoed throughout the cavernous garage.

A ramp led the way up, glass and steel replacing concrete as she emerged into McCormick Place at street level.

"Julianne!"

She hesitated only a moment, wondering if she had imagined the urgent whisper. A cursory glance at the people surrounding her showed no familiar faces, so she continued on.

"Julianne!"

The call this time came from ahead, loud and certain. Tyler Stern waved at her, trying to get her attention.

Julianne waved back, closing the distance between them. "Did you call me a second ago?" she asked.

"Isn't that why you waved back?" he teased, nudging her with his elbow.

"I mean before that."

"Nope. Just the once. Maybe there's another Julianne nearby."

Julianne shrugged. "Or just my imagination. Where's the exhibit?"

"Follow me."

The morning passed quickly greeting visitors to the trade show and hawking the virtues of Perkins & Stone. The convention hall ebbed and swelled as thousands of people milled around the exhibits. Tyler and Julianne took turns running for coffee and talking with the other exhibitors when the crowds thinned.

Reinforcements arrived at 11:30. Tyler and Julianne repacked their business cards and prepared for the return to the office.

"You want to get some lunch?" Julianne offered.

Tyler paused a moment without turning to address her and then closed his briefcase. "I better not. Jack might not appreciate it."

Julianne screwed up her face, but bit back the retort. She didn't want to go back into the garage alone. "Maybe I could give you a ride back to the office. I've got my car."

Tyler wheeled around. "Look, Julianne, it isn't as if I have something against you personally, but I'm just not comfortable with the way you showed up at the office, you know what I mean?"

Julianne shrunk back, hoisting her pack. "I'm sorry."

Tyler dropped his shoulders and scowled. "It's not really your fault, but you have to understand, it isn't that easy for the rest of us."

"You're right. It isn't my fault." She shouldered her way past the afternoon shift.

"Hey, aren't you the Hayden girl?" a woman asked, blocking her escape.

Tyler pushed past her. "See you back at the office,"

Julianne forced her smile back into place and turned to the woman. "Yes, I'm the Hayden girl."

"Cool!" The woman had purple streaks in bleached blonde hair. "How can I get into commercials?"

Julianne blinked, attempting to formulate an appropriate response that wouldn't offend. "Get a modeling agent?" she finally suggested.

"Cool. Who do you use?"

"I'm not really a model," Julianne explained. "I just had the look the client was looking for." Purple streaks weren't likely to get the woman on television.

The woman nodded and said, "Cool," and then walked away.

In spite of an invigorating morning with the crowds, Tyler's departure left Julianne frustrated. It was Kimball Brothers all over again.

Julianne marched down the ramp to the parking garage, one hand holding tightly to the strap of her backpack. Echoes of footsteps, horns honking and voices rebounded underground. In spite of the reverberating din, Julianne hastened her pace, squinting at every dark corner along the way. She slowed when she located her car and reached into her pocket for her keys.

"Look, Julianne. . ."

Julianne let out a little gasp when a hand touched her shoulder. She spun around to face the man standing behind her.

"Tyler! You scared me."

He smirked and tilted his head. "Sorry. I just wanted to apologize. You look like you're about to jump out of your skin."

"My mom always taught me it was dangerous to be alone in the city. I guess I'm still just a little nervous. Old habits die hard. What are you doing in the garage? I thought you took the bus."

"Like I said, I wanted to apologize. It isn't your fault."

Julianne looked past Tyler to survey the garage. "Thanks," she said, narrowing her eyes to read his motives. "Do you want a ride back to the office?" Her cell phone rang and she held up one finger.

Reception underground was weak, but Julianne could make out her mother's garbled voice.

"I can hardly hear you Mom, can I call you back in a few minutes?" Julianne continued to watch Tyler while she listened for her mother's broken speech. "You need me there?" she repeated. Julianne rubbed her forehead, trying to interpret the conversation and finally ended the call. She shrugged. "I guess I have to run home for a few minutes. I'm sorry, I won't be able to give you a ride back to the office after all."

"Everything okay?"

"Not exactly sure what's going on, but I guess I'll find out when I can get a clear signal."

* * *

Julianne randomly punched the buttons on the radio, hoping to ease her irritation before she reached her mother's house. News that Suzanne was there and "had to talk to her right away" couldn't be good. Imagined conversations of being left out of Julianne's wedding played out in Julianne's mind. Everything was a crisis with Suzanne, and now she felt it necessary to include her mother in whatever today's rant was going to be.

Julianne pulled off the expressway to the sound of her stomach growling. When she looked up, she saw the restaurant she and Steve had referred to as "their" place. After a moment of indecision, she turned in to pick up some lunch.

Rita had waited on them hundreds of times over the years. Tall and gawky, she had curly black hair and thick, dark-rimmed glasses, but what she lacked in appearance she more than made up for in personality. "Hey, it's Steve/Julie, Julie/Steve," she greeted when Julianne walked through the door.

"Just Julie," Julianne replied with a smile. "Can I get a sandwich to go?"

"Absolutely. Hey, it's been a long time since the two of you have been in here together." Rita nodded toward the bar. "Steve's over there."

Every muscle in Julianne's body tensed. Her eyes darted to where Steve sat nursing a beer. He rose from his seat and crossed the room.

"Give us a couple of minutes," Steve asked Rita, flashing her one of his brightest smiles.

The waitress nodded and hurried off toward the kitchen where she pointed out the couple to some of the other waitresses.

Steve and Julianne stood in awkward silence. They looked at the hearth in the middle of the room, the open bookshelves that created a dividing wall, the suit of armor in a corner. Anywhere but at each other.

Another waitress breezed up to them, a voluptuous young girl with flowing dark brown hair. "Hey guys. You two tie the knot yet? It was so romantic that night he proposed to you."

"No, Geri, we haven't tied the knot," Julianne answered politely. "And we won't be getting married."

Geri straightened and looked back toward the kitchen, blushing. "I guess I'd better pick up my orders. I'll talk to you more later."

"It can't be much of a marriage," Steve argued. "What with you sleeping in separate bedrooms."

Julianne watched Geri whisper by the kitchen window to the other waitresses and nod in their direction. As each waitress looked over, Julianne shuddered.

"My sister doesn't know everything," Julianne reminded him.

Steve's fingers played the side of his beer stein. "It isn't as if you would care anyway. It's not like you really had much interest in sex."

Julianne shuddered, aware of the overexerted muscles between her legs. "I would expect such an experienced man to take more time to pique my interest."

"Maybe if you were more interested I wouldn't be so experienced."

She smiled politely as Rita gave her the thumbs up to indicate she had placed her lunch order.

"Just another notch in your belt," Julianne commented.

"Excuse me?"

"There must be something missing in the equation. Otherwise you wouldn't need to add me to your score card."

"I haven't had any complaints."

"No compliments either, I'll bet."

He blanched, his blue eyes flashing. "You know, Julianne, it isn't as if you ever took the time to find out for yourself."

"I knew all I needed to know about you."

He threw his beer mug, drawing the attention of the sparsely populated restaurant. "So now you're an expert? You know, if you just wanted a little action, you didn't have to go and marry someone else to get it."

"I think the point here is that I didn't marry you."

He grabbed her wrist, twisting it in his hand. "I don't believe you're sleeping with him. Suzanne said your things were in a separate bedroom. She said the bed was unmade and that it was fairly obvious that he slept somewhere else."

"I don't care what you believe," she said, fighting to free herself.

"It can't be legal." He pulled one hand over his head, ruffling his usually perfect hair out of place. "You didn't have enough time to get the license. I don't know what little game you two are playing but I'm going to find out. You're supposed to be my wife, Julianne."

Julianne continued to struggle in his grasp. "Let go. You're hurting me."

"Admit it, Julie. You still love me and you know it."

"Let go of me!" She yanked her hand away and cast a sideways glance at the lunch crowd. In a lower voice, she continued. "I told you I didn't want to marry you, Steve, and I meant it."

"Because of the women? So why him? You want some antiseptic. . ." he waved his hands in the air, "anti-sex relationship? What?"

"You don't get it, do you? You can't go out with my sister and expect me to forget it. You know what kind of relationship she and I have."

"At least she's interested."

"You're welcome to her."

Steve closed his eyes and drew in a deep breath. "This isn't how I wanted this to go at all."

"You expect me to say let's put it all behind us and start over? Is that what you wanted?"

"If you'll just give me another chance."

"I gave you another chance. And another. I'm married now, Steve. And I don't intend to alter that."

"I don't believe it. Not that guy." Steve threw a fist full of money in the direction of the bar and wrenched Julianne's arm. "I don't believe it," he growled, pulling her out of the restaurant.

They stood outside the doors nose to nose in combat.

"What were you thinking following me to that banquet?" she shouted. "You could have killed that man. And you didn't even know who he was."

"If I wanted to kill him he'd be dead now."

Julianne stepped back, her anger replaced with horror.

Steve pinned both her arms to her sides. "Dammit, Julie, if you'd just have slept with me everything would have worked out."

"You're kidding, right?"

"Maybe if you loosened up a little you might not mind me having fun once in a while."

"You are sick!" Julianne tried to step away from him. She'd never seen him so angry, so out of control.

Steve pushed her into the parking lot.

"Let me go!" she cried out.

"You have to listen to me. I know you love me."

"Somebody help me!" Julianne cried out.

Steve opened the door of his black Trans Am and pushed her down. "Get in."

"I don't want to!"

He held her tightly while she pushed away, trying to free herself. "I said I wanted to talk to you, Julie. I'm going to ask you nicely to get into the car. I don't want to hurt you."

"Then let me go." She scanned the parking lot for help while tears spilled down her face.

"I can't. Even if he isn't sleeping with you yet, he's got to be human. Even a queer like him couldn't live with you and leave you alone forever. You're so beautiful." He pulled at her hair, jerked back her neck and placed a kiss on her lips.

"Help me!" Julianne screamed.

Stars flashed in front of her eyes from the blow that landed on the back of her head.

"I don't want to hurt you," he repeated in a calm, quiet voice.

"You don't want me," she cried. "Please. Just let me go."

"You're mine. You promised to marry me, Julianne."

"You know I can't do that now."

"I don't believe it." He pushed her again into the seat of his car. She rebounded with the effort to get up while he tried to close the car door and her hand rebuffed the heavy metal.

Julianne pulled back in pain and Steve slammed the door closed.

He was beside her before she could regain her equilibrium and the car screeched out of the parking lot.

"Where are you taking me?" she cried, holding her swelling hand.

"Shut up!" Steve swung the back of his hand across her face. "I know you're not really married to that guy. I'm going to prove how much I love you, Julianne, and then everything will be okay again."

* * *

He sat on the edge of the bed, stroking himself furiously in an attempt to bring himself to life.

"Please stop," Julianne moaned.

"I'm ready, I'm just distracted."

"Please, Steve, you don't want to do this any more than I do."

Again his hand crashed across her face, producing a waterfall of stars against the darkness of her predicament.

"Maybe you'll get pregnant," he said in a half-choked voice. "Then you'll come back to me."

"You couldn't be sure it was yours," she mumbled.

With her wrists tied to the headboard, he grabbed hold of her shoulders with both hands. "I don't believe you. You didn't sleep with him."

"He didn't have any trouble getting hard," she taunted. "And it didn't take him long to come back after he was done."

"You're lying!" he shouted.

"Then how do I know what I was missing?" She turned her head away from him and pulled once more against the ropes that held her to the bed.

"Whore!"

"He's my husband!"

"LIAR!" The back of his hand crashed against her jaw.

She tasted fresh blood where he broke open the split on her lip. Her nerve endings seemed to have stopped telegraphing the pain. Nothing seemed quite real. "Do you ha' this mush fun wi' all your women?"

"Put it in your mouth! he demanded, kneeling over her. "Make it hard."

"You put that piece of spaghetti in my mouth and I'll bite it off."

"You don't think I can do it? It's your fault. I'll show you." He got up, pulled his pants on and walked out of the bedroom.

Finally alone, Julianne closed her eyes. Searing heat prickled her bruised skin. She tried to lick her lips, gingerly avoiding the offended sections.

She tested the ropes around her wrists, hoping to loosen them and somehow break free before he returned with whatever he hoped to prove to her. The hand that had been slammed in the car door throbbed, sapping her strength.

The bedroom was dark and she wondered if anyone had noticed that she hadn't returned to the office.

Would he notice? Jack was always so absorbed in his work. "My God, the man thinks fax machines are sexy, " she said out loud.

Every muscle ached and still her body warmed at the thought of Jack Guilder.

Her mind drifted; the reality of her situation became more hazy. It was inconceivable that Steve could do such a thing to her. She tugged at her bonds again, not quite understanding why she couldn't pull her hands down. She wanted to tuck one hand under her head, to go to sleep. If she could just get some sleep, maybe she would wake up from this nightmare.

CHAPTER 31

"Omigod! Julianne, are you okay?"

Julianne tried to open her eyes, but only one cooperated. "Suzanne." Her voice croaked with the effort.

"I can't believe he did this to you!"

"Help me."

Suzanne crept to her sister's side. "He told me he had something planned. I wasn't even going to come over, but when you didn't show up at mom's . . . Oh, God, Julianne!"

Numbness tingled through Julianne's arms while she struggled to free them. "My arms," she whispered. Julianne ran her tongue across swollen lips and tried to swallow.

The knots tightened with Suzanne's efforts. "I can't get it."

"Help me. Call Jack, he'll know what to do."

Tears slid down Suzanne's cheeks and splashed onto Julianne's forehead. "I'm so sorry."

"Call Jack," Julianne repeated, finding her voice.

"What if Steve comes back? Where did he go?"

Julianne's arms strained against her bonds. "Untie me. Get a knife or a scissors or something. He'll kill me if he comes back. Don't let him come back! Get help. PLEASE."

Suzanne stood up and pulled her cell phone from her purse. She looked from the phone in her hand to the bedroom door. "Should I call first or untie you first?" She stared at the phone blankly. "Wait, I don't know his number."

"Bill," Julianne suggested.

"I can't tell Bill. He'll leave me for sure," Suzanne sobbed. "Oh, I shouldn't have come."

"He doesn't have to know why you came. Please, Suzanne. Help me."

Suzanne stared at Julianne for several seconds, then pressed a button on her cell phone. She took a deep breath, closed her eyes and waited for the answer. "Bill. Oh thank God. Julianne's in trouble. Can you call Jack?" Suzanne looked away from her sister while she waited for his reply. "She's at the apartment." And then, as an afterthought, "Bill, maybe we should call the police."

"Call 911," Julianne shouted.

Suzanne swung back around, her eyes wide. "He hung up on me!"

Tears slid from the corners of Julianne's eyes. "Untie me, Suzanne. Get something to cut these things off me."

Both women stared at the door when they heard the key in the lock.

"Help me," Julianne begged one more time.

"I'm sure Bill called the police. I'll take Steve to the arcade," Suzanne said. "Tell the police he's at the arcade." She hurried out of the bedroom and met Steve at the front door.

"When did you get here?" Julianne heard Steve ask sweetly.

"Just a second ago," Suzanne said evenly. "Why don't we go to the arcade for a drink?"

"You're gonna love the surprise I have planned," Steve purred.

"You're always full of surprises, but really, can't we get a quick drink first?"

Julianne closed her eyes, willing Steve to go with Suzanne.

"You know how we talked about doing a threesome?"

"Maybe we can find someone at D&B's."

The silence was deafening, and then Julianne heard Steve chuckle. "You are so hot!"

"So what do we need a third for?"

He hesitated a moment again and Julianne worried he wouldn't go.

Suzanne heaved a loud sigh, then her voice was deep and sultry. "Really, if you want to do a three, I think we should get a drink first. It will relax both of us. I bet that Roxanne that's always there will come back with us."

"Not Roxanne," Steve answered.

"Whoever, then."

He laughed again. "You are such a whore. I love when you do that to me."

"You know how much you love it in public. Buy me a drink. I'll be all over you at the bar. I promise. Then we can come back and do whatever you want."

"I guess one drink won't hurt anything."

* * *

It was almost worse waiting. Were the police coming?

She wondered how much of what happened to her was a dream. If she could just get up and go to her computer in the next room. . . .

But she couldn't move. She was more tired than she remembered. It felt as if she were tied to the bed. She struggled to open her eyes. The room seemed hazy through the one eye, while the other seemed determined to remain shut.

She sighed. Was it all just fantasy? The trip to Mexico? The job at Perkins & Stone? Her head ached with the images that crowded in on her, daring her to believe the truth.

Jack Guilder was just a man on the other end of the modem, a disembodied name on the computer screen.

"Steve?" she called out, the sound of her voice produced white spots behind closed eyes. Everything was such an effort. Why did she feel so lethargic? If she could just get out of bed. . .

Someone pounded on the apartment door. Julianne swallowed hard, trying to wet her throat enough to call out, but all she could muster was a weak rasp.

Keys jangled in the lock and someone fumbled with the door. Was Steve drunk? Julianne could hear voices, but she couldn't discern where they were coming from. With a deep breath, she gathered strength to focus on the bedroom door. In that instant, a policeman appeared, one hand on his gun. They gasped at the same time.

"We're going to need an ambulance," the cop called over his shoulder.

Everything seemed disconnected. Jack was there, except he didn't have a beard anymore. Julianne smiled and felt a trickle on her lip. The coppery taste of blood made her crinkle her nose.

Jack intermittently wiped at the tears falling from his eyes and reached for her hands, freeing them from where they seemed paralyzed over her head.

"Sir, we can't have you contaminating the crime scene," the policeman told him.

Julianne cleared her throat and attempted to sit up. Jack put an arm behind her for support and wrapped his arms gently around her. She licked her lips slowly, wincing across the split. "I dreamed I was in a commercial."

"And you were magnificent." Jack's voice was a choked whisper.

"How did you find out where I live? I didn't think I'd ever see you in person."

"You're mother gave me your address."

Julianne closed her eyes and looked. "How do you know my mother? She wouldn't like it if she knew I met someone I'd talked to online."

"But we met at the college."

Julianne shook her head, opening her one good eye to look at him. "Yeah, but I don't really know you, except for online."

Jack smiled. "Do you remember the wedding?"

Julianne's brow creased and she swallowed hard. "You'll probably like Suzanne better. They all do."

Jack shook his head. "No. Not all of them."

"Steve's really mad at me. Does he know I'm here?"

Two paramedics rushed into the room. One tapped Jack gently on the shoulder and nodded for him to move away.

"He's so nice," Julianne told the paramedic, looking at Jack as if he were an apparition. "But you can't believe anything he says. You know those ad men, slinging shit is their stock in trade." Her tongue went gingerly across her lips once more while the paramedics checked her vital signs.

"I feel like I'm looking through clouds," she complained.

"Just relax," one of the paramedics urged her. "We're going to take you to the hospital and you'll be good as new."

"Why am I so tired? Why can't I open my eye?" She tried to sit up again. "And why does my head hurt so much?"

"You just need a little rest," the paramedic reassured her. The two men lifted her onto a gurney and wheeled her into the dining room. She recognized the landlord standing just inside the door.

"It's like I told this other guy," he said to the policeman, "they fight all the time. I don't mess in people's personal lives. It's none of my business, domestic problems. I thought she was marrying this Montgomery guy."

"Well she didn't," Jack told him.

The landlord nodded his head. "She deserved better than that low life."

"I could kill him," Jack growled.

"Wouldn't do her any good in jail," the first policeman pointed out. "She'll need you by her."

The second policeman took his hat off and stood beside the gurney. "Will you press charges, ma'am?"

"Assault and battery," the first officer suggested.

"Might as well wait for him," the landlord said. "I expect he'll be home any time now."

Jack put out a hand and reached for Julianne as the paramedics wheeled her out of the apartment. "I love you, Julianne," he said, his voice thick with emotion.

"I shoulda known that guy was bad news," the landlord sighed. "But I never saw her beat up before."

* * *

"Hey." Through veiled eyelids, Julianne could smell Alec's Old Spice after shave, but her eyes refused to cooperate. She was barely aware of Jack, slumped in a chair beside the bed.

"Let's go down to the cafeteria. You need a break," Alec suggested.

"I want to be here when she wakes up."

"She knows you're here."

Julianne smiled, or at least she thought she smiled.

"Go on." Julianne heard her mother's voice. "I'll tell her where you've gone."

"Will you call me?" Jack asked.

The shadow of her mother crossed the room as Julianne tried to focus. "She'll be fine."

Julianne felt Jack's hand on her shoulder. "I'm just going to the cafeteria, I'll be right back."

Julianne wanted to reach out and pull him back, but she gave in to the relentless sleepiness.

* * *

The voices kept calling her out of the black nothingness. Unable yet to open her eyes, she listened to the soothing cadence of men's voices beside her.

"Makes me remember another time you and I were at the hospital," Alec said quietly. "With your mom and dad. She's not going to die," he added quickly. "Although her face will probably turn all kinds of funny colors. Did the doctor say anything more about her hand?"

"He said the surgery went well, her hand should heal normally. How is it we ended up with that same doctor you had?"

Alec laughed heartily. "Jealous, is it?"

Julianne heard Jack's impatient exhalation.

"C'mon. You're a little strung out, lad."

Julianne's forehead creased when her brother-in-law's voice joined the other two. "I just wish I'd seen this coming."

"I don't understand why she went with him in the first place," Jack said.

It was Bill that answered. "According to Suzanne, Steve tried to convince her you guys had framed him - made him out to be the bad guy. He even had Suzanne believing him. And then when Suzanne . . ." Bill paused a moment, then sighed. "I'm going to be sick again." A chair scraped across the floor and she heard footsteps leaving the room.

"You don't think she really . . ." Alec said.

"Yeah, I do. Did I tell you she made a play for me?"

"You didn't . . .?"

"No. And she was none too pleased about it, either. She decided I was gay. And then when she visited the condo she was sure of it since Julie and I were sleeping in separate quarters."

"And now?"

Julianne smiled and rolled her head to one side, but the effort sent her back into the dark oblivion of drug induced sleep.

* * *

The first thing Julianne saw when she finally opened her eyes was Barbara DeAngelo's hands, busily knitting while she spoke quietly.

". . . . Of course I realize that now, now that everything's happened." Barbara bobbed her head to one side, concentrating on the project in her lap. "But Suzanne is going to counseling now. I didn't know what was happening." The hands stopped and she laid the knitting needles down. Barbara stared straight ahead toward the open door. "I never would have believed it."

Julianne looked around the room to see who her mother was talking to, but no one else was there with them. Tears streaked her mother's face. Julianne raised an arm to signal that she was awake but Barbara hastily wiped at her eyes, distracted when someone else entered the room.

"I'm sorry," Suzanne whispered, taking Julianne's hand.

Julianne nodded her head. Everything seemed dark and uncertain. Her forehead furrowed as she tried to remember leaving Oliver's.

Barbara gasped and rose to her feet. "I better go get Jack."

Suzanne turned to stop her mother. "No, wait a minute. I don't think I'm ready to see him just yet and I wanted to talk to Julianne."

Julianne felt detached from the bandaged hand her sister held. She met her sister's eyes.

"I really believed Steve, Julianne. I never thought . . . I guess I didn't realize until . . ." Her words tumbled out.

"And then Steve called me. I wasn't going to go. Oh, Julianne, if I hadn't gone. . . " Her lower lip quivered and her eyes were bright.

Julianne looked away. *"I'll show you."* The words flashed in her memory with a picture of Steve, his face contorted with rage. She squeezed her eyes shut to push the image away, but it grew larger. Like slides flashing against a wall in a dark room, she saw Steve, his hands raised in fists, his face that of a wild man. She felt her pulse quicken, fought to keep the images away.

Suzanne backed away while the doctor pushed past, a look of alarm on his face. "How are you feeling, Julie?"

"It hurts," Julianne cried, putting her hands to her head. She thrashed in the bed, fighting to push the memories away.

The doctor reached for Julianne, trying to hold her still. He looked over his shoulder. "I'm going to have to ask you to leave," he told Suzanne. "How long has she been awake?" he asked Barbara.

"I don't know."

Julianne rolled to her side and curled her knees up to her chest.

The doctor shot an impatient look at Suzanne. "Where's her husband?"

"Jack?" Barbara called, moving toward the door.

Julianne pushed against the mattress. She sobbed, the shadows of pain striking fresh blows. The doctor called to a nurse while Julianne batted him away, pounding against him with her fists.

"No!" she shouted. "Johhhhn!"

Jack ran into the room, moved in front of the doctor and wrapped her gently in his arms. "I'm here, Julie," he told her breathlessly. "I'm here."

She relaxed in his embrace and gave way to cleansing tears.

"He - he tried to kill me," she choked.

"It's all over now," Jack whispered gently, fighting to control the emotion in his own voice.

"Don't let me go," Julianne sobbed, holding tight to Jack's strength.

Jack brushed the hair off Julianne's face and she saw a bandage wrapped around his hand. "What happened?"

He pulled his hand to his chest and looked away. Alec stepped in, fighting a tightlipped smile. "Tell her."

Jack shook his head.

"Then I will." Laying a hand on Jack's shoulder, he smiled at Julianne. "It seems that when they were putting Steve into the squad car he started kicking and fighting. Jack had a few unresolved issues with the man. Let's just say the police didn't rush to stop Jack from helping."

"Look at what he did to her!" Jack growled.

Barbara gasped. "You hit Steve?"

Alec turned to Barbara. "Steve only got back a little of what he gave."

"But Jack seems such a nice man."

Jack turned on Barbara, his hands on his hips. "It doesn't bother you? What he did to her?"

Barbara let out a long sigh. "Of course it bothers me. I'm just surprised. That's all. She's lucky to have you to defend her. I don't think she's ever trusted anyone the way she trusts you, Jack. Except maybe her father."

"Suzanne." Julianne looked around Jack's broad chest. Her sister stood cowering in the corner.

"I'm so sorry Julianne."

"You saved my life."

"You're confused," Jack said gently. "Suzanne was with Steve when the police arrived."

"I know," Julianne told him. "She went with him to keep him away from me."

"Is that true?" Bill stood in the hall outside Julianne's room.

"Yes," Suzanne answered quietly.

"Yes," Julianne echoed. "Thank you."

CHAPTER 32

Jack looked over the railing, alerted when Julianne stopped typing. Since returning from the hospital, he seemed sensitive to every sound she made, or didn't make. He watched her study the cast on her right hand and understood her frustration at only being able to type with her left hand. "Are you ok?" he called down.

"Yes," she answered impatiently. "You're such a mother hen."

Jack smiled. "How's the copy coming?"

"I'm almost done." She put her left hand back over the keyboard and began picking out letters once more.

A "ding" brought Jack's attention back to his own computer. He smiled at the instant message that greeted him on his screen. "I love you, too," he whispered, and put his words into type. "It's ok to say it out loud," he called down. He sent the instant message back to his wife and then turned to look at her once more.

She looked up, a shy smile lighting up her face. The bruises had nearly disappeared. Only a couple yellow blotches remained as testament to Steve's abuse.

Jack rose from his desk and walked down the stairs. "You need to finish your presentation so we can go on that honeymoon."

"It's done," she rose to meet him with a smile.

He wrapped his arms around her. As much as he wanted to squeeze her tight, he couldn't bear the thought of another bruise anywhere on her body.

"I won't break," she said as if reading his thoughts. She pulled him closer. "And I'm ready for that honeymoon cruise."

Jack leaned down and planted a kiss on her lips. "You know, in a lot of ways holding you in my arms is a lot nicer than talking to you online."

"You're not afraid to look into the face of the woman who knows your most intimate thoughts?" she teased.

"You are my most intimate thoughts."

"I love you," she whispered, brushing her lips against his neck.

Jack lay his hand against her cheek and felt her flinch. He cradled her head in the crook of his neck. Remembering her tied up to that bed, bruised and battered, produced a sharp pain in his chest. "Promise me you won't go off with any more old boyfriends."

"How many times . . . ?"

He held her out to look into the amber eyes that captured him so completely. "As many times as it takes to convince me."

"I've already told you. I didn't know he was there." Julianne didn't shy away from Jack's demanding gaze. "And I never really believed he intended to hurt me."

"But the banquet . . ."

"Steve said he didn't do it. Alec had never seen him before. It was easier to deny the truth."

Jack looked away from her, hunching his shoulders under the weight of guilt from all the lies they told.

She nodded, unsettling him again with the way she seemed to read his thoughts. "You need to understand, Steve never lied to me. With you, it was our way of life."

Jack cringed, but Julianne touched his cheek bringing his attention back to her face. "Everything with you felt so unreal – like a fantasy. From that first meeting with Hayden to the trip to Mexico, everything. It was surreal. It excited me and frightened me and I knew I never wanted it to end. But it had to. It was only a fantasy we created online."

Tears welled in her eyes, each drop burning into Jack's heart. "I couldn't stay away from my computer," he confessed. "I used to fight the urge to see if you were online. I was sure you were really just a part of my imagination and meeting you would only shatter the image I had created of you."

Dangerously close to tears himself, Jack swiped at the corner of his eyes. "I felt as if I'd ruined your life and everything you had planned for your future. All for one selfish moment with you." The tears refused to remain suppressed, clouding his vision.

"It wasn't one selfish moment." She brushed back his hair. "It was what I wanted to do. Where I wanted to be." Julianne gave an uneasy laugh. "I told myself it was to network – to get that job after I finished school." She shook her head. "But that was only a small piece of it." She took a deep breath and snuggled into him.

Jack held her close, breathing in the flowery fragrance of her auburn hair.

"I knew I couldn't marry Steve," she said. "What I'd found with you, even just online, was more than I'd ever known with him." She pulled back and looked at him with a silly grin on her face. "In more ways than one. I needed that lunch, too."

Jack brushed at his cheek. "You are . . . I can't even describe. We fit so well together. Intellectually, physically . . ." he drew her close to illustrate the effect she was having on him. "I don't ever want to be without you in my life."

Julianne lowered her eyes, showing him she hadn't overcome all her shyness. He marveled at the absurdity of it – she was so confident in her work, so sure of herself in so many ways. "You don't still think Suzanne can take me away, do you?"

The blush flowering in her cheeks charmed him. "No." Her voice was timid but she was still smiling. "Her loss." She poked at him playfully, tickling his sides with the fingers that extended out through the end of her cast, while her other hand pulled him toward the room she had once claimed as her own.

"Woman, your appetite is insatiable."

"Having trouble keeping up?"

The blood raced through his veins the way it did every time she touched him. "I just keep wondering why we waited so long to come out from behind our computers." He pulled her into his arms and pinned her to the wall. He kissed her hungrily, gently touching her face, feeling the silkiness of her hair against his hand.

Jack paused when the phone rang. Julianne put her hands to his chest. "Aren't you going to answer it?" she asked him.

"I'm busy."

She grinned and ducked under his arms. "It might be important."

Rolling his eyes and sighing, Jack followed her to the phone mounted on the girder beside the staircase and lifted the receiver. "Hello?" Julianne continued to kiss his face, distracting him from the voice on the other end. "Mr. Hayden," he said out loud, indicating that she should stop so he could concentrate on the conversation. But Julianne only smiled and continued to tease him.

"Guilder, I wanted to talk to you about the next commercial," the client was saying. "I want that wife of yours to do it again."

Jack smiled, proud of the woman he had married. He'd always known she was smart, even pretty. He hadn't realized just how talented she was and what a commodity she had become. "I'm sorry, Mr. Hayden, but she has other commitments."

Julianne stopped her exquisite torture and looked questioningly into his eyes. Jack shrugged his shoulders. "We never had a honeymoon, you know," he continued. "I'm afraid we're both going to be tied up for the next month or so, but after that maybe you can negotiate something with her." Jack leaned down and kissed his wife, oblivious to the complaints coming through the phone.

Julianne's eyes widened when she heard the man loudly asking, "Is she even there?"

Taking the phone from Jack's hands, Julianne addressed the client. "Hello, Mr. Hayden. I'm afraid this isn't a good time. Maybe we can set up a meeting on Monday at the office." Her eyes betrayed nothing, capturing Jack in her golden gaze. "Thank you, Mr. Hayden." She nodded and handed the phone back to Jack.

"Well?" he asked.

Julianne smiled. "He wants to sign a multi-year contract before we leave on our honeymoon."

Jack kissed his bride. "The most amazing thing, I don't care much what Ben Hayden wants anymore."

"That's only because you have him where you want him."

"Now how do I get you where I want you?" he asked, pulling her close against him once more.

"You have me for the rest of your life."

Also by Karla Brandenburg

The Treasure of St. Paul

"Author Karla Brandenburg presents a romance novel that strives to expand the genre and offer the reader suspense, mystery, mystic wonder and, of course, true romance... For anyone who enjoys romance novels, this book will not be a disappointment. It is well written and allows the romance to grow as a natural part of the narrative. Much in the same way that Nora Roberts crafts a good story first and allows the love interest to support but not overwhelm the plot, The Treasure of St. Paul delivers a well told tale that holds suspense until the very end." - A guest reviewer for the Chicago Daily Herald

"Karla Brandenburg weaves a surprising tale of suspense and romance in THE TREASURE OF ST PAUL. The historical value of this book is remarkable. The romance depicted is thrilling and satisfying. The characters are believable and well written. This reviewer can't wait for her next novel." - Tammy Falkner for *Road to Romance*

Watch for **Living Canvas** – coming soon!

Audrey MacDougall's well-organized life as an event coordinator is a series of lists and well thought-out plans – until she impulsively buys a painting. Her new piece of art takes on a new dimension when she finds herself inside the landscape, along with a man only she can see. When she meets Greg Ellison, the attraction stems from that sense of déjà vu – is he the man in the painting? Their paths continue to cross, but someone is trying to sabotage Audrey's job. Is it coincidence that Greg turns up every time something goes wrong at work? While considering wedding venues for her best friend, Audrey stumbles across the setting for her artwork at a bed and breakfast. Now Audrey has to decide if Greg is the one trying to get her fired or if there is something more to her painting than oil and canvas.